A Hard Land

P.C. Beck

ISBN: 978-0-9869165-1-9 (print)
978-0-9869165-2-6 (ebook)

Cover Design: Mary Baker

Interior Design: Patti Frazee

PURPLE MOON PRESS
Canada

Dedicated to women who seek social justice.

Dear Lynn,
Thanks for your support! I hope you enjoy! Cheers,
Michael

10/06/16

The devil keeps man from good with a thousand machinations spewed from his belly, so that when a person sighs to do good, he pierces him with his shafts; and when he desires to embrace God with his whole heart in love, he subjects him to poisonous tribulations, seeking to pervert good work before God. And when a person seeks the viridity of virtue, the devil tells him that he does not know what he is doing, and he teaches him that he can set his own law for himself.

– Hildegard of Bingen, 1166

1

Saudades

September 25, 1999

Saudades. *A beautiful Brazilian word. We don't really have a perfect equivalent in English. The word itself shows so much of the intensity of Brazilian culture – a culture where emotion is not stifled but free to be felt and expressed.*

Saudades. *The best way to describe it is longing for, or missing someone. But this does not really do justice to this word. It is that ache in your heart, that feeling of having lost a limb, when you wish so dearly you could be with a loved one. It is the loneliness, the emptiness. It is that lack of ability to take a full breath.*

Saudades. *This is the pain I feel right now.* Saudade. saudades, saudades. . . *through my entire being. No amount of yoga is helping me to breathe today. I am so, so sad.*

It is only through embracing *saudade* that I am able to embrace and rediscover my past. I will tell my tale of *saudade.*

I did very well in school. Graduated top of the class and had scholarship money from major universities in Canada and the United States. My parents (mostly my dad) had this vision of me being a doctor. I can hardly blame them as my older siblings were a veterinarian and a lawyer. The vet graduated from UC Berkeley and the lawyer from Osgood Hall, a prestigious Canadian law school. There was concern that the youngest child might go off track and not even go to university, so curious was I about the world.

A compromise of sorts was made when I decided upon Simon Fraser University and a degree in anthropology. I believe Dad thought the degree would eventually turn into a doctorate and the dairy farmer from Chilliwack could add professor to the list of accomplishments his refined daughters had aspired to.

Although my Dad does not play a major role in the beginning of my story, he was, and continues to be, a person who inspires and whom I love deeply. My mother says we are alike in many ways, although I definitely have my mother's emotional make-up. Like her, I wear my heart on my sleeve and am deeply affectionate to those I care about. My father does not show emotion very often and is a very private, closed man, but when I think of him as a younger person – way before the farm and the three daughters – I think of the Whitman poem, 'O Pioneers'.

In my eyes, he is the embodiment of a modern-day pioneer. He was a jet fighter pilot for the Canadian Air Force and flew in Korea and was stationed in Baden-Baden, Germany during the Cold War. When the Vietnamese war broke out, he enlisted with the Americans and flew gunship helicopters.

He says now that if he had fully understood the conflict, he would have avoided the carnage of that war, but he has no regrets and misses the camaraderie and the adrenaline rush of landing his 'bird' (he really does call it a bird) into enemy jungles. When he left Vietnam in 1968, he knew little about cows and nothing about dairy farms, but he had an uncle in Chilliwack who had no heir and was looking to sell his farm and keep it in the family. My dad did some research and believed he could do it. He did it. The farm was doing well when he took it over, but now it is thriving.

He is a multi-millionaire, owns his own bird, and continues to explore new things. He has got himself involved in cellular technology and swears that by the advent of the new century there will be something even kids as young as ten years old will have. The man is in many ways a visionary but in others I think he is delusional.

He was very proud of me when I graduated university with a double major in anthropology and Latin American studies. He assumed I would go on with my studies and was taken aback when I said I was going to travel to Brazil and work for a non-profit organization. I could tell, though, he was also proud of me and respected my adventurous spirit. He became very disappointed in me and some of the choices he thinks I have made. Many, many times I have wanted to tell him the truth but the risk would be too great, for I know exactly what he would do. Although he is a brave, industrious man, he would be no match for the forces of evil he would be up against.

2

It was through my professor and Latin American department head, Richard Patterson, that I met Maryanne Lucas, the founder of an organization called Saints for Sanctuary, which she established to offer sanctuary to children in developing nations. Her concept of sanctuary was safe homes, safe schools and safe streets to underprivileged children in the cities of developing nations. She believed that in order to achieve her goal, there needed to be an influx of community organizers tasked with developing cottage industries that were profitable and sustainable, and simultaneously to develop community advocacy through grassroots political organizations. The first time I met her was at an honours students' reception at Richard's home in 1992.

I was talking to a guy whose name I can't recall. All I remember was trying to feign interest as he tried to explain how the Marxist-Leninist revolution could really happen in Canada. I noticed Richard (who was standing behind him), and I was trying not to look but couldn't help see Richard point to me while talking to a tall, blonde wealthy-looking woman. The woman walked toward me and said to the boy, 'Excuse me, hon, would you mind doing me a favour and freshen my drink?' Before he could answer, she handed him her wine glass and said, 'The Concha y Toro red, will do just fine.' He nodded and left.

She grabbed me by the elbow and turned us away toward the patio of

Richard's apartment. She said, 'I don't know why Ricky buys that Chilean swill for these soirées. I guess he just wants to keep up appearances.'

She got me out in the patio and lit a cigarette. I stood there as she seemed to be taking a physical inventory of my body. She said, 'So you are Madeline Saunders, one of Rick's aces. I am Maryanne Lucas. It's a pleasure to meet you.'

She extended her hand in a way that suggested I was supposed to kiss it. I gave her one of those effeminate upside-down female handshakes.

She took a drag from her smoke and said, 'I must warn you, you are in the presence of a head hunter.'

I said, 'Excuse me?'

She laughed and said, 'I am a head hunter. Not a corporate head hunter, mind you, but a head hunter nonetheless. The only difference is that unlike the corporate boys who come offering huge salaries, incredible benefits, perks, and signing bonuses, I come offering poverty, dangerous work and, what did Churchill say? "Blood, sweat and tears. Lots of tears."'

The guy came out onto the balcony with her refilled wine glass. He handed it to her and was about to say something when she said, 'Thank you sweetheart, we girls will be inside in a minute.'

This gave him nothing to do but retreat inside the condominium. She leaned into me and said, 'You know the only thing you have in common with that boy is that you both have eyes for our Ricky.' I felt heat rise into my face.

'You're blushing,' she said. 'It's okay, you are not the first student to look at him with, how should I put it, curiosity. The way you are twirling your hair with your finger is quite telling to an old flirt like me. The thing with your professor is he knows it and he revels in it. He also likes the boys, so the competition for his attention is even more cutthroat than most. Here's some advice, if you want him, play coy; he likes that. Go flirt with one of his TAs and he will be on you like white on rice. But darling, once he has enjoyed your company, he will move on – the man is the ultimate conquistador of young, nubile Latin American Student Union members. And I say, *Sandanista, ole* to old Richard.'

If I was blushing before, I was sure my face was now completely red. I said, 'I really don't care for the way you're speaking to me. Now, if you'll excuse me.' I turned to leave but she grabbed my arm.

She laughed and said, 'Oh you are a plucky little thing. Well, listen, darling, I will let you be but please humour me and take my card.' She handed me her business card, put her hand on my forearm and said, 'If you want him, go flirt with the TA in the green polo, but honestly darling, you are so much better than that.' She gave me a condescending pat on the shoulder and sauntered off the balcony and back into the room.

I watched her from the doorway of the balcony for quite some time. She milled about the room like she owned the place. She was flirting with young students, flattering old professors while making her way to Richard. When she got to him, she was all over him; touching him lightly, accidentally on purpose rubbing her ample bosoms against his arm. I thought, *you bitch, you fucking bitch with your saggy tits in a hundred-dollar bra.* She caught my eye, smiled, and raised her newly filled glass to me. I grabbed a beer from the cooler by my feet and toasted her right back.

I made my way to the TA in the green polo neck sweater and attempted to smile coyly, but all I could think about for the umpteenth time in my life was how much I wanted bigger boobs.

She was right, within ten minutes Richard was by side. I gazed into his eyes and nodded as he raved about Carlos Fuentes's novel *The Death of Artemio Cruz.* He spoke specifically about how Cruz was not only a great tycoon but a wonderful lover. As he spoke, I tried to find Ms. Maryanne Lucas with my peripheral vision so I could turn to her at a natural pause in our conversation and give her the look of victory that men rarely notice and that women never forget.

As Richard kept droning on, I noticed his ponytail had many strands of grey hair and that he had very soft hands, fleshy hands. He finally stopped yammering and I turned my head slightly to the right to make sure I was in her field of vision and looked at her with a look I knew would be interpreted as smug victory. I caught her eye and the bitch smiled a big shit-eating grin back and gave me the thumbs up. I almost dropped my beer bottle and quickly turned my attention back to Richard.

He had two tequilas and handed one to me. I took a sip and tried to forget about the woman who had spoiled my victory. Richard brushed some hair out of my eyes and said, 'Madeline you look a little flushed, there is a secondary balcony off of my bedroom. Why don't we make our way there and get you some fresh air?' He put his hand on my elbow as if to escort me to the direction of his room.

I said, 'Oh, I'm fine, Richard, but I should be going. Thank you for the wonderful party but I need to rest up. It is my twenty-first birthday tomorrow and my girlfriends are taking me out clubbing.'

With that I turned away, grabbed my coat and hurried out of the condo into the cooling Vancouver air. I headed toward the sky train station when I heard a voice from a BMW parked at the curb say, 'Madeline, let me give you a ride home.'

I looked into the car and there was Maryanne Lucas, smoke in hand, grinning face glowing and thumb erect. 'See,' she said, 'I told you you were better than that.'

I opened the door and got in. Thus began the ride of my life.

3

I know it sounds like a cliché, but if there was ever a walking and talking contradiction, it would have to be Maryanne Lucas. On the one hand, the woman was a total bitch – the epitome of the snobbish socialite: petty, superficial, and selfish. Her tongue was acerbic and could make a person feel like she was completely worthless. Yet, she was passionate about making the lives of women better. She was a supporter and board member of the John Howard Society, putting her money and time into ensuring incarcerated women had an opportunity to better themselves. She also provided free legal aid to women who could not afford to pay for their own counsel. She was able to do this because she came from money, her mother was the daughter of an Albertan oil man and her husband had made his fortune in rubber plantations in Indonesia and Brazil.

She was a widow and an only child, therefore the sole inheritor of two massive fortunes. Her husband died of a massive heart attack and since then she had taken over looking after their business. He had transitioned his focus away from the dying rubber industry and had moved into the oil refining and mining businesses in Brazil. Maryanne proved to be a ruthless and successful businesswoman and the company had shown exponential growth during her reign as CEO.

In my Latin American Studies courses, Maryanne would have been the target of much criticism – an imperialist capitalist exploiting the people and natural resources of the land in order to make huge profits on the back of the poor. In her case, it would be hard to argue anything different. Nevertheless, she also showed a great capacity for good. Her organization, Saints for Sanctuary, was not only providing immediate assistance to tremendously needy families, it was also attempting to organize the poor so that they could gain political power and better their standard of living. She was trying to develop a system that, if successful, would cut into the profit margins of her company as well as those of the people who were members of the many social clubs she belonged to, and put that money in the pockets of the cheap labour force that was making stockholders gleeful. As I said, a walking and talking contradiction.

She was also very persuasive. It took her very little time to convince me that doing a year stint in Brazil volunteering for Saints for Sanctuary would be a welcomed challenge and help me decide what I wanted to do with the rest of my life. Maryanne said she would waive my volunteer fee and airfare if I did three things: took intensive Portuguese language training, focused on being a community organizer versus a cottage industry organizer and agreed to go to the city of Salvador da Bahia in northern Brazil.

I accepted her conditions and began my Portuguese lessons immediately under the watchful and stern eye of one Senhora Brito, while the equally stern Senhora Vaz taught me the essentials of Brazilian government and strategies of how to best organize the uneducated and the impoverished. The work was grueling and intense.

The old biddies were ruthless slave drivers who harrumphed and tsk'ed and yelled and even on occasion smacked me if I was not progressing to their liking. The ideas of positive reinforcement and constructive criticism were foreign to them. I believe my language skills progressed at the rate they did partly because I was curious to find out what vile names they were calling me on any particular day. The summation of their most common insults would be that I was a *Branquelo* (untanned white person) who was a *babaca* (fucktard) and that I would fit in with the *Baiano* (derogatory term for the people of Bahia) quite nicely as long as I, a *saptao* (effeminate lesbian) found a *sandalhinha* (butch lesbian), to look after me but because I was such a *canhao* (very ugly woman) the chances were good that even a blind *sandalhinha* would sense my ugliness and leave me a victim of the streets. From day one the word *idiota* was sprinkled into every second sentence or so.

I was on the verge of tears constantly but knew it would be disastrous to show weakness in front of these women. I was resolved to show them Maddy Saunders could not only take it but could excel in their macabre learning environment. My graduation consisted of the shawlies (I called them that because they always wore black shawls) telling Maryanne they had tried their best and that I got the basic concepts but God help the organization if I was the best they could find.

Finally losing my temper, I called them a litany of Portuguese swear words and ranted in fluent Portuguese for about ten minutes of how I would make them eat their words. When I finished, both women were smiling. They nodded to Maryanne and left her office.

Maryanne said, 'Congratulations, you just passed boot camp and basic training with flying colours. I have never heard such rave reviews from Vaz and Brito before.'

I looked at her and said, 'You know, I have developed a good grasp of the language in the last three months.'

She laughed. 'You have done exceedingly well. I had a hundred-dollar wager with those two; they said they could break you in less than three weeks and send you home to your rich daddy and his moo-moo cows. I knew when they looked at you they would underestimate you.' She poured herself a drink and lit a smoke. 'Believe it or not, the fact that they said you had the basic concepts would be like getting a double A+ from lecherous old Richard Patterson. By the way – never, never trust a man with a ponytail if he is over thirty-five.'

I replied, 'Well, I don't understand why they were total bitches about the whole thing. I mean, at the risk of sounding like I'm bragging, I pick up things pretty quickly and could have done just as well without the taunting and insults.'

She sat behind her desk, put her feet up. 'They wear black shawls because their husbands died trying to defend the shanty town they lived in from hired thugs who wanted them out of the way because their homes stood in the way of a proposed truck route that would ship trees out of the jungle and cattle into it. There is more than an environmental cost to this type of progress.'

I stood in front of the desk and looked at my feet. Maryanne continued, 'I hired them as domestics with the intent to use them in the capacity I now see fit. Their job is quite simple. They are to teach the basics to the strong and weed out the weak. Only one in ten make it. They and I can't afford to have any nervous Nelly's having breakdowns over there. And know this, my dear Madeline, what they put you through is mere child's play compared to what you will soon experience. Those women would be the first to tell you that. Are you still up for it?'

I looked at her and nodded.

'Good,' she said, 'then I guess my presumptuousness paid off.' She took her feet off her desk and opened the top drawer and handed me an envelope. She stood up. 'You'll find your plane tickets and travel itinerary in this package. If you have any questions before leaving, please contact Joan at the front desk. When you arrive in Salvador, Luiza, your group co-ordinator, will be able help you. Congratulations, Madeline, and welcome to the Saints for Sanctuary family.'

She extended her hand, this time in a very formal, business-like way. I shook it and showed myself out of the office.

4

I must confess I knew very little about Brazil. My knowledge consisted of the iconic things most people associate with the country: the Amazon jungle, the Corcovado Mountain and the famous statue of Jesus that rests on top of it in Rio de Janeiro, Carnival, the beaches, Carmen Miranda and her turban of fruit, the *Girl from Impanema*, the talented and incredibly good-looking men's soccer team, and of course, the wax job loved by men the world over.

Flying into Rio did little to debunk any of my preconceptions. I could see the green, lush jungle, the surf-caressed golden beaches, and the outstretched hands of Christ the Redeemer welcome me to a nation that I would soon discover was so much more than what the glossy travel brochures and western popular culture made it out to be. I was entering one of the world's most sophisticated and complex cultures.

I arrived in Rio on Friday, June 12, 1992, for what was supposed to be a ten-month immersion in Salvador de Bahia before returning to the city for a respite and an ev*alua*tion of whether I was suitable to carry on the work for the organization in another part of the world.

After clearing customs, I found a driver with a sign that read: 'M. Saunders/Saints for Sanctuary.' The driver was a large African man, and beside him stood a short, stern-looking woman named Gretchen Levi-Meyer, Maryanne's principal associate and confidante in Brazil. Her blond hair was pulled back into a tight bun and, other than her plucked eyebrows, there was no sign of any cosmetics on her very serious-looking face. She wore a dark grey business suit and no accessories other than the wire-rimmed glasses that hung around her neck. Her brown flats did nothing to enhance her height.

She stood in front of her driver and protector Ali Haddad, who must have weighed at least 280 pounds and stood at a smidgen over seven feet. As I approached them, Gretchen made eye contact and immediately moved to greet me. 'Madeline, how very nice to finally meet you. Welcome to Brazil.'

I said, 'Thank you, very nice to meet you.' While I was saying this Ali had already taken the suitcase and backpack from me. Gretchen said, 'This is Ali, he will be our driver and ensure we arrive in Salvador de Bahia safely. We will leave on Sunday. I am a Jew and will not travel on Saturday and my Muslim friend here needs to be at mosque tonight for the Friday prayers.' She smiled and said, 'Oh Brazil, what a place. Imagine me a Jew marrying a German lapsed-Protestant and entrusting my life in the hands of a devout Muslim. What a country.'

Ali laughed, his voice sounding off like a fog horn, which made me jump. I said, 'Impressive. It is nice to see people get along.'

Any notion that all people get along in Brazil was quickly squashed only a couple of minutes after we got in the car. To me the drivers were rude and aggressive. Horns blared as tempers flared. These drivers would eat polite Canadians alive. Ali was unfazed by the racket and the cursing that surrounded him. He wore a serene smile and drove the new air-conditioned Volkswagen van through what looked to me streets of bedlam. Gretchen also looked unimpressed with the havoc outside our four-wheeled sanctuary.

Gretchen said, 'Ali will drop us off at my mother-in-law's place. She is in Europe right now. Tomorrow we will rest and on Sunday we will head north to Bahia.'

I yawned. 'Excuse me. Yes, that sounds great.'

'Yes,' Gretchen said, 'well, it is a sixteen-hundred kilometre drive and will take at least twenty-four hours. We will have lots of time to get to know each other. We usually fly up, but I have been in Rio all week at meetings with government officials. Unfortunately it seems they were a total waste of time. We will be packing the van with supplies that would cost three times as much to ship by plane. It will be a long day so rest up as best you can. This will be your last sleep in a comfortable bed for ten months. Luiza's place is fairly safe, but be prepared for very rustic conditions.'

She looked out the window and then back at me, and said, 'Not to worry, the crazy drivers tend to stay in Rio; once we hit the country there will be far less of them.'

I laughed and said, 'You must be clairvoyant. I was just thinking the odds of anyone traveling sixteen-hundred K and living to tell about it must be a rarity indeed.' We both laughed and Ali bellowed.

Unfortunately, I did not sleep well. The time change, an unfamiliar bed and the excitement of my adventure were a recipe for restlessness. I was hoping the extra day in Rio and the fact I was always able to sleep in cars would offer me some rest while traveling to Bahia and help me catch up with my sleep.

I woke from my three hours of slumber feeling very groggy. It took me a few seconds to remember where I was. I heard voices coming from the front room and decided to shower and freshen up before making a public appearance, although what I really wanted to do was have a big mug of coffee. As I made my way to the bathroom I could hear Gretchen talking to someone in a rather abrasive way.

She said, 'Really, Lievan, why would we do that? All you guys do is ensure the poor remain poor with your pathetic charity and bullshit about the poor inheriting the earth while the fat cats cloak themselves in earthly materialism.'

The other person replied, 'I am not an apologist for the past, Gretchen. All I'm saying is there are those of us who see the situation similar to your world view and that we could be a good fit for each other.'

'Hah,' she said, 'and risk being subverted by the likes of Matos and his ilk? No thanks, not while I am running this operation.'

I peeked out of my bedroom door and saw Gretchen facing a man dressed in a rust-coloured T-shirt and blue jeans and red Converses. His back was to me, and I noted his sandy blond hair with a slight hint of a balding spot on his crown. He was fairly small in stature but looked athletic. He said, 'I understand your mistrust, I do, but Gretchen there is a great opportunity here for us to combine our resources and actually make some change for once.'

Gretchen's voice softened. 'I believe your intentions are good, Lievan, but don't you see that you have no power? Matos could pull the rug from under you at any time and then what? I will give you a ride to Bahia, but I want no more talk of any coalition. Deal?'

I found it hard to believe as the man put his left hand behind his back and crossed his fingers, saying, 'Deal.' I had to stifle a giggle. He shook her hand and walked to the door. He turned slightly. I could see the profile of what looked like a handsome and gentle face. 'You will see, Gretchen, I'm not like the rest.'

Gretchen followed him to the door and I made my way from the bedroom across the hall to the bathroom. I took one last glimpse and noticed he saw me. He had gorgeous blue eyes. He looked at me and smiled. I smiled back and scurried into the bathroom, suddenly conscious of the unflattering flannel plaid nightgown I was wearing. I stepped into the shower and welcomed the soft water as it touched my skin. My grogginess had vanished and I felt invigorated.

When I finished showering, I got dressed and made my way to the kitchen and the alluring aroma of coffee. Gretchen was busy putting food out on the table. She noticed me enter the kitchen and said, 'Good morning. I have prepared you a traditional Brazilian breakfast. It is nothing much really, just fresh French bread, papaya, and *requeijão* – it's a cheese spread. There's also some cold cuts if you'd like. And, of course, coffee.'

I looked at the spread and said, 'It looks lovely.' I didn't realize this breakfast would mark the last gourmet meal I would enjoy for a long time.

While sipping a second cup of coffee I remarked, 'So I heard you talking to someone this morning.'

Gretchen said, 'Oh, him. That was just Lievan, one of these idealists who still believes you can work within the system and bring real social change. He just doesn't get it. In a heartbeat, his bosses would squash any real political organizing of the poor if it threatened their interests in the slightest way possible. It's a shame, because he is a fairly smart guy, although I think he could use some backbone.'

'So why was he here?'

'He was nattering about coalitions and solidarity,' she continued, 'but he does not understand that we do not want to involve ourselves with his kind. It is too risky. If we share power with them, they will subvert it, take over and turn us into another pathetic charity organization that just fuels poverty by keeping people on the edge of starvation and on the edge of homelessness where they will never escape. We would be better off aligning ourselves with the fucking communists. Pardon my language.' She smiled and said, 'And no, we want nothing to do with the jackass Marxists; their only plan is to tear down the old system so they can move into the master's house.'

I said, 'Well, maybe he'll come around and just join us.'

'And leave the comforts and security of his current employer?' she said. 'I doubt it.'

I briefly considered her comments and changed the subject. 'Well, that breakfast hit the spot. It was great. God, I needed that coffee.'

She said, 'No problem. Just a heads up, I have reluctantly agreed to give Lievan a ride back to Bahia. He can be of some use and drive part of the way. He promised not to talk about any coalition, so don't let him suck you into talk of such. He is a little liar. Apparently while studying in the States he learned that if you cross your fingers while making a promise it does not count. The little brat actually did it with me today, as I am sure you noticed.'

My face reddened. She smiled. 'I saw you peeking and the idiot did not see the mirror right by your door.'

I shrugged and said, 'He seemed like a nice guy.'

She said, 'No question, he might even be too nice. And just so you know, he is very much taken.'

I chortled, 'No worries there. I am just saying he seemed nice and kind of cute, but I am here to work, not fraternize with the enemy.'

She smiled and said, 'Right answer. Now Ali will be here in an hour or so. He insists on giving rookies a tour of the city if we have the time. If you don't feel up to it just say so, but if you have the energy he is an excellent guide and he seems to get great joy out of showing off our not-so-humble city. But listen carefully. You stay with him at all times. People in this town can smell a tourist from blocks away and they will rob you blind given the chance. Trust me.'

I said, 'I would love to see the sites, and believe me I will stay with Ali. I sense even if I was careless, he wouldn't be.'

She nodded, 'You are right. He is an excellent bodyguard, driver, poet and philosopher. A very talented man. Still, be careful.' She looked at her watch and said, 'It is only nine o'clock and I have already broken more *Sabot* rules than I care to admit. So Madeline, if you will excuse me I am going to retreat to the study. Make yourself comfortable. Ali has a key and he will let himself in.'

I said, 'Thank you, Gretchen, and thanks again for the wonderful breakfast.'

Moments after Gretchen left, Ali unlocked the door, knocked and let himself in. He smiled a welcoming gregarious smile and said, 'Good morning, Ms. Saunders. I hope you had a good rest, though I doubt you did. Most people find the first night in a new country after a long journey somewhat unsettling. I know there is jet lag, but I think it has more to do with not being in the familiar.'

I said, 'I think you've hit the nail on the head. You're right, even though I felt sleep deprived, I did not sleep well. I think my fatigue is trumped, though, by the excitement of finally being here and having this incredible opportunity.'

Ali said, 'Well, I am glad to hear you enjoyed your breakfast and are feeling refreshed. If you are feeling up to it, I would like to take you on a tour, admittedly a whirlwind one, of our wonderful city.'

I replied, 'That would be fantastic. As long as it's no trouble.'

'No trouble at all. The only thing I ask is that you stay by my side,' he replied. He moved closer to me and said softly, 'Gretchen would have a conniption if I lost you and the myth of Ali being a great bodyguard would be debunked once and for all.' He winked and smiled.

I laughed and said, 'Trust me, Ali. I will always be within arm's reach.' I looked up at him and said, 'In your case that will give me lots of room.' I smiled and winked. Ali laughed and escorted me to the van parked below in the underground parking.

He was right. The tour was a whirlwind. We covered a lot of ground, including a brief walk on Copacabana Beach, followed by a bubble car ride up Sugarloaf Mountain for an amazing panoramic view of the city, then through the city, stopping for lunch at one of Ali's favourite Bahian vendors. We were on the Cobal do Humaitá where we were served by a woman named Lili. We had *acarajé* (fritters filled with delicious beans) *doce de coco queimado* (a burnt coconut desert), and according to Ali, the best *doce de abóbora com coco* (a pumpkin and coconut desert) in the city. Lili seemed quite taken with Ali and his flattering remarks about her family's business. Ali seemed to enjoy flirting with her. We then had an exclusive tour of the Maracana soccer stadium with a guy Ali knew from his childhood who worked as an equipment manager. Before heading to the Tijuca Forest National Park and the famous statue of Christ perched on Corcavado Mountain, Ali took me to his alma mater, the Federal University. Our day ended at Ali's sister's home where I was treated to an amazing meal of what I can only describe as Morrocan-Brazilian fusion. It was a brilliant day.

On our way back to Gretchen's mother-in-law's place I asked Ali, 'So Ali, what did you major in at university?'

'Philosophy,' he replied. 'One that generally guarantees a long and fruitless job search.'

I nodded, I think he must have sensed my next question and continued, 'I am planning to go back and get my doctorate. In the meantime I want to learn more about my country and my role in it. It is a place of many tensions and contradictions. Working with Gretchen exposes me to many of those tensions, especially the dichotomy between the rich and poor, the polarity between the feminine and the masculine, the beauty and bane between the European and the African and the aboriginal, and as you will soon discover, the raw political divides between the haves and the have nots.'

'What an exciting way to gather data.'

He laughed and said, 'In other words, why not stick my head in books and learn the way most of my contemporaries do? I know they might do the odd field study here and there and I am not being completely fair. I simply don't learn that way. My process is quite different. I experience. I write poetry about the experience. I do nothing with the poem for as long as it seems fit. When ready, I revisit it and write down what I have learned.'

'That's fascinating, Ali. I wish I had the courage to approach my education your way. Falling into the traditional academia trap is so difficult to avoid. Perhaps we need more academics like you who are prepared to kill all their darlings. Do you plan on returning to university soon?'

'I am not sure. My poems will tell me when it is time. All I know is that they have yet to do so.'

We drove in silence for a while and then he said, 'Did you know I am a pacifist?'

I thought about this for a moment. 'Well, no, I assumed being a bodyguard would conflict with pacifist ideals.'

He laughed. 'Just like my country, I am a contradiction.' He pulled into a parking lot in front of the condo. 'I have never been challenged in any violent way. Perhaps it is my size, and I can look rather stern.' He made what I can only describe as boxer's face when he is face-to-face with his opponent before the match: a look of intimidation and pending violence. Even though I was acutely aware I had no reason to fear the man beside me, I still felt intimidated. Ali could look like one mean, scary dude in the blink of an eye.

He said, 'I feel like I am cheating. I am compromising my pacifist ideals, but the look is an effective tool. I have not used it since my basketball-playing days at university. It is there in my back pocket, but so far it seems that being respectful to people has worked.'

'As well as being seven feet tall and built like a brick shithouse,' I said.

He looked at me quizzically. 'A brick what? I am not familiar with that term.'

'Pardon me, Ali, I didn't mean to be rude. It's a colloquial phrase in my country. When someone says you are built like a brick shithouse they are saying you are sturdy, big, and immovable. It often is said in reference to American football players and in some cases basketball players; for example, Shaq is built like a brick shithouse.'

He smiled. 'As long as you say I do not smell like one.'

We both laughed. He said, 'It has been a good day, no? I have enjoyed your company, Madeline, and I hope you have learned a tiny bit about our city.'

'I've had an awesome time, Ali. You have been a most excellent guide and I really, really enjoyed getting to know you, your family and your city.'

'Very good then. Let me escort you to the front door. You can buzz and Gretchen will let you in, but before you go there are two things I would like to discuss very briefly. One, please do not mention to Gretchen my pacifist ideals; she feels safe with me and I would like to keep it that way. Two, I hear Lievan will be joining us tomorrow. This is a good thing as it will give us an extra driver and it will give you an opportunity to find out more about Bahia. Gretchen does not care for his ideas, but he is resourceful and seems to genuinely care for the women and children you will be working with. All I am saying is, give him a chance.'

I nodded and said, 'Your secret is safe with me, and I will take your advice in regards to our travel partner tomorrow.'

In a flash he was out of the van and had my door. He walked me to the condo and waited until Gretchen had buzzed me in, waiting outside until he saw I was on the elevator. Gretchen had a glass of wine poured for me and showed me to the couch. She said, 'You look exhausted, how was your day?'

'Amazing,' I said. 'You were right, the man loves to show off his city and my goodness, what an interesting character.'

'Not your typical bodyguard, is he?'

'Not that I have had any bodyguards, but other than his size, he does not seem to fit the mold.'

A wry smile crossed Gretchen's face. 'I guess in some cases, size does matter.' She immediately started to blush.

I laughed. 'I guess in some cases it does. This is the land of the anaconda, is it not?'

Her blush deepened and she tried desperately to regain her no-nonsense businesswoman demeanour but to no avail. She started to giggle like a school girl. She said, 'Can you imagine?'

When our laughter petered out I asked, 'How was your day?'

She groaned. 'Fine, but I succumbed to the temptation of work and prepared several petitions. I really suck at being a Jew.' She patted me on the knee and said, 'Well, time for some rest. Tomorrow will be an extremely long day and we will have to get an early start. That relentless little shit Lievan will be here bright and early and bushy-tailed or whatever it is you Canadians say. So rest up and don't allow him to suck you into conversations about alliances and coalitions.'

I said goodnight. I crawled into bed exhausted and tried to relive my day. The last thought I had was of the blond-haired, blue-eyed man with the impish grin.

5

Four a.m. came early. Gretchen woke me and we made our way down to the van. I automatically expected a chill in the air but discovered none existed. Ali stored my bags on the roof as the back of the van was chock-a-block with books, paper and other school items. Before stepping into the van, I yawned and scratched a mosquito bite that was located just beneath my armpit. While scratching, I sensed someone was watching me. I peered into the darkness of the van and saw those blue eyes I had thought about before falling asleep peering back at me. Most of the face was shadowed by a hoodie, but I could tell the mouth was smiling. I must have looked like a twit standing there apparently scratching my armpit.

I said, 'Thought the mosquitoes in Canada were nasty but these bad boys take the cake. More like birds than bugs I figure.'

He pulled off his hood. 'You must be Madeline. Hello. My name is Lievan. Lievan Van den Broeck. So very pleased to meet you.'

He spoke in Portuguese yesterday so I didn't notice an accent, but this morning he spoke to me in English and I detected a European accent. I said, 'Oh yes, you were the person visiting yesterday. I recall getting a glimpse of you as you were leaving. I am pleased to meet you.'

He motioned for me to sit down beside him. Gretchen got in the passenger seat and Ali started to drive. Gretchen said, 'I see you two have met. I am going to try and get some sleep as I am next on the driver's list.

Please excuse me.' She reclined her seat, put her earphones and nightshades on and relaxed. Ali poured a large coffee from a flask and offered us both some as well.

Lievan said, 'I understand you are a Canadian? I studied in the states, in Chicago. I met lots of Canadians there. I also enjoyed the ice hockey. Go Hawks, go!'

I gave a thumbs-down sign and said, 'Canucks all the way!'

Gretchen sighed deeply and loudly. Lievan smiled, then put his finger to his mouth and said, 'Hush, we must use our whisper voices or grumpy Gretchen will have our hides.' I looked at Gretchen, who clearly did not hear him or had decided to ignore his antics. I noticed Ali was stifling a laugh.

I smiled and whispered, 'Whisper voices it is. Go Canucks go.'

He laughed quietly and softly said, 'Welcome to Brazil and welcome to one of the longest car rides of your life, but believe me the journey will be worth every kilometre. Now if you wouldn't mind, tell me a little about yourself and how you ended up in this crazy country.'

I told him my story. He was particularly amused by my teachers from hell, Vaz and Brito. He was also impressed by my Portuguese and had a hard time believing me when I told him I had been studying it for less than four months. He seemed to care about every word I spoke and his eyes rarely looked away from mine. He asked interesting and direct questions about my life and my choices. It was nice to talk to a man who was interested in me as a person and was not like the cheese-eating frat boys or revolutionary wannabes who had populated my life at university.

After telling my story, I asked him about how he ended up in Brazil. I discovered he was from Belgium. He went to the United Nations University in Bruges, where he majored in religious studies. After graduating, he went on what he called a 'spiritual quest' and felt called to the peoples and causes of Latin America. He then went to the University of Saint Mary of the Lake located near Chicago, where he focused his studies on Hispanic cultures. Originally he had wanted to go to El Salvador but more by fate than design, he ended up in Brazil.

I was cognizant of Gretchen's warning not to talk about the organization he currently worked for as it might segue into some forbidden discussions regarding alliances and coalitions. Nevertheless, it became abundantly clear that this man was interested in improving the lives of the people who called Salvador de Bahia their home. I could feel his energy and passion grow as he discussed the beauty and the possibilities of the region. I discovered he was a great listener and wonderful talker. He was charming without being flirtatious and sexy with an air of someone unaware of his own sex appeal. I felt drawn toward his sublime charisma and good looks.

We stopped in Guarapari, a town close to the city of Vitoria, for a late breakfast and then continued on. For the next eight hours things were very quiet as I was asked by Gretchen not to distract the drivers by making conversation. For the first time, I noticed the beautiful land and seascape that complemented our trip. I tried to avert my eyes from looking into the rearview mirror for a glimpse of Lievan. I caught him staring at me from time to time, but I am certain he caught me staring at him more.

I dozed off a few times over the next eight hours. We had a pee, stretch and gas break just off the coastal highway. Then it was back to the van. We stopped in a town called Canavieiras for our dinner break. Gretchen, who seemed to dictate all activities, informed us we would have an hour for food and a bit of a walk if we so chose. We ate at a place in the harbour of this beautiful old colonial town. The pastel facades on the restaurants, bars, and hotels, the golden beach and the mingling aroma of international and local cuisine made the place seem like a honeymooners' paradise.

During dinner Lievan remarked, 'Great recommendation, Ali. How is it you knew of this place?'

Ali smiled and said, 'I suppose it comes from my two passions in life: people and food. I love both and want to savour them both equally. I find if you talk to people about their passion they will open up and if you show interest in their passion, well, then you have a friend for life. Take Fatima and Werner, the owners of this fine establishment. They are both passionate about their food. Talk to them about cooking and show respect for their interests and you will have made two good friends.'

Lievan said, 'Sage advice. So Gretchen, what is your passion?'

She laughed. 'You know, Lievan, we share a similar passion – it is our work. You are very good at what you do and I hope I do okay myself. However, at the risk of contradicting my good friend Ali, I would say there is more to it. Unfortunately, people may have the same passions but can never be friends, no matter how warm and charming one of them might be. I am referring to myself, of course.' She paused to let us laugh, and then continued, 'Seriously, sometimes different world views just get in the way, as do politics and other such messy realities.'

I was about to suggest such things could be overcome when Ali said, 'Okay, I don't know about the rest of you, but I need to stretch my legs. We are ahead of schedule so I am going for a half hour walk and will meet you back at the van. This is a very safe town but do not wander off by yourself.' The last sentence was directed at me.

Gretchen said, 'I will join you and I will pick up the bill since my friend Lievan here did such a great job driving.'

Lievan smiled and said, 'I am forever grateful, Gretchen. I would like to walk, but I think I need some more coffee first.' He looked at me and said, 'Would you care to join me for a coffee? My treat.'

I almost looked at Gretchen for approval but averted my eyes at the last second. I replied, 'Another coffee would be nice.'

We drank our coffee and made small talk and then headed off to walk the promenade. Lievan looked at his watch and said, 'We have fifteen minutes and we best not be late or Ali will start to fret and Gretchen will get pissed off.'

We walked in silence for some time and then Lievan said, 'You know, I really respect Gretchen. She is a straight shooter and a person of integrity. Disagreements aside, the people of Bahia are lucky to have her, and from the sounds of it they are lucky to have you as well.' He punched me lightly on the arm as he said this.

I smiled. 'Well, the proof will be in the pudding. I just hope I am up for the challenge.'

He asked, 'So what is the long-term plan for Madeline Saunders?'

I stopped dead in my tracks and said, 'I am not sure. Shit. Never given it much thought.'

He laughed. 'Nothing wrong with that. I can assure you after a year in Brazil you will have a clearer picture of what you need to do and where you need to be.'

I punched him lightly in the arm and said, 'Thanks.'

'For what?' he asked.

'For befriending a lonely Canadian girl who often feels out of her element.' I emphasized the word 'lonely' hoping he would interpret it as meaning single and available. I was thinking about what Gretchen had said about him being taken, yet he had not mentioned anything about a partner.

He said, 'Oh look, here comes Ali and Gretchen; we should walk back with them.' As we walked back to the van Ali sang a popular Bahian song that echoed my feelings. It was about a person falling in love and wondering if the feeling would be requited, it was about dancing the Xote dance down by the sea

I looked out toward the sea and for a moment thought about how nice it would be to dance in the night air with Lievan.

Gretchen was behind the wheel and Ali rode shotgun. Lievan and I were back in our old seats except this time I was by the window. I was feeling quite tired but wanted to continue talking. However, Lievan yawned and said, 'Time for some shut-eye.' I thought he was going to leave me and sleep on the bench seat behind us but he stayed. In a few minutes he was nodding off. His neck would bow and his chin would almost touch his chest and then his head would snap back up. This happened several times until finally his body conceded to sleep. He leaned in to me and before I knew it his head was resting against my shoulder.

His hair was fine and soft and smelled of butternut. I enjoyed the feel of his body heat mingling with mine. I closed my eyes and pretended to sleep. I leaned my body into his so that our points of contact increased. I felt warm and safe and at ease as we rumbled down the highway toward Salvador and the sunrise. Eventually I did drift off to sleep waking occasionally to savour the warmth and listen to the calm breathing of the gentle and thoughtful man who rested upon my body.

However, I was fast asleep when I heard Ali say, 'Wakey, wakey, we are here.'

I woke to find that Lievan was pulling open the van's side sliding door. When the door opened I felt confused, I expected to be greeted by Luiza, the woman whose home I would be living in. Instead we were in front of a church. A teenage boy was grabbing Lievan's bags. He said, 'Welcome back, Father Lievan. Father Matos would like you to meet him for breakfast. He said he appreciates you will be exhausted, but he will take very little of your time. He needs some information regarding the tithes of the Pelancchi family.'

'Very well, Roberto,' said Lievan. He turned to face me and I hope the stunned look I wore was mistaken for grogginess. He hopped back into the van and gave me a hug. 'Well, Miss Canuck, thank you for being a wonderful traveling companion. I am certain our paths will cross sooner than later.'

I was speechless and hugged him back. I was able to muster an idiotic grin as the sliding door slammed shut. The only word, the only thought in my head was Father ... Father ... Father.

My thought was interrupted by Gretchen, who pompously said, 'I told you he was taken.'

My eyes darted to the rearview mirror as I stared at her.

She held my gaze, not intimidated in the slightest and said, 'It is funny how he doesn't just come out and tell people. I think he thinks it separates him from us commoners. If it does, then why belong to such an elitist organization? I have no time for the Roman Catholic Church in this country and the bozos who run it.'

Ali interjected, 'Now, Gretchen, though the organization may have many flaws, it does not mean that all who work in it are incompetent. Lievan is a good soul and he means well. You need to give him a chance. One thing is for certain, he is not Matos's lackey.'

Gretchen said, 'I think the verdict is still out on that. For arguments sake, let's say you're right Ali. My question would be, so what? He is powerless to change Matos and the church from within. They need to blow the whole thing off the face of the earth.'

She yammered on about the ills of the Catholic church, but I had tuned her out and continued to wrestle with one thought: Father Lievan.

6

The ride from the church to Dona Aurora (the shanty where I was scheduled to spend nearly a year of my life) was a blur. All I could think about was Lievan and what an immature little fool I was to fall for someone so quickly. It wasn't like I had us walking down the aisle and planning our family (two girls and one boy) who would undoubtedly be traveling the world on our sailboat while we homeschooled them in what was really important in life. Us, a family of nomads avoiding pirates and the pitfalls of modern living while commandeering the high seas. It wasn't like I had had thoughts like that. Oh blessed youth!

In order to keep me awake, Ali tried to explain the local religion called *Candomble*; a polytheistic mixture of African belief systems with a good sprinkling of Catholicism. He told me the locals were more inclined to *Candomble* than Catholicism, much to the chagrin of the local parishes. My mind was still a million miles away when Ali slid open the door for me. My olfactory glands instantly brought me back to reality. The smells – a combination of sewer gas, diesel fuel and urine that hung like a wet blanket in the moist tropical air. Ali said, 'This is where Gretchen gets off. We will be unloading the supplies in our storage bin behind the office and then I will take you to Dona Aurora.'

I said, 'This is not Dona Aurora?'

Gretchen, looking haggard and impatient, said, 'No. As I am sure you can recall, Dona Aurora is on the outskirts of town, much more rural than this. We are in the city centre, where our administrative office is located. After we unload, Ali will drive you to Luiza's and I will cab home.'

I thought to myself, if this is the city centre and it smells this bad, I don't want to think about how bad the shanty must smell. I helped Gretchen, Ali and two young women unload the supplies into the stifling hot bin. After locking up, Gretchen came to me and gave me a hug, she said, 'Sorry if I am a bit grumpy. You have had a lot to take in and I should have been more patient. I do not do well when I am sleep deprived. I am also a constant worrier and that makes me fret too much.' She pulled back from me and put her hands on my shoulders, 'However, I am not worried about you. You will do us proud, I just know it.'

I hugged her and said, 'Thank you. I will try my best. I cannot tell you how appreciative I am to have been given this opportunity.'

Her cab pulled into the parking lot and she said goodbye. As she was walking away she pointed to Ali, then to her eyes, then to me. Ali laughed and shouted to her, 'Yes, dear Gretchen, my eyes will be on her at all times.'

I sat in the passenger seat in the now-empty van, feeling better now that the shock of discovering who Lievan was had worn off. As we made our way to Dona Aurora I noticed there were more shanty towns. Once again, I was seeing the contradiction that was Brazil, there were homes made of abandoned plywood and corrugated steel and odds and ends of other building materials that overlooked the bay, million-dollar views for certain. As we continued to travel, the landscape became more and more rural. Finally we arrived and Ali pulled over to the side of a makeshift road. To my surprise, my nose was not violated by putrid smells. In fact, the air smelt balmy and sweet with the scent of papaya and guava wafting through a gentle, warm breeze.

However, if my nose suffered in Salvador, my ears suffered in Dona Aurora. There was a woman playing a guitar surrounded by children. She was singing, or at least attempting to sing. It was bloody awful. Her singing voice was more akin to shrieking and the children would join in the chorus of her song, but instead of trying to make the apparent music somewhat tonal and redeeming, they would follow their choir director's lead and shriek along. It was like listening to a pride of cats in heat involved in some orgiastic ritual.

I stood and watched. They were oblivious that I was even there. In spite of the dissonance it was obvious all of them were having a great time. The children were trying their best to snuggle up to the woman, vying to be the closest. They all seemed to know the words and every child was smiling right along with the woman. I noticed she had stuck a lit cigarette between the strings on her tuning pegs and the head of her guitar like some female version of a Jimmy Page or Jimi Hendrix, although that was the only similarity between her playing and theirs.

Ali remained in the van until the song was over. When he got out pandemonium ensued. The children started yelling *Mr. Ali* and raced toward the giant. Ali produced candies from his trouser pockets as children clamoured to hug his legs. One little girl, perhaps four or maybe five, was continuously pushed to the back; Ali swooped down and picked her up with his giant hand. He said to the woman, 'Luiza, the Bible is like the Qur'an in many ways; both believe the last shall be first.'

I looked at the woman and must admit my first thought was, *Dear God I hope she does not have the sing-alongs every night.* I looked at her again and saw her watching the kids. She was smiling between drags on her cigarette. Her smile was beautiful and contagious. Ali pointed to me and said, 'Luiza this is Madeline. She will be staying with you.'

She looked at me and her face lit up. She stood up from the concrete slab that acted as her porch and made her way toward me. She said, 'Welcome my friend.' She held my face in her hands and looked into my eyes, smiling. I could smell the recently smoked cigarette and could feel her warm breath. She patted my cheek and turned her attention back to the kids and Ali. She said, 'Children, leave poor Ali alone, he must be exhausted. Now scram, back home the lot of you.' Without hesitation the children left Ali and headed in a multitude of directions to their homes.

I noticed that Luiza's home was located in the middle of the block. It looked a little bigger than her neighbours'. She said, 'Let me give you a tour of your new home.' Luiza took me by the hand and Ali picked up my belongings and put them by the front door. Before going into the house she took me to her backyard. It was fenced in by old pieces of wood, plywood, and some wire. The ground was compacted mud and was inhabited by seven chickens. There was a papaya and a guava tree growing out of the hardened, cracked earth. I noticed, sitting in a chair under the papaya tree, an old woman whose face was as hard and cracked as the earth. Large hairs, much like the papaya and guava trees, grew from moles on her face.

She was sleeping. Luiza said, 'That is my mother, her name is Dona Aurora, the same name as our neighbourhood. We shall let her sleep. She will awaken soon enough.'

I was amazed to find myself standing on earth that seemed so impossibly inhospitable, yet here I was surrounded by the smell of iron, of new growth, of fruit and life growing out of a hard, hard land.

Luiza guided me into the house. The first thing I noticed was there was no glass in the windows. The house was built from bricks made from red mud that was indigenous to the area. Later I learned that she and her husband Carlos built the place brick-by-brick. Luiza would never say so, but Dona Aurora told me that Luiza was both the brains and brawn behind the construction. There was a toilet that worked most of the time. The bathroom was the only inside room that had a door. The running water was pirated and made its way into the house via a complex and ingenious system of pipes and clay pots that acted as a filtering system. The water always tasted earthy and I was required to add iodine to mine before drinking it.

She led me through the kitchen that also served as a utility room. There was a simple cupboard and electric stove with two burners. Like the water, the electricity was pirated and worked most of the time. There were two rooms downstairs. Both were about eight feet by six feet. One room was for Luiza and her husband Carlos, the other was the sleeping/study/play area for her teenage son Fabricio. The inside walls had been plastered and the house was considered a villa compared to most of the homes in the neighbourhood.

Luiza took me back to the kitchen area and pointed to a homemade ladder that led to a hole in the roof. She said, 'Your room is up there. We just finished building it yesterday so the plaster might still be a little damp.'

I was shocked to think that she had built this entire addition just for me. I said, 'Oh my goodness, I did not realize I would be so much trouble for you.'

Luiza said, 'No trouble, when you are gone I will have a place to rent out or perhaps give singing lessons.' The look on her face suggested there was no irony or sarcasm to be interpreted with her assertion that she could be a singing teacher.

I said, 'Yes, well, renting the place would be helpful.' I asked, 'Where does your mother live?'

'She has a home next door. It is only one room so she eats with us and uses our facilities.'

When I went to get my things Ali was waiting at the front door for me, a couple of the older kids had returned and he was kicking an old soccer ball that was stuffed with rags and held together with duct tape. Ali grabbed my suitcase and backpack and entered the house. He had to duck the entire time but insisted on bringing my things into the kitchen. He was able to stand upright by putting his head through the hole in the roof that led up to my room. Luiza burst into fits of laughter when she walked into the kitchen to see what looked like a headless Ali standing in the corner. I could not contain myself and soon started laughing as well. Ali poked his head down to see what was causing the ruckus and asked, 'What's so funny?'

Luiza replied, 'I thought the calm and collected Ali had finally lost his head.'

Ali joined our laughter. After we stopped laughing he proceeded to pick up my stuff and was going to climb the ladder to my room. Luiza said, 'Please Ali, no. Your good manners must play second fiddle to practical matters. There is no way the ladder will support your weight, and even if it did I am afraid you might come crashing through our ceiling. The room was not built by engineers you know.'

Ali shrugged and said, 'Very well,' He looked at me, 'Madeline why don't you climb up and I will pass you your luggage.'

I climbed up the ladder, wondering if the roof would support me. I saw there was a blow-up mattress in the corner covered with a fresh sheet. The room was furnished with a few old wooden cartons that would act as my table, chair and chest of drawers. There was no electricity and only half of the area was covered with a roof. I was thankful I had remembered my mosquito net.

Ali passed up all my earthly belongings and I climbed back down. Ali said, 'Well, Madeline, you are settled in and in the safe hands of Luiza. Remember not to wander off by yourself. I will see you when Gretchen drops by, but if you need anything don't hesitate to call me. There is a public phone only a few blocks away and my number is in your orientation package.' He gave me a hug and left.

After Ali left, I went up the ladder (I could not wait to use that one when I wrote home to my friends and family) to my room. I spent a half hour or so arranging my living space and securing my mosquito net. When I descended, Luiza had made coffee from a creative filtering system that included a neck-less large coke bottle and a small piece of mesh that could have come from a screen door. It dawned on me that everything Luiza and her neighbours had, had come from their own hands. There were no electricians, plumbers, building inspectors to provide them with the expertise and guidelines of how to build their homes. Everything was improvised. I found it hard to imagine myself and my friends even knowing where to begin. The only person I could think who would thrive in this environment was my father, and he was the most intelligent and resourceful man I knew.

While drinking my coffee I laughed. Luiza asked, 'What is so funny?'

I said, 'I was just thinking of one of my old professors, a man named Richard, and how he would never survive in Dona Aurora.' Luiza started to frown. I said, 'Forgive me, Luiza, I meant no offence. I was just thinking that the home you have built is incredible. The fact your family did it all by yourselves. Few Canadians would be able to do this and Richard... well Richard... I would be surprised if he ever had a hammer and a nail in his hands. He would be like a little lost sheep.'

Her frown disappeared and she said, 'But didn't you Canadians build log cabins and clear the land and grow wheat in ice and snow.' She paused. 'Someday I will see ice and snow.'

I replied, 'Many years ago when Europeans settled, they did indeed suffer tremendous hardships and carved a vibrant country out of the wilderness. A wilderness that native people had survived in for centuries before their arrival, but my point is today, very few people from my country would have the ability to do what you have done.'

Just as I finished talking, I heard a loud cough from behind me. Dona Aurora had woken from her sleep and entered the kitchen. She seemed even frailer awake than asleep. She said, 'Luiza, you should have wakened me when our company arrived.'

I stood up and said, 'You looked so peaceful, I asked Luiza to let you sleep until I got settled.' I reached out my hand and said, 'Hello, my name is Madeline, but my friends call me Maddy.'

She smiled an all but toothless grin, brushed past by hand and gave me a kiss on each cheek. 'Dona Aurora welcomes you to Dona Aurora.' She laughed at her joke and motioned for me to sit down. She said to Luiza, 'Could you pour me a coffee, my love?' As Luiza went to pour the coffee

Dona Aurora looked around and said, 'Where is that useless husband of yours? And where is Fabricio? I hope he is not hanging around with his deadbeat father and his cronies.'

Luiza sighed and said, 'Please mama, not in front of our guest.'

'The girl will find out soon enough.' Dona Aurora looked at me and said, 'One of your first lessons in this country will be a simple one to learn: The women do most of the work during the day and the men do most of the playing during the night. My son-in-law is living proof of this. He is a bum, an oaf, and a drunk, as was my husband.' She crossed herself when she said 'husband.'

Luiza set the coffee in front of her, looked at me, and rolled her eyes. Dona Aurora continued after taking a sip from her coffee. 'I blame us women. For centuries, we have let them treat us like nothing more than a mattress, a fuck hole. They fuck us, take our money, spend it on the cock fights or booze or prostitutes, and what do we do? Nothing. We let them do it and simply bitch to each other.' She shrugged and pulled out an ancient tobacco pouch and started to roll a cigarette. Silence ensued. After finishing rolling she said, 'Take my daughter's silence as agreement with what I say.' There was another pause. She took a drag from her smoke and said 'Oh well, at least Brazilian men are experts at fucking.'

She said this as I was taking a sip of my coffee. I did a spit-take. As my coffee spewed across the floor, Dona Aurora cackled and Luiza burst into laughter. Dona Aurora said, 'We will have to get this *gringa* a Brazilian lover to prove my words are true, eh Luiza?'

Luiza said, 'Yes, mama, a lover, but not a husband.' Both women burst into laughter again.

Even the strong coffee could not stave off the fatigue I felt. I was having difficulty keeping my eyes open and soon surrendered to sleep. I said goodnight to Luiza and Dona Aurora and headed off to bed. I closed the trap door on the roof. My penthouse offered a spectacular view of the southern stars and I spent a few moments gazing skyward. The eastern part of the sky was shrouded in cloud but the western part was still clear. After my brief stargaze, I climbed into bed, making sure my mosquito net was well secured. Within seconds I was asleep; thoughts of Father Lievan barely making it to the forefront of my consciousness.

I awoke afloat. My bed was literally floating close to the roof. I heard Luiza's voice shouting, 'Wake up Maddy, the roof is flooding.' Luiza had removed the trapdoor and water was pouring into her kitchen. I heard a man's voice from below holler, 'You stupid fucking bitch, you are flooding the house. Close the fucking door.'

Luiza yelled back, 'If I close the door the whole ceiling will cave in! Get the broom and start sweeping the water out the front door.' I heard the man grumble and snarl. Luiza said, 'Maddy, are you okay?'

I was wet and startled but otherwise no worse the wear. 'I am okay. What can I do to help?'

Luiza handed me a tin can and motioned for me to start scooping water over the side of the roof. I did so, and did so with fervour, but realized I lacked the strength and coordination of Luiza. While my scoops were erratic and spastic, hers were efficient, mechanical, and effective. Thanks to her, we soon had most of the water removed. Luiza went to the hatch and called down, 'Carlos, pass up the frying pan and the rebar.'

After a minute or so a hand appeared, and Luiza grabbed a frying pan from it. A few seconds later a ten-inch piece of rebar appeared. Luiza passed it to me and motioned for me to follow her to the edge of the roof. She said, 'This little retaining wall was built to prevent you from taking a tumble in the middle of the night. I stupidly forgot to think about drainage. I want you to hold this metal bar where the wall and roof meet.' I put the bar where she told me to. 'Okay good, but put it on an angle.' She directed my hand until she had the angle she wanted. She said, 'Good. Now hold still, hopefully the plaster is still soft and we will bang through in no time.' She grabbed the frying pan and began to bang at the bar. I hoped she had a steady hand and a good eye. It didn't take long for a hole to appear.

We were able to make four drainage holes in short time. Soon the deluge of water on the roof was gone. Nevertheless, I was soaked. Luiza said, 'Good work, Maddy. You have nerves of steel. I was certain I would break at least a couple of your fingers.' I looked at her and began to feel faint. She laughed. 'Joking! I am the queen of the frying pan hammer. I never miss my mark.'

I smiled and she motioned for me to follow her downstairs. When we got to the kitchen, Carlos, her husband, snapped, 'I told you, you fool, not to waste your time building that wall. I knew there was a reason.'

From the door of the kitchen Dona Aurora said, 'The only reason you did not want to build it is because you are so fucking lazy and incompetent.'

Carlos turned and said, 'Shut up, you old cow.'

Luiza said, 'Mama, really, stay out of things. Why are you here?'

'The hammering and yelling – it woke me from my beauty sleep.'

Carlos turned around and for the first time noticed me. It took me a second to realize he was staring at my breasts. I had on a thin T-shirt and the wet cotton was clinging to my nipples. I self-consciously crossed my arms in front of my chest. Both women noticed where Carlos's eyes were focused and both shot him looks of disgust.

He seemed oblivious to their scorn. He smiled and said, 'Hello, Miss, I am Carlos and pleased to be your host while you are staying in beautiful Brazil.' He extended his hand and I reluctantly shook it. He did not even pretend to avert his eyes from my breasts while shaking hands. He gave my hand an extra squeeze. I sensed this was going to be a problem, perhaps a big one.

Dona Aurora said, 'Come with me young lady, you can spend the night in my mansion, it may be small,' she gave Carlos a cold stare, 'but it is safe.'

I looked at Luiza, she nodded and I went to the roof and found that the clothes on the top of my suitcase were damp but not soaking. I grabbed the driest things I could find and descended the ladder. I heard Dona Aurora say, 'Fabricio you must have a clear conscience to be able to sleep through that ruckus.' As I entered the kitchen, I saw Dona Aurora gently pat the cheek of a boy dressed in his skivvies. Luiza said, 'Maddy I am pleased to introduce you to my son, Fabricio. Can you believe he slept through the entire ordeal?'

One look at Fabricio and his wry smile and the way he shrugged led me to believe that he hadn't. I guessed he had feigned sleep until the work was done and then entered the kitchen as his curiosity got the best of him. He was a good-looking boy with dark curly hair and big brown eyes and a charming, radiant smile. He was at a lanky stage; wiry with feet and hands disproportionately bigger than the rest of his body. He shook my hand and said, 'Welcome to our country and our home, it is my hope you enjoy yourself, please let me know if there is anything I can do to make your stay a more pleasant one.' As he spoke I noticed his mother and his grandmother were smiling adoringly and focused entirely on their Fabricio. I believe I was getting my first lesson as to why the men in Brazil were able to maintain their firm grip on a patriarchal society. Doting mothers and grandmothers contributed greatly to a young man's sense of entitlement.

I left for the three-step walk to Dona Aurora's home. Her home consisted of one room; there was a wash basin, a bucket, and a mattress. I could see cardboard sticking out from underneath the mattress. The one small window was covered with chicken wire. There was no electricity and the only light came from a candle Dona Aurora had lit. I noticed a ratty-looking Bible beside the bed and a tin, six-inch crucifix nailed to the wall above the bed. Dona Aurora motioned for me to lie on the bed. I said, 'Oh, no, Dona Aurora, I will sleep on the floor, you take the bed.'

She smiled and said, 'Silly child, neither of us will sleep on the floor. You are my guest, you will take the bed.' I looked at her. The candle light accentuated the deep lines that crisscrossed her leathery skin and made her dark eyes shine brightly in the darkness. I realized I was standing in front of a survivor who in spite of her poverty and hard life revealed dignity, pride, and purpose. I made my way to the bed and lay down on my back. The old woman climbed in beside me and held the candle above my head. She said, 'My child, you are beautiful. Please be careful in this hard land, it can hypnotize you with its splendour but like the jaguar it can tear you to shreds if you do not pay attention.' She kissed my forehead and blew out the candle.

I began to cry and sobbed softly. In the darkness she turned toward me and motioned for me to lie on my side. She threw her arm around me and sang, as sweet as a bird, a Brazilian lullaby. The song was entitled, '*Se Essa Rua Fosse Minha* (If This Street Were Mine)':

On this street
On this street there is a garden
That is called
That is called loneliness
Inside it
In it there is an angel
Who stole
Who stole my heart

I fell asleep to a beautific soothing voice, a voice unimaginably emanating from this chain-smoking, toothless relic. Clearly the hard land of Brazil had not defeated her.

7

I awoke to the sound of yelling. I jolted upright but it took me some time to remember where I was. After getting my bearings I jumped out of Dona Aurora's bed and looked out her small window. I saw a police car parked across the street but nothing else. I put on my shorts and ran to the road.

The police car, a grey Volkswagen station wagon, had its front doors flung open. I heard the shrill voice of a man in pain but could see nothing as my view was blocked by the car and several men who had gathered on the side of the road. I moved toward the crowd and saw a cop with a submachine gun resting malevolently on his hip. The crowd of men seemed unconcerned with the exhibit of firepower, but they also gave the policeman a respectful distance. As I worked myself to the front of the crowd I finally saw the source of the crying. The other officer, a man with a vile-looking scar running down his cheek, had a young man handcuffed to the bumper of their car. The police officer was kicking the young man in the ribs. Every kick was followed by the dull thud of bones being fractured and the scream of the victim. The cop was saying, 'That will teach you, you dirty little queer, not to ply your trade in our town. You think you can come here spreading your fucking faggot disease on our streets, drinking our water, eating our food, and then spreading your AIDS like a plague? Eh, Inacio?'

The man on the ground wept. The cop mockingly said his name in a falsetto voice, 'Inacio. Inacio. Oh, Inacio, you faggot, are you going to continue to suck cock, fuck other faggots in their disease-festering assholes, and then fuck the monkeys as well as our goats and chickens?'

Inacio whimpered, 'I do not do such things.'

The officer holding the gun struck the man on the shoulder with the butt of his submachine gun. He screamed, 'You dirty whore, we know you sell yourself to every pervert from here to Rio.' He then said to his partner, 'Show me the faggot's pretty little face.' His partner grabbed Inacio's hair and yanked down, exposing the young man's face to the crowd and the barrel of the gun. The gun-toting cop then forced the barrel into his victim's mouth. He said, 'Suck on my barrel like you suck gay cock.'

Inacio tried to drop his head but the cop propped it up with the gun.

'Suck it or your decrepit brains will paint the back of my car.'

The other cop laughed and said, 'It would be a shame to see your pretty face blown to smithereens because you resisted arrest, Inacio.'

The young man hesitated and the cop put his hand on the trigger. Inacio's shoulders sagged and he started to simulate fellatio on the barrel of the gun. The cop said, 'Look at me while you suck my rod, Inacio. Let me see your pretty brown eyes.'

Inacio looked at the cop and the men who had gathered around began to laugh. For the first time I noticed that Carlos was in the crowd, evidently enjoying the show.

Tears started to roll down Inacio's face. The cop holding the gun said, 'Oh look fellas, our little princess is starting to cry, maybe I should cum in her mouth.' He feigned pulling the trigger and his partner screamed 'BANG!' Inacio yelped and pulled his head back, hitting it hard on the back bumper. He became hysterical and the cops and the men howled with laughter.

One man pointed at Inacio's crotch and said, 'Look, the little faggot has pissed his pants.' This brought more laughter.

One of Carlos's cronies came forward and slurred, 'Excuse me, officers, I, too, need to take a piss. He pulled out his penis and proceeded to urinate on the shell-shocked Inacio, bringing more applause from the crowd and the cops.

The cop said, 'Make sure you do not get your piss on my handcuffs, Raul.'

During the entire ordeal I remained gobsmacked, unable to comprehend what was happening to another human being in front of my eyes; however, watching one person urinate on another snapped me out of my shock. I opened my mouth with the full intent of expressing my outrage and disgust. Before I could say a word I was horse collared, pulled right off my feet and away from the crowd in a split second.

The arm that grabbed me spun me around and I stood face-to-face with Luiza. She no longer looked like the smiling Buddha, the saint of wayward children and Canadian do-gooders, her face was that of a stone-cold killer. She simply said, 'Be quiet, don't turn around and don't run.' Her hand had my arm in a death grip and she nonchalantly did a slow hustle across the street. She opened the front door and pulled me inside. My arm was hurting. Still holding onto my arm she closed the door with the back of her foot. She turned me toward her and said, 'Listen to me. Never gather where there are men only and never, ever raise your voice or challenge a cop in any way. They will make what happened to the gay boy look like child's play. They will leave you for dead only after they have raped you and taken away everything that makes you feel like a human being.' She shook my arm and said, 'Do you hear me?'

I bit my lip and did everything to stop the tears from flowing. I couldn't speak for fear of crying. I simply nodded. She looked at her hand on my arm as if it did not belong to her, as if she was thinking, *Whose hand is that that is hurting my poor Maddy's arm?* She let go and hugged me. She started to sob. She put her hands on my shoulders and pushed me back to arm's length. She looked at me and said, 'The school Maddy, the school and the children are all you can focus on, otherwise you will drown in the multitude of sorrows that exist on these streets of shame.'

A hard land indeed.

8

I went into the washroom and quietly wept. I didn't want Luiza to hear me for fear that she would think I cried at every misgiving that crossed my path. The sight of Inacio being beaten and urinated on was still on my mind when I heard Dona Aurora enter the house. She said, 'Luiza get a cloth and boil up some water, we have work to do. They have gotten to poor Inacio again.'

I dried my eyes and ran to the kitchen where I saw Dona Aurora guide Inacio into the kitchen and sit him on a chair. Luiza met me there at the same time. She said, 'Mother, perhaps we should take him outside, he's bleeding.'

'So what? There has been blood in this kitchen before. Now get this boy some water and give me that cloth,' Dona Aurora barked.

Luiza looked scared, she gave her mother a cloth and put a large tin can on the burner but neglected to give him a drink. I raced up to my room and brought back my canteen and filled it with water. I made my way to Inacio and tilted his chin upward and slowly poured water into his mouth just like they did with the half-dead cowboys found in the desert in the Westerns I watched with my father. One of his eyes was completely shut but the other stared up at me, the young man's eye looked dead, the expression on his face was one of complete resignation. His Adam's apple bobbed up and down as he accepted the water.

Dona Aurora used the cloth to clean the cuts of his face and arms. She whispered 'shhhsh' as she gently cleansed his body and attempted to bring back his dignity. When done, she motioned for him to stand. He did so and she unbuckled his urine-stained jeans. The young man winced and tried to stop her. Dona Aurora said, 'Silly Inacio, we must wash these pants; besides do you think you have something between your legs an old whore like me has not seen? Luiza has seen her fair share as well.' She paused. 'Perhaps you should be concerned about the *gringa*, look at her, there is a good chance she has never seen a man in his manliness before. And what a treat for her if you are her first, eh, Inacio?'

In spite of his pain and discomfort, Inacio smiled. Dona Aurora chuckled and said, 'That's the way, Inacio. Show us that your vanity, your spirit and your beautiful body is no match for those small-dicked thugs.' As she said this she pulled down his pants.

I hope Inacio was not looking at me as I am sure my eyes popped out. In spite of his beaten face and bruised ribs, a well-endowed Adonis was standing in front of me. I caught myself gawking and diverted my eyes to Dona Aurora. She winked and said, 'Too bad this fruit will only be tasted by other men?'

Luiza said, 'Momma, stop it. The poor girl is turning redder than the blood in Inacio's cuts.'

Dona Aurora laughed and said to Inacio, 'Wrap this blanket around yourself and come to my house. I do not want you here when my fool son-in-law returns.'

After they left Luiza poured most of the boiling water into a plastic wash tub and added some lime and then threw in the stained, stinking jeans. Using the broom handle, she frantically stirred the jeans in the tub. She then poured the rest of the boiling water into her table and onto the chair where Inacio had been sitting. She used soap and scrubbed both surfaces with all her might. I could hear her mumble under her breath.

I asked, 'Luiza, what are you doing?'

'Cleaning and praying.'

'Praying for what?'

'Three things,' she replied, 'That Carlos will not find out Inacio was here, that Inacio will be okay and that he does not have the AIDS and that he has not infected our house with it.' She looked at me and said, 'You should throw that canteen out.'

Her anxiety over having Inacio in the house was now starting to make sense. The misunderstanding of how AIDS was spread among the poor of Brazil was something I was not used to. I soon learned that the men of Dona Aurora believed that men who got AIDS did so by having sex with animals and the women were convinced a person with AIDs could spread it by being in the same room. The fear and loathing of homosexuals in such a macho society was compounded by the threat of the spreading of an incurable disease. This led to the murder of an average of three gay people a week in Brazil throughout the 1990s.

I asked Luiza, 'Why did the police beat that poor man, was it because he is gay or is it because he's a prostitute?'

She thought for a minute and said, 'Neither. Both.'

'I'm not sure I understand.'

She replied, 'It's complicated. Knowing those cops, they probably enjoyed every minute of the torture they doled out on that poor boy. They also did it because he is a prostitute but not because they think prostitution is wrong. Those pigs have left their mark in every whorehouse in their precinct. More than likely, knowing Inacio, he neglected to pay Maximo Pelanchhi his protection money. Pelancchi in return sent his thugs to send Inacio and all other hustlers and thieves a message. To make it clear that there is a price to pay for doing business on these streets.'

My look to her communicated incomprehension.

She said, 'Maximo Pelanchhi and his son Andres run the streets of Salvador. Every cop, politician and priest is on his payroll. The unions and the businessmen all pay homage to Senhor Pelancchi. His compound is only a few miles down the road and on any given day you will find senators, archbishops and police chiefs sipping rum and making backroom deals with the man they call the *Vagando Aranha* – the wandering spider. Are you familiar with the wandering spider?'

I shook my head.

'It is a deadly, silent killer that is at home in the jungle and the city. You never know when it will show up, but it is never too far away. Trust me when I tell you Maximo Pelanchhi comes by the moniker honestly. He is always in the shadows and always knows the goings on of these streets. Believe me, he knows you have arrived even though your arrival is trivial to him. If anything is to be done around here it has to have the approval of the spider. A missed payment, an illegal transaction or a government appointment not authorised by Pelanchhi will mean someone will incur the wrath of his venom. What happened to Inacio is nothing compared to what will happen to him if he does not smarten up and pay Pelanchhi his cut instead of spending it on heroin. The fool boy should know that the heroin comes from the Pelanchhis anyway. I believe Andres, the son of Maximo runs the drug enterprises.'

'Is Andres as bad as his father?' I asked.

Luiza said, 'In some ways, he is worse. The fat pig is a sadist whereas the father does what he does in order to protect his interests. Andres walks around this place like a pompous ass, whereas old Maximo could, as mother would put it, have you eating the corn out of his shit, he is so charming and smooth. If you are obedient and play by the rules, his rules, he will let you be, but Andres, that is another story. He goes looking for trouble. On top of that, he is a complete moron.

'I am sure Daddy Maximo must fret about what will happen to his empire in the hands of Andres. From what I hear Andres is much more inclined toward the Inacios of the world, so there is only one heir to the fortune. However, Maximo is a total health freak and will most likely outlive his son who spends most of his time smoking, gambling, drinking and eating. Those that call Maximo the wandering spider very quietly call Andres the *bugio*, a howler monkey, because he is fat and so obnoxious and you can hear him before you see him.'

Luiza laughed at this and stopped suddenly. 'However,' she said, 'they are careful to whisper the nickname. One of the Pelanchhi henchmen got drunk and called Andres howler monkey. He ended up on the steps of the church where his daughter was to be married that afternoon, dead, naked and with his cock in his mouth. They found a banana in each of his hands.'

I thought about this for a moment and began to wonder if I could survive this place. I asked Luiza, 'So in order to get the school built, will we have to deal with Maximo Pelanchhi?'

'Will we have to?' she asked. 'We already have been, but that is at the uppity levels. Gretchen is the only one who talks to him. We are too far down the food chain to deal with the Pelanchhis.'

'I see,' I said. 'Well, it is only eleven in the morning and I think I have received more education since arriving at your doorstep than I did in all my university courses, along with the crash course on Brazil through

Saints for Sanctuary and those angels from hell, Senhora Brito and Senhora Vaz.'

Luiza said, 'You have so much more to learn. But no more of this awful talk. Let me show you some good Bahian cooking and then we will go on a visit to the homes of the women who want to see their children become educated. When you see the kids your worries will disappear.'

Luiza walked to the stove and lifted the lid from one of the pots. A delicious aroma escaped and it lured me to the pot. Luiza was smiling as she took a spoon, scooped up some of the food and offered it to me. I blew and then had a taste. It was delicious. Luiza smiled proudly, evidently pleased with the expression on my face. I said, 'This tastes fantastic. What is it called?'

Luiza replied, 'It is called *feijoada*, it is a simple mixture of beans, some sausage and my special spices.'

'My God, it tastes great!' I said.

'It is a good thing you like it,' Luiza said, 'because you will be having variations of it just about every day. It is what we eat. It is served either over or on the side of rice.'

I said, 'You'll have to show me how to make it, including the secret spices. I know it would be a hit in Canada.'

Luiza beamed. 'Perhaps, but it will be near the end of your trip. I do not want my secrets getting out.' We both laughed. Luiza said, 'Because there is no fridge and usually not enough money for meat, we usually have a vegetarian version, but if the veggies are good it can be even tastier.

'Oh, and one more thing, Dona Aurora thinks she can make a better dish than me. She can't, but I play along and tell her nobody makes better *feijoada* than the Dona Aurora of Dona Aurora.'

'I'll play along.'

I surprised myself by how easy I was able to lap up my bowl of *feijoada* after witnessing the traumatic beating just an hour earlier. I believe I had made a subconscious decision to go with the ebb and flow of Dona Aurora and roll as best I could with the community's ups and downs.

After we ate, Luiza took me around the neighbourhood and introduced me to the women whose children would be candidates for the school. As we made our way further from Luiza's house I began to realize that Luiza's home was one of, if not *the*, nicest pieces of property in the community. It became evident that the most impoverished of the poverty stricken lived on the outskirts of Dona Aurora. I saw homes that were barely more than the discarded boxes my family threw away on Christmas morning. I saw children dressed in rags, and malnourished mothers looking desperate as they tried to breastfeed their colic and weak babies. Pre-natal care, vaccinations and accessible nutritious diets were not part and parcel of the norms for these women. I had learned through Saints for Sanctuary that the infant mortality rate for Brazil was fifty per thousand; in Canada it was seven.

Gretchen told me the Brazilian figures were more than likely low due to the fact that many indigenous infant deaths were never recorded and that many of the women in places like Dona Aurora were also unaccounted for. She did, however, tell me the government was investing in the healthcare infrastructure to improve the likelihood of a child surviving its first year. She believed that by the end of 1990s the number would be cut, at least, in half.

As we went from home to home, we invited the women to meet us with their children at the local beach: Itapau beach. Saints for Sanctuary would be providing hot dogs and milk for the kids, and the women would be making banners and signing petitions to get the school built. I believe most of the mothers were more enticed by the prospect of getting food into their children's bellies than becoming political activists. Nevertheless, these women who were born into hardship and gave birth into hardship were full of resolve and spirit. They were determined to make sure the lives of their children were better than their own, and though many struggled with the concept that education was a key in escaping poverty, they were willing to listen to optimistic, ideal and naive *gringas* such as me, because they refused not to believe in hope.

It was clear that Luiza had the respect of the other women. They joked with her and called her an angel of Yemaya. They explained to me Yemaya was the Candomblé goddess of the ocean and the protector of women and children. At every house, the children gravitated to Luiza and the mother listened intently as she described what needed to be done in order for the school to become a reality. She said most of the pieces of the puzzle were in place. The Canadian embassy had come through with funds, the Saints for Sanctuary organization had made a large donation and the Brazilian Ministry of Education had made funds available. The only thing that needed to be done was to convince the local politicians that municipal land in the centre of Dona Aurora could be used and that there were enough children for a school to be operated there.

The mention of local politicians led to a series of guffaws and rolled eyes in just about every home we entered. I garnered from the conversations we had there was little confidence in the corrupt local government to warrant much hope of the school being built unless there was money for a bribe. From what I witnessed earlier in the day with the beating of Inacio, it was hard to argue with their well-earned cynicism. If Luiza was correct in her assessment of things (and I had every reason to believe she was), inevitably the building of the school would be contingent on the blessing of the *Vagando Aranha*: Maximo Pelanchhi.

We returned to Luiza's and I went up to the roof to reorganize my room after the night of the great flood. One thing I was discovering about living in poverty was that when you have few belongings, there is little to worry about. It took me less than five minutes to reorganize everything. I scooted over to Dona Aurora's to check in on Inacio and grab my blanket.

Inacio was gone. Dona Aurora said, 'The boy has a few cracked ribs, bad bruises on his face and a couple of loose teeth. He will survive as long as he remembers who he is and where he lives. I suppose Luiza filled you in on the street politics of Dona Aurora and Maximo?'

I nodded.

She said, 'Maximo, is what the kids call 'old school'. He is a horrible man but a horror that old cranks like me can live with, for we are used to it and the way he keeps order. I know you will find this hard to believe, but there is less chaos and violence in these parts because of Maximo Pelanchhi and his iron fist than if he was never here. The day he loses control will be the day blood will truly flow in this godforsaken ghetto.

'There is something else I want to tell you but I can't remember. Ah, must have been a lie.'

I said, 'With all due respect, Dona Aurora, after what I saw them do to that young man I find your analysis hard to believe; having said that, you know these streets better than anyone so I'll take your word for it.'

She smiled and nodded.

I paused and asked, 'Dona Aurora, how come you didn't seem afraid of contracting AIDS when poor Luiza seemed petrified?'

She thought for a moment. 'Luiza is more concerned about our Fabricio and his health than herself, and knowing my daughter, more concerned about her asshole husband. Me, well, you should know, I was a prostitute in my younger days. I am sure that even before I was married, I had caught every sex disease known to man. If not before marriage, certainly after as my fiend of a husband was a scapegrace and thought himself a Don Juan of every whorehouse in Bahia.' She crossed herself when she referred to her husband. Then she smiled. 'But he did have a certain charm and he was good to Luiza, even though we were uncertain if she was even his. I swear she must have been the offspring of some fallen saint I fucked because she has compassion – something that neither me nor my husband possessed.'

I said, 'Ha! I saw how you treated young Inacio; it's clear where Luiza gets her kindness from.'

She looked at me sternly, her dark eyes seemed to get darker. 'Believe me, my child, the compassion I know has come from my daughter. She taught the mother. Before Luiza came along, I was nothing but a whore whose only interest was to become a madam so I could set up my own shop. I was well on my way too. I am certain Maximo Pelanchhi would have approved as he knows talent when he sees it.

'I remember one night, when I was so much younger and Maximo would have still been a boy – at a casino his uncle, Americo Pelanchhi, commented on my business acumen and said I would be a great proprietor of a men's social club when my extreme beauty faded ever so slightly.' She smiled.

I thought, *this place is becoming more bizarre with every passing hour.* I could not believe I was listening to a woman fondly reminisce about the night a ruthless gangster complimented her by suggesting she would be an excellent host for whoremongers after her days of whoring were over.

Dona Aurora continued, 'Then I got pregnant and for some reason I knew I wanted to keep the child, although an abortion would have made more sense. It changed everything. I started to see the young girls in the business differently. They no longer looked like a commodity. I questioned the role of the pimps and decided to get out of the business. So I married the man who thought there was a chance he was the father. He had been a regular at the brothel for years and was only too glad to leave his hag of a wife for me after she had lost her inheritance when her father, a retired general, decided to run off to Cuba and work for President Fulgencio Batista in 1957.

'The general took the family fortune and word has it he invested it in the casinos owned by American gangsters – Jews and Italians, a prosperous group I am sure – along with a tobacco plantation. Then came Castro and the revolution and everything was lost. The old general ended up in the USA working as a spy. Last I heard he was strangled in his sleep while helping the Americans and Portuguese combat communist insurgents in Angola or maybe Mozambique in the early sixties. Wouldn't be surprised to find out it was his bitch daughter who did it, she would have followed him to the ends of the earth to exact her revenge.'

I said, 'What a story. So Luiza changed things for you?'

Dona Aurora paused for a moment. It seemed that she was trying to regain her stream of thought. She said, 'Yes, yes, she did. Even as a child she was full of kindness. She would share the very little that she had. She never complained and always had a smile on her face. At first I thought she was retarded, but when it came to figuring out numbers, even words, she was quicker than kids twice her age. There was an old priest who took an interest in her, said she was a special kid, a gifted child.

'Oh, that was what I was meaning to tell you; that young, weird priest was here to see you. He stuck around quite some time helping me with Inacio. I think he might have the hots for the boy. He looks the type.'

'Do you mean Lievan?' I asked.

She said, 'Yes. Yes that is it. Father Lievan, a young European fellow. He is a strange one. I can't figure out what his angle is. Not sure if he likes the boys or the girls or maybe both.'

I noticed a small quiver in my voice when I said, 'He is a priest, Dona Aurora. Perhaps his interests are not carnal in nature.'

Dona Aurora replied, 'Ha! Everyone is carnal in nature!' You know, many people around here, including that sourpuss Gretchen, give priests a bad name when most of them are good men who are trying to do what is right by God, even if they are off their rocker with some of their ideas. Having said that, there are the few who hide behind their frocks and crucifixes and take advantage of the most innocent and vulnerable. Believe me, I saw it when I was working the streets and the bordellos.

'There is something not right with this Father Lievan; he doesn't give me the creeps the way his boss, the Archbishop Matos does. But there is something phony about him, I know a salt-of-the-earth priest when I see one and that guy is not one. Anyway he said he might try to get to the rally this evening down at the beach, but if he couldn't, he wanted me to say hello to you from him. Considered it said, now my dear it is time for my nap. Walk back with me to Luiza's backyard and my chair.'

I walked her to her chair and went into the house to find Luiza fluffing the rice. She smiled and said, 'You look flushed, Maddy. Don't tell me you have fallen for a despicable Brazilian man already. They are nothing but trouble.' She winked at me and said, 'Trouble that can be lots of fun.'

I conjured a smile and said, 'No worries, at least not yet Luiza. I think I am just flush with anticipation of more of your delicious *feijoada*.'

This compliment brought about an even bigger smile. I excused myself and went to my penthouse suite to make myself presentable for dinner and the rally at the beach.

Carlos and Fabricio grabbed their dinners first. There seemed to be little consideration regarding the amount of food left over for Luiza and myself. There was no mention of the beating of Inacio. Carlos bragged to his son about how much money he had won the night before at the casino. Luiza asked for some and he begrudgingly gave her a few reals, saying he would save the rest for when they really needed it. Everyone at the table knew this was a fallacy. I left the table hungry and grumpy.

9

It would not be until the next visit that I would realize what a beautiful spot Itapau Beach was. I was too consumed with the thought that Lievan might actually show up for me to pay much attention to anything else.

I am ashamed and embarrassed to admit I was not as focused on the cause as I should have been. I am not suggesting that my first rally with the women of Dona Aurora was not a success. It was, but I also know that I was distracted by the thought of Lievan being there. I could not prevent myself from scanning the beach, looking for him while we were setting up for the rally. Gretchen was there before I arrived and had some teenage boys mount a banner on the sand near the red-and-white-striped lighthouse, which was a landmark and natural gathering place along the beach.

As I said, I did not notice the true beauty of the beach until I returned by myself a few days later. Suffice it to say it was an oasis from the poverty that Dona Aurora swam in. The half hour walk from Luiza's house was transformational. I would go through the worst of the ghetto to get to the beach.

Although I found peace at the beach, it was also a place full of life and energy during the day and the night. The exception was the early morning; the time I most preferred to venture to my new-found haven. In the morning there was myself, the surf and the fishermen who quietly prepared their colourful boats for a day of mining the ocean well beyond the breakers.

In particular, I used to love to watch an old man prepare his boat. He had an ancient *Saviero* – a vessel made in Bahia and used for cargo and fishing throughout Brazil. It was about seventeen feet long with a high bow and low stern. It was green with a bold purple stripe running horizontal along the hull. It had a purple canopy. Every morning the man went through a ritual. He would load the boat with his nets and other fishing paraphernalia and then circle the vessel three times and then kneel by the stern. He would then say the following prayer to Yemanja, the Candomble Orixa (saint) of the sea:

Yemanja you are purple and green
You are every colour in between
You are an endless wave on the sea
You are everything to me

After a few visits, I asked the old man why he and he alone was the only person that performed the ritual.

He said, 'Because I invented it. The sea has yet to claim me or my beautiful Rain.' He laughed and said, 'I am too scared to stop something I started forty years ago when I was drunk and out of my mind for the unrequited love of a woman. A girl I nicknamed Baby Rain, because every time I thought of her tears flowed from my eyes like those of a babe crying for its momma. On that day of drunkenness and debauchery, I sold my soul to Yemanja. The deal was she would keep me safe and prosperous and I would commit myself to no other but her and the sea.' Faded on the purple paint I noticed the boat had a name, *Bebe Chuva*, which meant Baby Rain. The name was written by coarse hand onto the stern of the purple and green beauty.

When I made it to the beach before the boats left I would always make sure I quietly recited the prayer of adoration with my romantic fisherman friend. He, too, would look for me and after finishing his ritual he would come to me and whisper, 'If I had met you forty years ago, I would not have made the deal with my beloved Yemanja.' He would kiss my hand in the most chivalrous way and then place a cowrie shell in my palm. Those shells have remained with me since. They hearken memories of peace, memories of soft sand, coconut trees, ocean waves and blue, blue skies that always soothed a suffering soul, memories of my own Bebe Chuva.

However, my first visit to the beach was very different. Making my way to Gretchen at the lighthouse meant wading through herds of soccer players ranging from grade schoolers to old men, and schools of Capoeira circles who were practicing the ancient African martial art form that made its way from the Portuguese outpost in West Africa to Brazil via slave ships. To me, this beautifully violent dance was the Southern hemisphere's physical embodiment of the Negro spirituals that rose from the plantations of Mississippi and Alabama. Its actions spoke of freedom and endurance in the face of oppression. Because the smells and the images of Bahia are so strong, I often forget about the sounds. Yet forever part of my auditory memory will be the *berimbau* – a one-stringed, bowed instrument made from a stick, wire and a gourd – played by the musicians who provided the soundtrack for the Capoeria dancers, along with the *pandeiro*, the tambourine-like instrument that provided the rhythm.

As Luiza and I made our way to Gretchen, I scanned the crowd looking for Lievan. I wondered if he would be dressed as a man or as a priest. He was nowhere to be found.

Upon spotting us Gretchen smiled and waved. Ali was entertaining a bunch of kids who had arrived early with their mothers; he did not seem to notice us as he was so busy being a walking, talking jungle-gym. Gretchen was wearing a grey business suit and a white starched shirt but did not seem to feel uncomfortable among the ready-for-the-beach attired. Her watchful eyes were making sure the charcoal-fuelled barbeques were set up and started and that the banners were well-placed.

She was holding a massive bullhorn; I would have been surprised if she would have been able to lift it to her mouth. When we got to her she said, 'Hello ladies. I trust your first night at Luiza's was a good one Maddy?' While speaking she handed me the bullhorn. I wasn't sure if I could lift it to my mouth. Luiza and I both laughed and I explained to her the great flood and the consequences. She did not see much humour in the situation. Neither Luiza nor I mentioned the beating of poor Inacio.

I asked Gretchen, 'What's the bullhorn for?'

She replied, 'Why, for you, of course, when you address the crowd. They will need to hear every word.'

I said, 'Oh, I can get lots of volume out of this voice. I won't need it, besides I would feel silly using one.'

Gretchen smiled and said, 'Perhaps you have a loud voice, but we want to make sure that everyone hears you, not just the women who show up. That is why we picked such a public place. We want to preach to more than just the converted. You will be surprised how many of these people not affiliated with our movement will sign the petition after you speak, Maddy.'

From behind a voice said, 'Is that before or after you give them a free hotdog Gretchen?'

Gretchen turned and said, 'Lievan, my dear, shouldn't you be saying your vespers or something? Well, I admit the food might act as a bit of temptation, but at least we are not damning people to hell if they don't do what we want them to. We are also giving out free condoms. Would you like to help distribute them?'

Lievan laughed and said, 'Oh Gretchen, you are something. In good conscience I cannot help distribute the rubbers as my word is my word and as long as I remain in the priesthood I must obey Rome. Having said that, the rational, twentieth-century part of my brain applauds your efforts.' He smiled at me and nodded, he then said, 'There are days I wish the Holy Father himself came here, or to Manila or Kinshasha and saw the impact of teen pregnancy and sexually transmitted diseases, including AIDS, on the people of developing nations. Perhaps he would rethink the ban of contraceptives, particularly condoms.'

Gretchen replied, 'Perhaps, or perhaps he would see that continuing the ban would help propagate poverty thus propagate ignorance thus keep himself employable and relevant.'

'Ouch,' I said. 'As a somewhat lapsed Catholic I must say that I find your comment is a little on the harsh side.'

Luiza piped in, 'Gretchen, there are many priests who do their best to do the best they can. For example, when I was very young child a priest, Father Griffin saw potential in me; he even suggested I was gifted. If it wasn't for Father Griffin I would never have learned how to read. He taught me that the way to free oneself from poverty was through knowledge. Now, granted, he did leave the priesthood, but even so there was him and many like him who have helped. Remember Gretchen, it was Father

Griffin who turned me on to Paolo Freire and his masterpiece "The Pedagogy of the Oppressed".'

Lievan chuckled and said, 'Well, it is nice to see that chivalry is not completely dead and that these two damsels have come to my rescue.'

Luiza said, 'Father Van den Broeck, you are not entirely off the hook. More work and less pontificating by many of your colleagues would be greatly appreciated. Now, why don't you make yourself useful and help poor old Ali set up those tables.'

Lievan saluted and said, 'Yes ma'am.' Lievan made his way to Ali and the van where the tables were in need of being set up. If not for his blond hair he would have fit in with the beach bums – he was wearing frayed khaki shorts and a yellow T-shirt and, I almost hate to say it, Jesus sandals.

I looked at Luiza and said, 'Paulo Freire? Really? You are full of surprises Ms. Academe!'

Gretchen laughed and said, 'Never underestimate our Luiza and her IQ. I swear it is off the charts. If given the chance she could run this town better than the collective assholes that do it now. But seriously, why is Matos's right-hand man here? I know he is usually out there spying on us, but he does not make a habit of coming right out and introducing himself.'

'Really Gretchen,' said Luiza, 'he is not spying. He has come to show support for our ideas. And I do not think he is Archbishop Matos's right-hand man. I think the Archbishop respects his intelligence and uses Father Van den Broeck's ease with people to do his bidding, but mostly he keeps him close to keep an eye on him and control his, in the Archbishop's estimation, radical ideas.'

I asked, 'Who is this Archbishop Matos?'

'About the biggest asshole you will ever meet,' said Gretchen.

Luiza shrugged and said, 'I concur.'

Gretchen said, 'Showtime. Show us what you got, Maddy.'

While we had been speaking, a crowd of women – many of whom I recognized from our visits earlier in the day – had congregated in front of us. They stood, milling about, chatting as their children played a variety of games on the beach, some opting for soccer while others engaged in a high-energy game of tag. I smiled at them and tried to make eye contact but most continued to chat. I thought about putting my hand up like my grade teachers did in order to get silence, but thought that I might insult people. I raised the bullhorn and spoke into it. 'Hello.'

Gretchen came forward and said, 'You need to pull the trigger in order to amplify the sound.'

'Oh.' I looked down to see that the contraption did have a trigger. I pulled and a terrible squelch noise came out. This got people's attention, momentarily at least. Gretchen came forward again and turned the volume down halfway. I pulled the trigger and said, 'Hello, welcome.' I paused. There was no reaction from the group gathered just feet in front of me. I looked at Gretchen and said, 'Is this thing working?' She nodded. I tried again. 'Hello folks and welcome to our Saints for Sanctuary rally. We are here to discuss the possibility of getting a school built for the wonderful children of this community.'

Nothing. The children kept playing and the women kept yammering amongst themselves.

'Hi,' I said, 'could I please have your attention?' I felt invisible. It seemed like Lievan was the only person in the crowd acknowledging my existence.

Luiza came up to me and said, 'May I have a go?' I shrugged and handed her the bullhorn.

She turned it up a little and then screamed, 'Good evening ladies, it is time to quit being gossipmongers and give your attention to this lovely lady in the front. She has come all the way from Canada and is here to help us get what all children in her country are entitled to – a free education with no strings attached. Now sisters I know you have heard it all before...'

At this moment one of the women had the audacity to start talking to the woman standing next to her.

Luiza said, 'Excuse me, am I bothering you, Dona Rozilda? I did not mean to interrupt you. Please, why don't you come up here and share with us what important information you were sharing with Dona Flora. I am certain it must be of great significance if it trumps the future of our children.'

I noticed Flora was inching herself away from poor Rozilda who had inadvertently made herself a scapegoat for all the women who were chattering while I was speaking. Luiza held out the bullhorn toward Rozilda. Rozilda smiled sheepishly and shook her head. Luiza waited until the women were silent and attentive. Luiza said, 'Okay ladies, please welcome a new friend, but fast becoming a good friend of mine, Dona Madeline Saunders.'

There was a smattering of applause from the chastised crowd as Luiza handed the bullhorn back to me. It was the first time anyone had called me Dona in Brazil. I noticed Luiza was keeping an eye on the crowd as I started to speak.

I said, 'Thank you for the warm and lovely introduction Luiza. Though it has only been a short time, I, too, feel as though I have already made a very good friend.' I paused, then said, 'I also realize it will be in my best interest to pay attention to every word you say.'

This got a laugh out of the crowd and broke the ice. From that moment on, I had them. I spoke with passion, explaining the benefits of a school. I provided them with a plan of action and spoke of fraternal solidarity. I convinced them of the possibility of change and invited them to become active participants in determining their own fate and the fate of their children.

Things were going swimmingly; I even attracted a sizable amount of the sun worshippers and soccer players. I could tell they were feeding off my words, my pacing and my gestures. In fact, they seemed to be overtaken by some sort of rapture, laughing and clapping at my pontificating. I knew I was a good public speaker, but I didn't realize how good. I was guessing I had never found my audience. Lievan was in hysterics, even Gretchen was smiling and Luiza was trying to look stern but had tears of what I assumed joy rolling down her cheeks. I had them, all of them, eating out of my hand.

I finished by saying. 'Thank you, thank you for being such wonderful listeners and for greeting my words with such a positive response. In Canada we would say you were A-OK' and for the final time I held up, what I thought was the universal symbol for A-OK – the thumb and the index finger making a circle with the other three fingers fanning out. This brought the greatest crescendo of laughter and backslapping. I smiled, shrugged and returned the bullhorn to Gretchen.

While Gretchen made an announcement about the petition and the hotdogs, Ali approached me and put one of his massive arms around my shoulder. He explained to me that the A-OK sign I had used from the beginning of my speech meant something completely different in Brazil. It meant asshole. I said, 'Oh dear God. I make the sign all the time. I hope

I didn't ....' then it dawned on me why the crowd was laughing and were so attentive to my presentation; I was inadvertently calling them assholes the entire time.

I was so embarrassed I wanted to turn and run, but before I could Lievan had his arm around me and said, 'Well done, Maddy I have seen many politicos, priests and idealists give speeches on this not-so-hallowed ground, but that was definitely a topper.' He said, 'Oh, don't even think about crying. It was great. You have endeared yourself to a bunch of women who are very skeptical to anything to do with political and social action. Trust me, you just did your cause a great service.' He hugged me.

I inhaled him. He smelt like comfort. I giggled and said, 'Now something just clicked.'

He said, 'What?'

I smiled at him and said, 'These snarky old women who were hired to teach me Portuguese would surprise me every once in a while by saying my pronunciation was *perfeito* and give what I thought was the A-OK sign to me. Come to think of it, it was the only time the hags ever smiled.' I laughed and said, 'Those bitches.'

Lievan laughed loudly and said, 'Oh Maddy, you are something.'

I looked into his eyes. The blueness was alive and they drew me in. I brushed my hair out of my face and said, 'Thank you, Lievan, and thank you for coming this evening. It is nice to have your support; it means a lot.'

He said, 'You're welcome, Maddy.' He brushed the few remaining strands of hair from my face and turned and walked to the hot dog table.

As he walked away a soccer ball crossed his path. He chased it down with the ease of a natural athlete, then he brought it from foot to knee to head and back down to the other foot, juggling the ball before passing it back to the teens playing soccer. They beckoned him to join them and he couldn't resist. His quickness and agility was on par with the Brazilians who some would say were born with their cleats on. Watching him and watching them play soccer as the sun set was akin to watching a beautiful ballet accompanied by the surf, the *berimbau*, the *pandeiro*, and the laughter of children.

I did not hear Gretchen come up behind and jumped a little when she said, 'Too bad the good ones are married, gay or priests, or gay priests.'

I did not turn to face her. I muttered 'whatever' and went to greet the women who were already calling me A-OK Maddy, a moniker that would stick for the rest of my stay in Dona Aurora.

***

The rest of the rally went really well. Luiza and Gretchen were thrilled with the response we got from the crowd. Luiza told me she had never seen so many names on a petition. Gretchen had explained she would be using the data to show business leaders and local politicians that the fully funded program was supported by the locals. After the crowd dissipated and Gretchen and Ali had packed up the van, Luiza and I were invited by Lievan to join a group of *Capoeria* dancers who had lit a fire on the beach. We obliged and were treated to an incredible exhibition of dancing. Bodies were leaping millimetres from each other as the music drove the blue flames into the darkness of the night.

I sat by Lievan. Every once in a while our bare knees touched. I was entranced by the dancers and exhilarated by the heat of the priest's skin.

10

By looking at the journal I kept from my first month in Dona Aurora it would seem like the month was incredibly eventful, and it was. However, the incredible soon became the norm and I settled into a routine of sorts. Nevertheless, there are some things I would like to share.

My Saints for Sanctuary predecessor, an effective young woman from Emo, Ontario, had started a program called Comics for Kids, in which she distributed comic book versions of abridged children's classics to families. When I heard of the program I thought it was a great idea until I saw how the graphic novels were being used.

In one home *Heidi* was neatly cut and folded and used as rolling papers, in another home *Gulliver's Travels* was used as fire starters for an ancient Dutch oven. However, Johanna Spyri and Jonathan Swift got off easy compared to Canada's very own Lucy Maud Montgomery, as *Anne of Green Gables* was economically being used to wipe the ass of a three-year-old.

I had an epiphany and realized that my stupid gringa, naive, do-gooder, first-world, idiot self was part of an organization that was making the same mistakes that the missionaries had made – we were in many ways a top-down organization.

I recalled on one of my return visits from the beach, in one of the poorest streets in Dona Aurora, I came across an evangelist giving out

Bibles to families who looked malnourished and beleaguered. He wore pressed khaki shorts, a garish plaid shirt, knee-high grey socks and an Aussie slouch hat complete with corks. He gave the mother a cheaply bound bible and promised the kids a 'Jesus Rocks My World' bookmarker if they prayed with him. The kids, looking at the shiny bookmarkers of a cool-looking Jesus playing guitar a la Pete Townsend, obliged. I watched as he laid his pink, fleshy hands on the heads of the little boy and girl and prayed that they would come to Jesus. Before I knew what I was doing I approached the postulator and asked, 'May I see your Bible?'

He smiled and handed me a copy of what was called an 'Evidence Bible.' He said, '*Maranatha* sister.'

I looked at the Bible and smelt it and said, 'Looks tasty.'

His smile disappeared and he walked away crestfallen until he reached the next house where he perked up when he saw there were at least four little ones to lay his hands upon.

I thought the fucker could have at least brought snacks for the kids, and then caught myself as I realized I was beginning to sound like the rather bitter and cynical Gretchen. I almost wanted to run after the man and apologize, but I didn't as I thought I would just get angry at his inane cause all over again. That was a week or so before I saw Prince Edward Island's most famous icon being used as an ass wipe. I realized organizations such as the one I volunteered for needed to take more time to figure out what the people wanted, because what they wanted was more than likely what they needed.

The other disclosure I need to make is that my infatuation for Lievan was becoming stronger. I made a point of traveling into downtown Salvador da Bahia to hear him deliver a homily. He was preaching at the Basilica Cathedral, a seventeenth-century church that was built by slaves and financed by the sugar barons of the region. The church was a testament to Catholic European dominance of the area. A winged Christ hovered in the middle of a massive, eighteen-columned altar that was covered in gold. Although the altar and the sculpture of Christ were very European in design I could not help but notice that the enslaved craftsmen had added fishtails into the motif. I thought of my old fisherman friend and his pact with Yemanja.

Lievan's homily was part of a special mass that was to commemorate the death of Pedro Fernandes Sardinha, Bahia's first Archbishop. Archbishop Sardinha's ship was cast ashore by a violent storm well before it entered the Atlantic. The good Archbishop and his crew were massacred by the local inhabitants.

The organ played and the congregation rose as the priestly procession walked in. The altar boys came first with their incense. They were followed by Lievan who wore a cream-coloured vestment with a light blue stole that bore intricate gold designs of various fauna that tapered into an organic-looking cross. I could not help but notice that the blue and the gold were almost an exact match to Lievan's eyes and hair. I was sitting at the aisle end of the pew and noticed Lievan notice me as he walked by. He smiled a serene smile. Even though I was mesmerized with Lievan I could not help but notice the man who followed him.

Archbishop Matos was very large, perhaps not Ali large but at least six foot five. His white miter made him look like a giant. He was not obese by any means, but the man looked very fleshy. His eyes were those of a bloodhound; looking at them made me feel like I wanted to take a nap. He had bushy eyebrows, a hooked nose that would rival the dignity or malevolence of Cosimo de Medici and an unwavering mouth firmly set as a thin line just above what was once a square jaw but was now rounded by the extra flesh that hung ever so slightly from the jowls. As the Archbishop walked past I shuddered in spite of the soft peach-coloured chasuble that cloaked his pure white alb. I imagined that the six-foot crozier would be used as more of a weapon to keep his flock from straying than a staff to ensure they did not get lost. The man certainly had a presence.

Even though he did not look at me or show any signs of pomposity or arrogance there was something about him, something untenable that made me believe right there and then that Gretchen and Luiza were right: The Archbishop was an asshole of the highest degree. I noticed that as he continued toward the altar the congregation averted their eyes from him.

The Archbishop's presence didn't seem to intimidate Lievan. His homily focused on the superciliousness of the founding church and how he hoped that modern Catholics would be less likely to perceive themselves as being above another culture but would instead see themselves as being immersed in a culture. He reflected that immersion in a culture was the only way to truly transform it. His arguments were convincing in their logic and passion. He used humour and gave anecdotes and cultural reference points that the average parishioner could relate to. Although the altar from where he preached was perched so high above the pews that he did not come across as aloof; instead his words and thoughts closed the distance between the people on the terra firma and the celebrant in his lofty roost.

The congregation laughed and nodded during his fifteen-minute reflection. The only person who remained stoic was the Archbishop. His poker face indicated neither approval nor censure for the words of the young priest. I would have a hard time being convinced that Archbishop Matos would share Lievan's philosophy toward what it meant to be a modern Catholic and I got the sense that the Archbishop would pine for the days when men like his first predecessor, Archbishop Sardhina, were able to rule with an iron fist and would be kowtowed to by everyone from the slaves to the sugar barons. Yes, I am sure he would have rather had it that way, in spite of the threat from hostile heathens lurking on the outskirts of the civilized world.

When the recessional hymn was sung and the service ended, Lievan joined the recession and greeted the faithful as they exited through the massive doors. I lingered until the crowd was gone and made my way to him. He welcomed me with a hug and said, 'Maddy, thank you so much for coming. I am honoured you would risk the wrath of Gretchen to hear me ramble on about the relevance, or perhaps the irrelevance of Brazilian Catholicism.'

I said, 'What the hey. Gretchen is my boss six days a week but Sundays are mine and I haven't been to church for a long, long time – my parents will be happy when my next letter includes the fact I went to Mass. They will also be reading about how the homily was one of the most relevant and engaging I've ever heard. You are a great speaker, Lievan.'

'Thanks Maddy, that means a lot from a person such as you.'

I gave him a quizzical look.

He said, 'You are educated, obviously intelligent and very aware of the world you live in. Most people of your ilk would find little relevance for the church and for the power of Christ's love. It is obvious to me that you are a spiritual person who is willing to allow for the possibility of a power greater than ourselves. Your mouth speaks for the oppressed Maddy, and I am sure you will not rest until there is Shalom.'

I stood and stared at him. I wanted to push him into the vestibule and take him then and there right under a statue of the Holy Mother. I breathed deeply and said, 'Wow, thank you. That is perhaps the most beautiful thing anyone has ever said to me.'

My carnal thoughts dissipated immediately when I heard a voice from the shadows of the vestibule say, 'Excuse me, Lievan, do you know where I put my glasses? I seem to have misplaced them.'

'I have them in my coat pocket, Your Grace.'

The Archbishop came out of the shadows and said, 'Please forgive, I did not know you were conversing with someone. My apologies.' His voice was deep and rich. He bowed slightly and humbly toward me and began a slow retreat.

Lievan said, 'Archbishop, you are never an intrusion. This is my friend Maddy, the young Canadian I was telling you about.'

The Archbishop looked at me and smiled and then looked at Lievan quizzically. Lievan said, 'You know the young woman who works for Saints for Sanctuary.' I looked to see if the Archbishop's face would reveal anything about his thoughts toward Saints for Sanctuary. It remained blank. Lievan continued, 'Remember? The woman who inadvertently offended an entire crowd but at the same time had them in hysterics. The A-OK woman?' I looked at Lievan and gave him a gentle swat on the shoulder.

The Archbishop revealed a small smile and said, 'Ah yes, now I recall the rather amusing anecdote.' He stepped forward and offered his hand.

I took it and said, 'Your Grace.' His hand was massive. I thought it would be soft but there was a hardness to it. It reminded me of my father's hand; a hand that loved work and relished challenges.

The Archbishop said, 'I am impressed by your formality my dear, but I prefer to be called Father Thiago. I am not sure if Lievan has invited you to join us for lunch, but if he hasn't I would like to extend an invitation. I believe we are to be treated to *muqueca* this afternoon. Our cook is famous for her shrimp *muqueca*.'

Before either of us could respond, the Archbishop said, 'Come.' He walked back into the church with Lievan and me in tow.

After crossing ourselves, we entered a door behind the altar and Lievan turned to me and said, 'Please wait here, Maddy. Father Thiago and I will change and join you shortly.'

The men left and I sat on a plush velvet chair in the small hallway. I thought no matter where in the world you were there are certain smells that encompass all Catholic churches. I could smell the communion wine and the lingering aroma of incense.

The men returned from their changing room. I was somewhat shocked to see Lievan in black slacks and a black shirt with the traditional white collar. I hoped he could not read the disappointment on my face. The Archbishop wore a purple shirt with his white collar and black slacks.

We left the back door of the cathedral and walked down a small alley and entered the Pelourinho, the old city centre, so called because it was where the original pillory was located to tie up newly arrived slaves. The Archbishop walked briskly across the main square to the Palácio Arquiepiscopal, the traditional palatial home of Bahia's reigning Archbishop. We entered through a small, almost hidden door located on the side of the building. We walked into a beautiful open courtyard flanked by three stories on each side and the back of the façade on the fourth. The courtyard smelled wonderful. Papaya and mango trees were interspersed among flower beds that housed a multitude of exotic-looking and fragrant flowers. I recognized a few azaleas but the rest were foreign to me. Grapes were growing on their vines, entwined around intricate lattice work made from freshly cut cedar, a smell that reminded me of the mills that dotted the Fraser River back home. About a quarter of the courtyard was still under construction. An old table saw was in the corner and lumber was neatly piled beside it.

It was clear that more flower beds were being manufactured and that other projects were underway involving the left-over cedar. I breathed in and smiled.

Father Thiago said, 'Aromatic, no?'

I replied, 'Very much so. The scent from the flowers is incredible, and the cedar, it reminds me of home.'

Father Thiago said, 'It should, the lumber was imported directly from British Columbia. A small indulgence I permitted myself to have on this project.'

Lievan said, 'The frugal Father Thiago has saved much money by building this Eden with his own hands. He, however, could not resist the temptation for Canadian cedar.'

I said, 'Well, at least he didn't eat the apple, right?'

Both men looked at me. I realized I had perhaps been too forward with the Archbishop but was surprised to see that Lievan did not even crack a smile. Lievan said, 'Father Thiago has undertaken the reconstruction of the entire palace. He has dedicated a portion of his time to not only supervise but to work alongside the craftsmen.'

'Please Lievan,' said Father Thiago, 'you make it sound like such an onerous chore. Madeline, I come from a family of carpenters and builders. It is in my blood. I feel as comfortable, perhaps even more so with a hammer or saw in my hand, than I do with a crozier or chalice. Believe me, this work gives me more time to ponder the ways of the world than the silent meditation that others participate in. It is here where I feel closest to God and what God wants me to do for his children.'

I nodded… politely.

Lievan said, 'Would you like a tour of the palace, Maddy? We can leave Father Thiago to order our lunch.'

I said, 'That would be great.'

We left the courtyard and headed toward the first floor. When we had entered a long, dark hallway and were out of earshot, Lievan said, 'My apologies, Maddy. I did not mean for you to be put in this situation.'

I said, 'What situation? I came here under my volition, and I am very happy to do so.'

He looked at me and smiled. He said, 'I understand, but Thiago can be quite…' he was searching for words, 'forceful. Often he makes assumptions that people, especially Catholic people, will simply follow his command.'

I laughed and teased him by saying, 'Are you one of those people?'

Lievan smiled, shrugged and replied, 'I suppose I am. Priest training is similar to military training in the sense that chain of command is drilled into you.'

I thought about how desperately I wanted to have him court-martialed, thrown out of his corps and banished forever into my arms. I said, 'Between you and me, the Archbishop is not my cup of tea as far as the direction the church must take to stay relevant, but I am glad priests such as yourself have his ear. He obviously thinks highly of you and, who knows, perhaps he will gravitate toward a more progressive, modern view.'

Lievan said, 'His heart is in the right place.' Lievan put his hand on my shoulder and said, 'Thank God, and I mean that literally, that you showed up in Bahia. It is so incredible to talk to someone who understands my perspective. May I have a hug?'

I nodded. In that dark passageway, Lievan opened his arms to me. I embraced him. I pushed my body hard against his. My hug was not the kind one would give a good friend. My crotch found his upper thigh and I pressed harder against him, feeling the warmth spread through my loins as well as up into my stomach. Lievan said nothing. His body did not repeal against my advances. In fact he held me tighter. A door opened at the end of the corridor and we both jumped out of the hug.

Three young boys came bounding down the hallway. They were laughing and horse-playing. When they saw us, they came to an immediate stop. Their faces grew serious. They looked terrified. Lievan said, 'Boys, why are you here?'

When they recognized it was Lievan at the end of the hallway they gave out a collective sigh. The boys approached us and Lievan said, 'Gentlemen, why are you here today?'

A boy with a military brush cut who appeared slightly larger and older than his friends replied, 'Our mothers have gone to Aracaju to work for the weekend so his Grace said we could stay here.'

'I see,' said Lievan. 'Well, enjoy the rest of your day, boys, and no roughhousing, especially in the areas still under construction. Which as you know is everywhere.'

The boys walked to the door Lievan and I had entered. The smallest one, an Afro-Brazilian boy, grabbed hold of my hand and held on with what I can only describe as desperation. He looked at me and made guttural noises, and when his friends tried to pry his hands off of mine he clamped down all the harder. The oldest boy said, 'Teodoro, let go of the lady's hand and stop with the noises already.' The other boys tried to pull him away from me but this just made his grip tighter, more frantic. The guttural noises became high-octave screeches, an 'awk-awk-awk' sound akin to some exotic bird either courting or in distress.

Lievan bent down and said, 'Teodoro, hush. It is okay; you are safe here.' He gently rubbed the boy's back and made soothing sounds. The boys 'awks' diminished and his grip on my hand loosened. He looked up at me with big brown eyes that seemed to plead for me to take him with me when I left. He hugged my waist and gently sobbed into my belly. The boy with the crew cut picked up on Lievan's cue and said, 'It's okay, Teodoro, come. Let's go find your soccer ball; I think it is in the courtyard.'

Teodoro let go of my waist and allowed the two other boys to gently escort him through the door. When the door closed behind them Lievan said, 'Poor little Teodoro. He has seen too much for one so young.' He paused, gently grabbed my elbow and directed me down the hallway. He said, 'Teodoro and the other boys, their mothers are prostitutes. There must be something big happening in Aracaju, for no doubt their pimps have taken them to work the streets and brothels. Last year Teodoro saw his mother raped by three men. They beat her to within an inch of her life, and then had a go at Teodoro's twelve-year-old sister. The boy tried to fight them off and he, too, was beaten. He has never been the same.

'We offer this place as a sanctuary for the kids during the week and their mothers take them on the weekends. Teodoro latches onto young women like you all the time; the child has not said a coherent word since the incident. The other boys try to support him, protect him, speak for him. The only time he seems at all happy is kicking around the soccer ball.' Lievan smiled whimsically, 'Believe it or not he is the best player in the neighbourhood by what you North Americans would say, a country mile.'

I asked Lievan, 'Where is his sister?'

He looked at me and said, 'Aracaju.'

11

The rest of the tour of the palace seemed irrelevant. I was in a haze as Lievan pointed out the many renovations and adaptations the Archbishop had made to his home. Lievan saw the renovations as a metaphor for a redefining of the church in the heart of Bahia. He spoke of how the palace would be a refuge for kids like Teodoro.

All I could think about was a mother and her twelve-year-old daughter being whored out to sweaty, overweight men on the streets of Aracaju.

I would have to take Lievan and the Archbishop's word that the shrimp *muqueca* was delicious as I had completely lost my appetite. Lievan walked me back to the bus stop. Many parishioners politely nodded and smiled. One woman gave me a scurrilous look; it was as if she could read the guilty thoughts that had been ruminating in my head only hours earlier. I knew she knew.

Lievan waited with me at the bus stop until the old diesel showed up to take me back to the ghetto. Before I boarded he said, 'I know Teodoro's story and the incident that happened with him has upset you, Maddy. I hope you never get used to stories such as his, but this land is full of such stories.'

I nodded and said, 'I know, Lievan. I know.' We hugged a decidedly dispassionate embrace. I got on the bus and contemplated the fact that a church worth billions would babysit the sons of whores and do little to prevent the daughters of these same women from being raped and sodomized. My bus passed the spires of several churches on my way back to Luiza's.

I shuddered each time I saw one.

12

My experience at the Archbishop's palace strengthened my resolve to contribute to the betterment of Dona Aurora's poor. I realized that change could only come from the people and all I could do was support them as best I could. I spent countless hours canvassing the streets of Dona Aurora, campaigning for the school the mothers so desperately wanted for their children. The 'A-OK' girl developed a reputation for being a tireless organizer and a bullheaded worker who was relentless in her quest to accommodate the women of the slums.

I threw my heart and soul into my work mostly to serve the cause but also to try and forget about Lievan. I could not get out of my head the cold stare of the stranger as she passed me and Lievan the night he escorted me to the bus stop. In my mind, she had become God's judge and jury and she would meet me at the gates of heaven to deny me entrance for my harlotry if my earthly desires and passions overpowered and seduced the innocent servant of the Lord.

I didn't notice, but others started commenting on how much weight I was losing. Luiza and Dona Aurora told me that I would never get a Brazilian lover if I continued to shed pounds. Their lighthearted comments were reinforced by Gretchen and Ali's concern for my health. At the time I thought they were over-reacting, but when I look back at the photos I collected, I realize my figure was almost boyish and that my face was gaunt and drawn. I didn't notice because I was obsessed with my work and willing to do anything to get the school built. 'Anything' showed its face the day I met Andres 'the howler' Pelanchhi.

I heard him before I saw him. He rode a big Harley that had customized straight pipes with the baffles removed. The noise reverberated off the tin roofs of the houses on Luiza's street. He wore silver, mirrored aviator glasses and sported a Fu Manchu. His hair was permed and hung in medium-sized ringlets to his shoulders. He wore a black Sepultura T-shirt that promoted their 1987 album, Schizophrenia. The shirt stretched over a substantial beer gut and clung tightly to meaty but powerful-looking arms. He wore tight black jeans and scuffed motorcycle boots. If one was to typecast a biker for a B-movie they would have to look no further than the image Andres Pelanchhi conveyed on the dusty streets of Dona Aurora. I was surprised he didn't don one of those ridiculous World War II German army helmets and have a cigarillo clenched between his lips, strategically placed at the corner of his mouth.

The motorbike cruised by me at a snail's pace and Pelanchhi looked me up and down like I was a piece of meat. He then sped up and did a half donut fifty yards up the road. He cruised back toward me, stopping twenty yards ahead of me. He put down his kickstand, pulled out a smoke from his saddle bag, struck a match off the heel of his boot and lit it with dramatic flair. The idle of his bike was deafening. As I got within feet of the bike, he switched off the engine. Just before I passed him he said, 'You must be the Canadian they are talking about.'

I gave him a look of disdain, and though I was certain I knew who he was, I pretended to ignore him. As I walked by he said, 'I think it is admirable what you are trying to do for the kids of these streets.'

I kept walking.

He called out, 'I thought Canadians were supposed to be polite. Are you sure you are not a Yankee? I simply want to contribute to your cause.'

I stopped and turned around. I looked him the eye and said, 'Who are you? And why would you assume I would talk to any cowboy who rides around these streets?' I noticed he liked being called a cowboy.

He said, 'My apologies, ma'am. My name is Andres. Andres Pelanchhi, at your service. I am just a local yokel who would like to contribute to your noble cause.'

I said, 'Well, Mr. Pelanchhi, my name is Madeline Saunders, but my friends call me Maddy. I'm Canadian. My apologies if I presented myself as less than cordial, but you must admit these streets are alive with rogues and bandits and a woman must be careful of all strangers. Would you not give the same advice to your sister?'

He smiled, revealing yellow, nicotine-stained teeth, and said, 'I would, I would indeed. But alas I do not have any sisters, no brothers as well for that matter. And God bless her soul, my mother departed this earth many years ago. So forgive me if I seem coarse on the ways of women, but know I will try to be a gentleman, even if I lacked the feminine influence while growing up.' He tried to produce a sad puppy dog look. There was nothing to suggest he felt actual remorse for the loss of his mother, he appeared to be caught up in the cowboy movie he was enacting in his head. I played along.

'Oh my goodness,' I said. 'My condolences for your loss. I am so sorry if I have stirred up heart-rending remembrances. You have behaved like a perfect gentleman; it is I who has been the boor. Your rather... rugged appearances did move me to feel somewhat... insecure.' His faint smile indicated he liked this. I continued, 'However, as the adage goes, "don't judge a book by its cover" and I have learned my lesson. If you are willing to contribute to our cause I would be remiss in not accepting your help.' I smiled.

He smiled back and reached into the back pocket of his jeans. He pulled out one big-ass wallet – I could hardly imagine it fitting in any normal pocket – and grabbed a fistful of dollars. He started to count it and then did a 'pshaw' and handed me the entire wad.

I looked at it with what I hoped was a look of extreme astonishment and said, 'Thank you, thank you. On behalf of the children and their families of this community, I thank you.'

He shrugged and said, 'Think nothing of it. I appreciate guests such as you in our country who are here to help make Brazil a better place for all Brazilians. Perhaps at some other time, you would allow me to take you on a tour of either our city or our beautiful countryside. That is, if you are not intimidated by motorcycles.'

I smiled and said, 'I have never ridden on one before. Are they safe?'

He said, 'Think of a bike as a horse. As long as you can control it, it is safe. I assure you, if you decide to take me up on my offer, you will have a safe and enjoyable ride.'

'Well,' I said, 'if that is the case, then I will consider it. However, I don't ride off into the sunset with just anyone. Beg my forgiveness, but what was your name?'

'Andres, Andres Pelanchhi,' he replied. 'People in the neighbourhood know who I am. May I be so bold as to ask where you are staying?'

'Do you know Luiza and her mother Dona Aurora?'

He said, 'Ahh Carlos's beautiful wife and his, how shall I put it, rather colourful mother-in-law. I know Carlos well. He is a good man, a hard-working man with a fine son. Before accepting my offer I urge you to speak with Carlos, I am certain he will vouch for my reputation.'

I smiled and thought to myself that I was sure Carlos would indeed give 'the Howler' a glowing reference. I said, 'Well Mr. Pelanchhi –'

'Please, call me Andres,' he interjected.

'Well, Andres,' I said, 'let me think about this. You know where I am living. May I suggest I get back to you via Carlos?'

He smiled and nodded, 'Certainly Madeline. Now I will let you get back to your important work. It has been a pleasure meeting you, and I hope this is not our only acquaintance. If you would excuse me, I do need to be on my way, but before I go let me ask, would you be interested in attending an event hosted by my father this coming Saturday? I believe there would be some very good contacts there for you to meet and perhaps shed light on the fine work your organization is doing. I will give the details to Carlos and you can see if it fits your schedule.'

'Of course, I can't commit here and now, but I will be interested to hear what Carlos has to say,' I said. 'It has been a pleasure. Thank you so much for your generous donation; be assured Saints for Sanctuary will put it to good use. Enjoy the rest of your day.'

I turned and walked away. When the bike started, I jumped. I thought someone had shot at me. I hoped he didn't see my reaction For years after, I cringed every time I heard a bike roar.

I continued my long walk home and tried to figure out how I could use Andres Pelanchhi to ensure the building of the school would happen. I recalled the conversation with Luiza and Gretchen and how the entire town was run by Maximo Pelanchhi and that every rally, petition and bureaucratic hurdle to overcome would be for naught if Pelanchhi did not approve our plan. Perhaps the best way to the father was through the son.

I wondered what Gretchen would say. Would she demand that I back off, thinking I could destroy the countless hours she had spent trying to get Maximo Pelanchhi to the table, or would she exploit me, gambling my involvement with Andres would help the cause? I also wondered what Luiza and Dona Aurora would think.

13

'Are you out of your fucking mind?' howled Dona Aurora. 'You are not to be left alone with that animal. Trust me, my very stupid child, he is a bad, bad man, and you are no match for him. You will get nothing from this except perhaps a disease or a coffin.'

I said, 'But Dona Aurora, Luiza herself said that the Pelanchhis' hold the key to the kingdom as far as getting the school built. I'm not stupid. I just want to befriend him, see where it leads in terms of furthering our mission.'

Dona Aurora rolled her eyes and raised her hands to her head in an act of exasperation. Luiza said, 'Maddy, you are right the Pelanchhis are, at the end of the day, the ones who will decide our fate, but this is ludicrous. I agree with mother, you should have nothing to do with that man.'

'I'm not an idiot. I think I have proven myself to be capable on these streets. I have dealt with the come-ons and the jeers and leers of men; I have become savvy at negotiating my way around. Luiza, you said yourself, Andres is a dimwit. I know I can handle him.'

'What you have become, young lady, is full of yourself. You are a complete and utter fucktard if you think you can handle the howler. He may not be the sharpest knife in the drawer, but he is miles ahead of you when it comes to understanding the rules of the game and he knows you are nothing but a pawn, and that is being complimentary, and he is, at the very least a knight. The only ones more powerful than him around here are the Archbishop Matos, and his father who is King and since the death of his wonderful wife, he is by proxy the Queen.' She walked up to me and got in my face. She said, 'Your pride and ambition are getting the best of you. Don't fly so close the sun my child.'

I said, 'Whatever.'

She slapped me hard across the face and grabbed me by the front of my T-shirt.

Luiza gasped, 'Mama.'

Dona Aurora ignored her and said, 'Listen to me you silly little bitch. Nothing good can come from this. I am an old whore and I know men. If you are in the business you develop a sixth sense about the sickos. You have to if you want to survive. I have only had one, just one encounter with that man and I can tell you for certain he is a sick fuck. Heed my words child or pay the consequences.' With that she gave me a shove, spat on the ground and retreated to her chair in the kitchen.

My face still stung, and the shove from a frail old woman had actually pushed me back a few feet – I had become a ninety-pound weakling. I was just about to load up with all the vitriol I could muster when Carlos burst through the door. He said, 'Luiza, Maddy.' He gave a cold stare at Dona Aurora and continued, 'Great news. You will never guess who I ran into. None other than Andres Pelanchhi.' He smiled at me and said, 'Maddy, I believe you met him earlier today.'

I nodded.

'Well,' he continued, 'he has asked that I escort you to his father's compound this Sunday for a special luncheon honouring the Senator's wife's birthday. He says he would like to have an opportunity to speak to you more about your project and that it will be a perfect opportunity for you to share your ideas with his father, and, of course, the senator himself. He says I am to let him know tomorrow.'

Still angered by the harsh words, the slap and the push, I looked indignantly at the old woman in the kitchen and said, 'Tell Andres I would be happy to join him.'

Dona Aurora flinched. I thought for a second she was going to break down and cry, but instead she sighed, got up slowly from the chair, and said to me, 'The sun down here is far too hot for you my child.' She slowly walked out the backdoor to return to her one-room abode.

Carlos smiled and fawned all over me. 'Never mind that crazy old bitch. She has no idea how much good you could do by going. And not to worry, I will be accompanying you and will help guide you on how to act in the company of refined Brazilians.'

Luiza guffawed.

Carlos snarled at her, 'Shut up, woman, and make sure my best clothes are ready for Sunday. This could be a great chance for us, too, you know.'

He returned his focus to me and smiled, 'Now, I would suggest you get Luiza to prepare your clothes as well.'

'I will do no such thing,' I said. 'I will get my own things ready.'

'No problem,' he said. 'You would probably do a better job anyways.' He gave me a knowing wink and a look indicating he thought very little of his wife's domestic skills. Not seeing the reaction he was hoping for, he said, 'Joking, of course. Luiza is a great wife and does tremendously well at making a cretin such as me look presentable.'

I continued to stare blankly at him and he said, 'Well, I'm off. This is good news and the kids and the hospital you will help them build will be forever grateful.'

I was going to correct him, scream at him it was a school we were building but could not muster up the might to do so. I felt that I had just made a deal with the devil.

Luiza shook her head and walked slowly to the door, indubitably making her way to console her mother.

14

I woke up early the morning after my encounter with Andres Pelanchhi and my row with Dona Aurora. The rest of the night had been awkward to say the least. Luiza was cordial but much more reserved than usual. Carlos came home early, a little drunk, which was unusual as he was typically inebriated. He added to the tension by fawning all over me, oblivious to the discord between his wife and me. I kept waiting for Dona Aurora to show her face but she remained elsewhere. Part of me thought the old biddy was behaving like a pouty little brat and that she had no business treating me the way she did. However, I was mostly feeling sad and guilty. I had brought added strain into someone else's home. I had insulted an important community matriarch and had shown disrespect by not acknowledging her wisdom. I knew I had to make things right.

I decided to head down to Itapau Beach, but before doing so snuck over to Dona Aurora's home and peeked in the window. She was there, lying on her back sleeping peacefully. I stood and watched her breathe. Perhaps it was gravitational pull, perhaps it was the relaxation that comes with sleep or perhaps it was my imagination, but the old woman looked years younger as the deeply embedded wrinkles on her face seemed to have faded and revealed the beauty of a proud woman.

As I looked beyond the wrinkles and the age spots I thought of what this beautiful woman had done to survive. How she had raised a wonderful daughter and made certain her girl was spared the life of a whore. How she, in her own quiet and steady way had become an advocate for women's and children's rights in her community. It was clear that her opinions were highly regarded by the younger women and that her validation of me gave me credence in a neighbourhood where women were inherently cynical and wise to the misanthropy that plagued their world. I thought of how I had ignored all her experience, defied her credibility and cheapened her status as a wise woman with my dismissive 'whatever'.

I knew I had to make things right. I just didn't know how other than to refuse the invitation to the Pelanchhis', an opportunity I could not refuse. Part of me thought, now that I had accepted, I couldn't refuse in the same way characters in *The Godfather* would be wise not to refuse offers made by Don Corleone. I thought a walk to the beach would give me some perspective, some time to think things through. Before I got to Itapau I had already decided I would need to check in with Gretchen. I imagined she would either see it as a coup and an opportunity for Saints for Sanctuary to make some headway in the building of the school or she would see me as a threat to all the work she had been doing; an amateur who would jeopardize everything.

I arrived at the beach and sought out my old friend with the purple and green boat. I found his boat, but there was no sign of him. His boat, Baby Rain, was tipped to her port side and sat silently, awaiting her owner and her Candomblé blessing to Yemanja before her daily baptism with the sea. I sat and looked out toward the breakers. My hand rubbed the cheek Dona Aurora had slapped. There was no lasting mark, but the rubbing brought back memories of the smack and that still stung.

From my left I heard a voice say, 'You look troubled my child.'

Startled, I turned quickly to see the fisherman standing a few feet from me. He held an impressive mango in one hand and a machete in the other. He smiled and said, 'I forgot my machete at home and on my way to retrieve it, this beautiful mango showed herself among her lesser brothers and sisters. I could not get her out of my mind so on the way back to the beach I had to climb her tree and claim her as my own. At the time I wasn't sure why I had to have her but now it is all making sense. She has given herself freely to me so that I can share her with you.'

I smiled and said, 'Thank you, but couldn't you eat it yourself while at sea? You must get awfully hungry out there.'

'Hah,' he replied, 'hunger is what I am used to. Besides to eat a mango such as this by myself could cause, how can I put it, great discomfort at sea. No, it would be best if I was to share. Yes?'

'Well,' I replied, 'if you insist. It looks delicious. Thank you for asking.'

'My pleasure.' He stood above me and deftly split the mango, using the machete like a surgeon would use a scalpel. His leathery hands worked the knife not only with expert precision but with the speed and efficiency of a man who saw the machete as nothing more than an extension of his hand. After cutting the fruit he turned the machete into a serving knife and offered me three perfect symmetrical slices. I thanked him and tasted the sweet fruit. There are few things better than freshly picked mangoes, especially served on a beautiful beach before the rising sun in the company of an old, schooled gentleman.

He said, 'As mentioned once, you look troubled. Is there something wrong?'

I shrugged. I hesitated.

He said, 'My apologies if I am prying. It really is none of my business. Here, have a few more slices.'

He handed me more of the delicious fruit. I gratefully accepted and thought about how I would share, with this sweet man whom I hardly knew, my burdens. I blurted out, 'I have been rude and arrogant toward the people who have welcomed me into their home, made me feel a part of their family and shared the little they have to share. I came here thinking I knew how I could help make the lives of the disadvantaged better, only to find out that I had not a clue and the people I was here to help had much more wisdom than I would ever have. I have betrayed them by not following their advice, now Dona Aurora has no respect for me.'

He laughed softly and said, 'My child, I am sure you have not offended an entire town.'

I replied, 'Although right now I feel like an offence to the whole community; I did not mean Dona Aurora the town, I meant Dona Aurora the old woman.'

I heard the rest of the mango make a gentle thud as it hit the sand and heard the clang of the machete as it struck a large stone buried beneath the sand. When I turned to face the fisherman I saw that his sun-darkened skin had become ashen. I knew then and there who his 'Baby Rain' was.

His knees wobbled and buckled ever so slightly, but he regained his balance by putting his hand on my shoulder and pushing himself upright. I caught his eye for a second but he quickly diverted his gaze away from mine. He almost gained his balance but had to place his hand on my shoulder again when it looked like his knees would give out. He rested his weight upon me for a few seconds, breathed deeply and then stood tall. I waited until I was sure he was okay and then got up and faced him. I reached for his hand. He let me take it. I have never felt a hand so rough and calloused. I said, 'My Dona Aurora is your Baby Rain?'

He nodded.

'Please, tell me your tale,' I asked.

He shook his head and said, 'Not now, my child. There is no time. I must get to the sea.' He let go of my hand and made his way to his boat.

'Let me come with you.'

He stopped dead in his tracks and without turning around he said, 'Fine.'

I walked a few paces behind him and stood at a respectful distance as he said his prayer to Yemanja. His voice was full of lamentation.

The tide was almost to the bow of his boat and it took little time to drag it into the froth of the sea. Still, it was hard to imagine that the old man in front of me possessed such strength. Once the boat was afloat he motioned for me to join him. I hesitated. Then felt my feet cooled by the Atlantic as I reached out for that hard hand. He stood in knee-deep water and, like a gentleman assisting a lady into her landau, guided me onto the weather-worn planks of the vessel named after the old woman who held me in her arms and sang to me, soothing me to sleep on my first night in the ghetto.

He started the tiny motor and skillfully navigated the breakers until we were in calm waters. He cut the engine, hoisted the sail and allowed the wind to pull us toward the horizon. He said nothing for the first hour. He kept his keen eye on the birds ahead of us and followed their path, eventually getting a little ahead of the flock. He then dropped his net, rolled a cigarette and offered it to me. I smiled and shook my head. He nodded, lit it with an ancient lighter and then grabbed a jug of water. He offered it to me first. I took it from him and he broke the silence by saying, 'My apologies, I am not used to company on my boat and do not even have a cup to offer you.'

I replied, 'What you lack in materials you more than compensate with good manners and better company.'

This got a smile from him. He said, 'And they say Brazilian men are charming; I am not sure we could hold a candle to Canadian women if you are an example of how enchanting they can be.'

I took a large swig from the massive jug, wiped my mouth with my forearm, and let out a modest belch. 'Speak up, for God's sake. I didn't hear what the hell it was that you said.'

This made him laugh. He said, 'Ah, that's better. Now I feel like I am on familiar ground, like I am in the company of a Bahian woman.'

I said, 'We Canadians are often considered to be the most polite people on the planet, but believe me our reputation is often grossly exaggerated. We can drink, fight and carouse with anyone and our men aren't much better.'

This got another laugh out of him, he was returning to the happy-go-lucky fisherman I had met on the beach. It dawned on me that during our morning interludes I had never asked him his name. As if reading my mind he said, 'My dear girl, here I have you on my boat and I do not even know your name.'

I said, 'You see, I told you we Canadian girls have few scruples. Imagine going on a gentleman's boat without even knowing his name or him knowing yours. Scandalous!'

He chuckled. It felt good making someone laugh, especially after all the upset I had caused back on terra firma. I said, 'My name, sir, is Madeline Saunders, but I prefer my friends to call me Maddy. And may I ask what is your name?'

'I am called Luiz Cardoso.'

My smile faded as I wondered if there was a connection between his name and that of Luiza's.

'Does my name upset you, Maddy?'

'No, of course not.'

A gentle breeze caught the sail, making a comforting flapping noise as the boat bobbed gently in the calm Atlantic. He finished his smoke and began rolling another. He said, 'You know, Dona Aurora was not always called Dona Aurora.'

I looked at him and shrugged. He finished rolling the cigarette and lit it. He took a drag. It was evident he was a man who spoke little to others. His face suggested consternation; I got the sense he was having an internal debate as to whether to tell me more of his tale. He took another drag and then said, 'Aurora is her middle name; as a girl she went with her first name. She was called Lorinha Badaro.' He stopped talking and sat silently at the stern of the boat, subtly guiding the rudder.

I thought that was all the information I was going to get into what was becoming a curious mystery about his history with Dona Aurora. I didn't want to seem nosy and push him for more information, but I was intrigued. He flicked his smoke into the sea and said, 'I think she adopted Aurora when she settled in the neighbourhood.' He smiled. 'That would be my guess anyway, the woman has always had a keen sense of humour peppered with vanity.'

I chuckled.

He said, 'I first laid eyes on her when I was fifteen. It was in the city of Ilheus, about four hundred kilometres south of San Salvador. She was there with her sisters and her drunkard of a father. Her mother had died of the fever a year before. Ilheus was booming as cocoa was king in this region. It was like every drifter, grifter and greed-ravished gambler in Brazil was making his way to Ilheus in order to establish his own cocoa grove, which he would expect to turn into a plantation and become a land baron. I was a fifteen-year-old kid – no family and no future, so I became a deckhand on a steamer that made its way from Bahia to Ilheus, taking prospectors to the land of chocolate gold. Each man told a yarn of how he was going to make his fortune and become a colonel of high regard. None of them ever did. They became slaves to the ruthless who had already made their mark on the land. The poor bastards would go to the plantations, and by the time they had bought their tools, paid for their room and food, they had unwittingly become indentured servants to the powerful men who had captured the promised land and made it their own. The vast majority of these prospectors would die penniless, and the only cocoa they would own would be the sap that stained the soles of their feet.' He looked at me and said, 'I am sorry my child, I must be boring you with my history lessons.'

I quickly replied, 'On the contrary, please continue. I am genuinely fascinated.'

He handed me the water jug. I took a swig and passed it to him. He took a sip and continued. 'Although I was only a fifteen-year-old punk, I considered myself a hard man in a hard land. We dropped off the duped in Ilheus and picked up the dead to bring back to Bahia. Some succumbed to the fever, others to firearms and machetes. I realized cocoa fortunes were a sham and that I was better off working the boats. But I, too, was hungry for fame and fortune and soon realized the men who were making money off the cocoa boom were the merchants and the hired guns who aligned themselves with the "colonels" who owned the plantations.'

I noticed his eyes darken as he said, 'By happenstance I became a trusted shot for the Pelanchhi family.'

I said, 'You worked for Maximo Pelanchhi?'

'Ah, you know of "the spider",' he replied. 'I worked first for his uncle and his father. Maximo was a boy of maybe seven or eight when I worked for his family.' He chuckled, 'Imagine, his poor mother, a classy lady from a fine Bahian family, thought her little Max would become a doctor, lawyer or engineer and bring honour and sophistication to the family name. He turned out to be almost as ruthless as his father.'

He wiped his brow with an ancient cloth and said, 'I met Americo Pelanchhi on a trip from San Salvador to Ilheus. He was playing cards in the state room of the steamer. Americo was Maximo's uncle. He had a well-deserved reputation as a womanizer and a gambler. He lacked the business acumen and the ambition of his older brother Estefan, but like his brother he was ready to kill and die for the growth of their plantation in the backwaters of Ilheus. Americo played the swashbuckler; his brother said he created most of the hijinks he found himself in. He lived up to his brother's analysis that night on the boat. He was gambling with three other men: a mulatto who I looked up to because he was one of the few of us who had the money to sit and gamble with the very wealthy, an Englishman who was a military engineer and a hired gun of the Pelanchhis' who surveyed and mapped out the massive plots of the virgin jungle to be scorched and then planted by the aforementioned fortune seekers, and a lawyer named Armando Peres.

'Peres was known as a freelance swindler who would finagle the law in order to add credence to a large land baron's contention that smaller landowners did not have proper deed to their land. He was a regular on the steamer and I hated him. He was a fat braggart who gleefully described how he was able to steal the land that had been hard-earned by men who may have been greedy and bloodthirsty but at least put their lives on the line for what they wanted. He was also a poor gambler, a terrible drunk and a dirty coward who would have a tantrum if he lost at cards. Did I mention I hated him?'

I nodded. He sighed and said, 'He was also the first man I killed.' He rolled another cigarette and continued, 'We were about three hours from Ilheus and the card game was coming to a close because Americo was cleaning the table with the lawyer. Lawyer Peres was becoming morose, the alcohol that had fueled the frivolity that had started the game had changed into a dark, sullen rage. It was dawning on him that the fortune he had just made by evicting two cousins from their entitled land by twisting the law and making sure the magistrates were greased was now lining the pockets of Americo Pelanchhi, a man who already owned a massive plantation.

Americo was not being a gracious winner. He taunted Peres, saying it was too bad he wasn't as good at cards as he was at pushing papers and making up laws. He suggested that the money the lawyer had lost was real justice and that the cousins he had ripped off would be having a bit of a laugh at the lawyer's expense. I was enjoying the show. I hated that son-of-a-bitch lawyer and made sure I pretended to be busy cleaning up the room so I could watch him have his face rubbed in it.

'Americo got up, bowed to the lawyer and thanked him for adding to his coffers, then informed him the whores would be getting extra tips thanks to Peres being such a terrible poker player. Americo turned and walked to the door, the engineer and the mulatto were not paying attention as they, too, were enjoying Peres's humiliation. Only I noticed Peres pull out a pistol and aim it at the back of Americo's head. I do not recall thinking at all, all I remember is reacting. I grabbed the engineer's pistol, which he placed by the makeshift bar in the room, and fired it into the face of the lawyer. I hit him on the eyebrow. I will never forget that, right in the thickest part of his bushy eyebrow. He dropped to his knees and then fell forward onto the floor.

'The smoke from the pistol filled the air and after the sound of the shot dissipated silence, and smoke consumed the room. Americo was the first to do anything. He walked over to the lawyer and with his fine leather riding boot kicked the lawyer before declaring him deader than a doornail. He picked up the gun, an American Smith and Wesson, a beautiful widow maker, and handed it to me. He also gave me the money he had won from the lawyer and told me to keep it or consider it a bonus plus my first month's pay.

I became a gun for hire. The youngest one in the territory and lived up to the moniker the British engineer gave me – "Cardoso the Kid".'

He finished his smoke, looked at the sun and started pulling in his lines. I helped him, or at least attempted to. He appreciated my efforts, but I think things would have gone faster without my attempts. He said the catch was pretty thin but not the worst. He efficiently killed his meager bounty. I got the sense he felt more remorse for the fish than he did for that son-of-a-bitch lawyer. When he had put the fish into the plastic tub he pulled on the sail and the boat made a neat one eighty and we headed back toward the land. He said, 'They say men who are born for the sea should stay on the sea or their life will lead to tragedy. Such was the case with me. I soon discovered I was extremely good at killing, and like most assassins I was treated with respect and adoration from my bosses and their men, and from my enemies – fear and loathing. To my credit I never let the "Cardoso the Kid" go to my head. I remained humble with my notoriety... for the most part. I did, however, have one weakness and that weakness was Lorinha Aurora Bodaro, my one and only true love.'

As he said her name a whimsical smile crossed his weathered face. 'The first time I saw her I made an ass of myself. It was a few months after I had worked for the Pelanchhis, and my first time in Ilheus. We had been involved in a messy affair over a particularly lush parcel of jungle land. I had proven myself to be an effective sniper, killing two gunmen and several workers as a rival family vied to clear the land. They were no match for us. The Englishman had fought in the Boer War and upon his release from the army he became a soldier of fortune, making his mark in the Cocoa Wars of the Gold Coast in Africa. He was our field marshal and used tactics learned in Africa to annihilate our enemies. I will not tell you of how he and the older Pelanchhi extracted v*alua*ble information from our captives, but he said he learned it from the Belgians in the Congo; he regarded them as the most effective torturers in the world. I hated it and would not partake. I could tell Americo had no stomach for it as well, although he readily admitted its effectiveness was unquestionable. His brother, on the other hand, seemed to not only have a stomach for it, he seemed to revel in it.'

I interjected, 'Forgive me, this is Maximo's father and therefore Andres's grandfather. I can't recall his name...'

'Yes, that is correct,' he nodded. 'His name was Estefan and he became the heir to the Pelanchhi fortune. My apologies, I have digressed. Please forgive the ramblings of an old man.'

I replied, 'Again, there is no need to apologize. I could sit and listen to these fascinating stories all day.'

He smiled and said, 'Well, after a victory such as ours it was customary to celebrate in Ilheus. The town, at that time, was abuzz with gambling halls, beer parlors and whorehouses. Americo insisted we all ride horses into town. I had never been on one and could hardly handle a mule, never mind what turned out to be a Mangalarga Marchador, a huge black beast. Before what was to be our victorious ride through the streets, the Englishman gave me lessons, and I soon became the comic relief for men who had spent the last few months wondering from which direction the bullet that had their name on it was coming. Men could not believe that "Cardoso the Kid" had no aptitude for horsemanship. The Englishman said my...' He scratched his beard and looked toward the land that was barely appearing on the horizon.

I said to him, 'Mr. Cardoso, you are holding me in suspense.'

He looked at me sheepishly, and said, 'I am trying to find a way to politely tell you what the Englishman said.'

I chuckled and said, 'Must I remind you again, that we Canadian girls are used to bawdy talk.'

He shrugged and said, 'Okay. The Englishman said my balls would be bluer than the deep blue sea by the time the Mangalarga Marchador was done with me and that I would be spending my time with the doctors and not keeping company with Ilheus's finest whores.'

I laughed and laughed. Partially because of the story, but mostly because of the way the poor man told it. He laughed with me. When my hysterics were over he rolled another smoke and continued.

'I know now I never truly had that horse under control,' he said, 'but I thought I did. When we rode from our camp to Ilheus he stayed with the pack and my anxiety lessened as my confidence rose. Being fifteen and allowing myself to be a little cocky, I thought that I had become master of the monster. I soon discovered the beast was just biding its time, lulling me into a false sense of security. We rode down Ilheus's main drag and then into the red light district, which was lined with newly constructed bars and whorehouses. We stopped to hitch our horses outside of Americo's favourite gambling establishment. The prostitutes were already gathering. That is when I spotted the beautiful Lorinha Aurora Badaro. She was gathered with the other hookers, but she did not look like them. She possessed neither the hardness of the experienced ones nor the frailty and fear of the younger ones. Of course, at the time I would not have been able to make that analysis. All I saw was the most beautiful girl my eyes had ever had the pleasure of setting themselves upon.'

The whimsical smile returned to his face. He said, 'I did something very uncharacteristic for me to do – I made an obnoxious catcall to her. I had always been quiet and respectful around women; mostly because I felt awkward in their company. Lorinha looked at me and sneered, saying she did not entertain little boys and that I should go and play with the other children down by the river. The other men laughed, as did the whores. I was enraged and in a fit of fury pulled out my pistol and aimed it at her. She stood and smiled saying, "I bet that is the biggest gun you got." I knew not what to do. I could not shoot something so beautiful and brave. Foolish, mind you, but brave nonetheless. Americo suggested I return the gun to my holster and he, as a treat, would buy the services of the bold lady for me to use for whatever pleasures I wished.

'At the time I did not appreciate his attempts to help me find a diplomatic way out of blowing the head off the woman I had already fallen in love with. The stupidity of a mannish boy was in full force. I aimed my pistol at her head. She did not look away; in fact, I swear I saw a tiny smile cross her lips. Then she yelled "BANG!"

'The skittish Mangalarga Marchador had had enough. He neighed wildly and reared, almost throwing me, which in retrospect would have been the best thing. I grabbed the reigns and panicked, digging my spurs into his sides; in doing so I dropped my gun. It discharged. The horse turned violently and headed down the dirt road we had so eloquently processed up only minutes before. He then bucked and threw me; however, my foot was stuck in the stirrup and he dragged me down the road. I was knocked out in seconds. Americo told me later it was the Englishman who had saved me by riding alongside the horse and grabbing the reigns.'

He reached for the water bottle and took a swig. He said, 'Forgive me, my child. I do not think I have spoken so many words to one person in years, perhaps decades.' He took another swig and said, 'I woke up with a cool towel on my head and stared into the eyes of my Lorinha. She kissed my forehead and tenderly gave thanks for me sparing her life. From that day until the day I killed her father, she was mine. Imagine a boy not quite sixteen having his very own kept woman. Ah, the crazy days of Ilheus during the cocoa wars.'

I must have looked at him with a look of shock for he said, 'I have offended you.'

I replied, 'No. Her father? You killed her father?'

'Oh, that, yes, I will explain the circumstances to you sometime, but for now I need to focus on getting our vessel over these swells. Forgive me, but that is enough talking for one day.'

The ride back to the beach was a quiet one. It became clear that Luiz was done with talking about the past and I was left to speculate why and how he had killed Dona Aurora's father. When he had secured the boat and unloaded his paltry catch, he asked, 'So you have not told me what it is that you have done to upset my Lorinha so much.'

As I explained the dilemma I found myself in with the Pelanchhis, I noticed the concern on his face. He said, 'I agree with Lorinha, or should I say Dona Aurora, that you should have avoided the Pelanchhis, but you didn't, so now what? From what I hear about this Andres fellow he would take offense if you did not accept his invitation, and I understand he does not like to be offended. I think you should go back to Canada immediately.'

My jaw dropped and a small gasp of air whistled through half-pursed lips.

He said, 'I get the sense you will not heed my advice, though I am absolutely certain it is the best advice you will get. If a return to your home is out of the question then you should go to the function.' He scratched his forearm and said, 'Go, be cordial, but somehow find a graceful way to distance yourself from that lot. Nothing good comes from Estefan Pelanchhi's offspring.'

I said, 'I cannot leave. I will not leave.'

How I would learn to regret those words.

He said, 'You can leave, but I respect and understand why you will not leave.'

I said, 'Thank you for understanding.' I gave him a hug and said,

'We must get together soon, and I insist you tell me the rest of your story. Goodbye for now "Cardoso the Kid".'

He said softly, 'Goodbye, my dear girl. Thank you for listening to my ramblings, and yes, I will tell the rest of my tale if you so wish. Now I must get this catch to market. Come visit anytime. May the gods be with you. Please, I beg of you, keep my identity a secret from your Dona Aurora.'

I looked at him, nodded and said, 'I will. I promise.'

I walked down the beach and heard, 'Maddy! Wait!'

I turned to see him jogging down the beach. I walked toward him and when we met he said, 'I have something for you. You need to be very careful with it, but try and keep it with you at all times.' He handed me a beautiful ivory-handled knife. He said, 'The Englishman gave me this. It was a souvenir from the Boer War; a weapon belonging to a young Boer woman who used it on the Englishman's major when they raided her home looking for her husband and his men. Cut his throat with it. The Englishman was forced to shoot her, though I recall him telling us the woman did them all a favour and perhaps inadvertently saved the lives of many British soldiers by killing the fool of an officer.'

He handed me the knife, belt and the sheath.

Luiz said, 'Apparently the woman had it under her skirt. The belt it comes with is designed to be tied around the lower hips and the sheath sits just above the buttocks. She waited until the captain was in striking distance before revealing it. It is a small but powerful weapon and is incredibly sharp. I have been waiting a long time to give it to someone. Promise me you will keep it with you at all times, even if it is just to appease the worries of an old man.'

I looked at the knife and the decorative leather sheath it slept in. The sheath had been inscribed with what I guessed were Afrikaan words. I picked out what I thought must have been a couple of names – Lettie and Koos. I also was able to decipher what I was certain was love (liefe) and God. God was spelled G-O-D. Later I was to find out the inscription read, *Lettie, may this knife protect you when God can't. Love, Koos.* I was reluctant to promise Luiz I would keep the knife with me as I did not believe in weapons and certainly could not see myself carrying one around on a daily basis. I knew if I gave my word I would keep it. I struggled, trying to find the right answer. I thought of how I had disregarded the advice of two wise sages in less than twenty-four hours and decided to make a vow to become a knife-toting pacifist. I said, 'Thank you my friend, I promise to keep this knife with me at all times.'

He nodded and we once again hugged. I made my way to the road that would lead me back to Luiza's and thought about the craziness that was becoming my life: Here I was in a foreign land, the owner of a weapon that for all intents and purposes was used to protect apartheid. On top of that I was falling in love with a Priest while hobnobbing with the elitists and living in a slum with women whom I had openly defied although they were trying their very best to protect me from forces I did not understand. Brazil.

15

I had walked maybe fifty paces on the road when a van came racing toward me. The large man driving was easy to identify. Ali rolled down his window and said, 'Maddy, are you okay?'

As he was speaking, Gretchen dashed out of the van and slammed the door behind her. She darted in front of the vehicle and grabbed me by the shoulders. She said, 'Are you safe Maddy, did anyone hurt you?'

I said, 'I'm fine, why would you think –' I stopped mid-sentence and rolled my eyes. I said, 'You have spoken with Luiza and Dona Aurora, haven't you?'

Gretchen and Ali both nodded. Gretchen asked, 'I know it is your day off, but may ask where you have been?'

I said, 'Just walking along the beach and clearing my thoughts.'

'Really?' she asked.

'Really.'

'That's funny,' she said. 'We, along with several others, have been scouring this area for hours and none of us caught a glimpse of you.'

I shrugged and said, 'Well, I walked quite a ways. I didn't realize I was obligated to give you an hourly account of my whereabouts on my day off.'

Ali erupted, 'Cut the crap, Madeline, you had us worried sick! We had thought something terrible happened. Day off or not you have no business wandering away without letting someone know. I thought you were much more considerate than that. Luiza, Carlos, Gretchen, myself and even Father Lievan have spent the day looking and fretting about you.' Gretchen was staring at Ali like he was a total stranger. The man who was the epitome of serenity looked like an angered prizefighter.

I held it together for all of three seconds before I started bawling like a blubbering child. I kept saying 'I'm sorry' between massive sobs. I grabbed onto Gretchen and tried to bury my face in her scrawny shoulder. I felt her stiffen and then accept my hug. I could tell she was trying her best to be physically comforting. She was well out of her comfort zone and I could hear her whisper, 'Ali.'

Ali stepped out of the van and Gretchen maneuvered herself toward him, pivoting me into his waiting embrace.

He said, 'I am sorry, Maddy. Truly I am. There, there it is okay. You're safe and that is the main thing.'

I sunk as deep as I could into his massive frame, smelling the scent of fresh, plain soap. I sobbed and sobbed. First Dona Aurora and Luiza and now Ali and Gretchen. Who else could I offend? I thought about what the fisherman had said and the idea of going home seemed like a very good one. Then from somewhere in the back of consciousness came the voice of my father. He said, 'You're no quitter, Maddy. Suck it up, for God's sake.'

Within seconds the tears stopped and I said, 'I am such a fuck-up, but I am going to make this right.'

Gretchen patted my shoulder and said, 'Okay then, good. Let's get in the van. There is much to discuss.'

When inside the van she handed me a tissue and said, 'We need to get to the office right away. Maryanne said we were to call her as soon as we found you.'

I thought *great*. Perhaps I would have no say on whether or not I was going home. Maryanne Lucas had warned me before my sojourn began that she did not suffer fools. I was feeling very foolish.

Ali interjected, 'Gretchen, I know Ms. Lucas insisted we get Maddy to the office as soon as possible, but we need to find the others first and tell them the search is off.'

Gretchen glowered at him but said, 'Okay, fine, but make it quick, Ali. The first one we see will be responsible for telling the others. Maryanne does not like to be kept waiting.'

No sooner had she finished talking than Carlos appeared on the street with a couple of his cronies. Ali honked the horn and beckoned to him. He saw me in the van and crossed himself. I gave the disingenuous bastard a glare, but he did not pick up on it. He came to the window and said, 'Oh, thank God you are safe Madeline. I have been worried sick. Not that it is that important, but I hope you are still up for our engagement tomorrow.'

I snarled, 'Listen to me, when I get home tonight I better find out that you have told all who have been searching for me that I am safe and sound. If you don't I will be going to the Pelanchhis by myself.'

He said, 'Of course, of course. I will personally make sure everyone gets the message. You have no worries there.'

We sped off. I was certain if I had not made the threat Carlos would have gone off and not told a soul I was found. I sat back in my seat and felt a dull jab from the sheathed knife that was down the back of my jeans. My thoughts turned to Maryanne Lucas, the president of Saints for Sanctuary and my boss, and what she had in store for me.

16

We arrived at the office around five in the afternoon, making it noon in Vancouver. Gretchen dialed the second she sat at her desk. After a brief exchange of pleasantries she handed the phone to me.

'Hello Maddy. I hear you have caused a bit of a ruckus.' The sharpness in her voice made it clear she was understating the obvious.

'Unintentionally, but yes, I suppose I have.'

'I also hear your billet was very distraught today. In fact, worried sick about you. We don't like to upset our billets, Maddy, as they have been gracious enough to let workers such as you stay with them.'

I replied, 'The last thing in the world I would want to do would be to upset Luiza and her family.'

'Yet, you did,' was the cold reply.

'Yes, yes I did.'

There was near silence on the other end, but I was certain I heard the click of a lighter followed by an intake of breath. Maryanne eventually said, 'Well, hopefully for all involved your billet will let bygones be bygones. Otherwise it will be hard for you to be effective, don't you think?'

'I am sure there is nothing that can't be fixed,' I replied.

'Are you certain?'

'Positive.'

'Good,' she said. 'Now tell me about this little pickle you have got yourself into with our good friends the Pelanchhis.'

'Well, first let me say, I had no idea I was even in a pickle and I have never met Maximo Pelanchhi. I did meet Andres and through my billet's husband he invited me to attend some birthday party for the wife of a senator.'

'And when is this soirée to happen?'

'Tomorrow afternoon.'

There was an audible exhale on the other end. I imagined Maryanne done to the nines, sitting in her office discharging smoke through her nostrils, her professionally coloured black hair and black eyes giving her a dragon-like quality.

'My, my,' she said, 'that is very soon. Did you ever consider checking in with Gretchen before making a decision? I am sure Gretchen would have had lots to say on the matter.'

'No,' I said. 'I just accepted. I thought it would give me an opportunity in a very exclusive forum to do the job I signed up to do. I think of it as a golden opportunity to promote the cause.'

'Indeed,' she said. 'Well it sounds like you have everything under control. I'm glad you're so confident in your skills. A less confident person would be concerned about the disastrous position he or she could be putting our cause in. A less confident person would be thinking that one faux pas could set our cause back substantially. A less confident person would be thinking about how they would be surrounded by political and ecclesiastical sharks all vying for the same thing: Maximo's blessing. A less confident person would have thought I will stick to what I do best, be a community organizer with the women and children I have come to know and not meddle in affairs that are beyond my jurisdiction, because that, in my own humble way, is how I can best help the cause.'

Silence ensued. I grappled with my emotions and vowed not to show weakness. I was through with crying in front of these people. I was quite sure I heard another cigarette being lit. I said, 'Well, thank you for recognizing I do not lack confidence. Nevertheless, if you feel it would be best I cancel my invitation, I will do so.'

'Unfortunately,' she said, 'it's too late for that. Andres would be very offended and the ripple effects might do more harm than good. I'm sure you'll know exactly what to do.'

'I am open to advice.'

'And here I was assuming you needed nobody's help,' she said, baiting me with her sarcasm.

'I would be foolish not to ask for advice from people with much more experience than I. Please, tell me what you think would be best.' I could tell she was trying not to snap. She wanted to make my punishment one of a thousand cuts, but knowing Maryanne she was close to giving into her urges and screaming bloody murder down the telephone.

She said, 'In your case you need to find the balance between seeming quiet and demure; someone who wants to stay in the background. I know you will struggle with this. You also need to appear intelligent; hopefully the others will interpret your silence for someone who is a deep thinker and not just a simpleton. Stay away from political and theological discussions and never ask for anything either for yourself or for Saints for Sanctuary. If you talk about your work, emphasize the fact that you are here to help the poor, stay away from all clichés that have to do with transformation and empowerment. Do not drink, and fight your natural tendencies toward flightiness and naiveté. Last but not least, dress nicely and eat all that is put in front of you and again, as hard as you might find it not to, avoid drawing attention to yourself. It is not the Madeline Saunders show.'

I thought, *you bitch,* but said, 'Sage advice, thank you so much Maryanne. I will take it to heart. Is there anything else?'

'Yes,' she said. 'Andres is a sociopathic asshole. He also likes to show his power. He might offer to help us in ways that would otherwise take months, maybe even years. There will be a personal cost to you, even though I would bet dollars to donuts he will never follow through with his promises.'

I asked, 'What will the personal costs be?'

'He will want to fuck you.' I could almost hear her smirk.

'I have fucked for less.'

Gretchen dropped the coffee cup she was holding. Gravelly laughter bellowed from the other end of the phone. I bit my lip and pictured myself punching Maryanne Lucas in the face. Maryanne said, 'Oh Maddy, you are something else. It seems that you have become a hard woman since the last time we spoke.' She paused and laughed some more. Then she said, 'I know you didn't think that what you have done was a big deal. I get it. But you have unintentionally put all the work Gretchen has done in jeopardy.

You have also put yourself in harm's way. Andres is a bad, bad dude. There is too much at stake to have you screw this up. When you go tomorrow, keep your wits about you at all times and try to avoid any conversations that seem controversial.'

'I will be like an obedient child,' I said dryly.

'Good,' she said. 'Brazilian men seem to like that. Let me speak to Gretchen.'

I handed the phone to Gretchen and took a seat on the couch in the office.

I had never met a woman who was so proficient at bating me, however, I was sure this was part of her test to see how I would perform at the party the following night. I felt like I had acquitted myself quite well with the exception of the 'I have fucked for less' outburst. She was also right – I had no idea of the significance of accepting the invitation. I got the feeling that Luiza, Dona Aurora and Luiz were very concerned for my safety and that Gretchen and Maryanne were concerned about the organization's welfare.

17

Gretchen continuously nodded and kept saying yes a lot while on the phone with Maryanne. She kept looking at me while doing so. She hung up and said, 'Okay, let's get you back to Luiza's.'

She picked up her cell and called for Ali to bring the van round to the front of the building. He was waiting for us when we hit the pavement. Gretchen could hardly look at me. When the doors of the van closed I said, 'So are you angry or are you hurt?'

She looked at me through the rearview mirror and said, 'Neither.'

We rode in silence for some time. I tried to keep my mouth shut and let her stew. Ali was humming some indecipherable tune that I would usually find soothing but was currently finding agitating. I could stand it no more and said, 'Well, if you are neither angry nor hurt then what are you?'

She stared at me and said, 'Worried. Extremely worried.'

I said, 'Ali do you know where the old fishermen live?'

He said, 'Yes.'

'And do you know Luiz, the one who owns the purple and green boat?'

He nodded again and said, 'Ah, the one the old timers call Cardoso the Kid? I know of him.'

I said, 'I need to find him before we go home.'

Gretchen said, 'We will do no such thing. Maryanne said we were to drop you off at Luiza's safe and sound and that you were to stay there until you go to the Pelanchhis.'

I said, 'Either we go and find the fisherman or I jump out of this van at the next light. I am not some indentured servant working in a post-colonial cocoa plant.'

Gretchen looked at Ali. Ali shrugged. Gretchen said, 'Maddy I have no idea what you are talking about. Indentured servant … in a cocoa plant … really? But whatever, it seems you are giving us no choice. So be it. Ali find the goddamn fisherman.'

Ali drove to the old man's shack. It, too, was painted purple and green and stood out among the grey corrugated steel and blanched plywood. Through the glassless window I could see his home was as rustic as that of Dona Aurora's and wondered how he had squandered the riches he had incurred while being an assassin of renown in his younger days. He was nowhere to be seen. Ali said, 'I know where he might be.'

We climbed back into the van and Ali navigated down narrow potholed streets until we came to the ocean. The only building was a dilapidated cannery. Ali pulled up beside homemade saloon doors and said, 'There is a good chance he is in here.'

I said, 'Stay here.'

Before I had a chance to move I heard and then felt Ali's massive paw on my shoulder. He said, 'Over my dead body. You want to go into that bar, fine. You want to talk to the old man, fine. You even want to play dominoes with him and discuss post-colonial history, fine. But there is no way that I am letting you go in there by yourself.'

The gentle pressure of his hand on my shoulder told me he had just about enough of my demands and that if I didn't agree with his request I would be shanghaied back to Luiza's whether I liked it or not. I said, 'Okay fine.'

We exited the van and walked toward the swinging half doors. I pushed through with Ali right behind me. It took a while for my eyes to adjust to the darkness. The abandoned fish processing plant smelt of oil, cigarettes and stale alcohol. When my eyes adjusted to the light – it was one single bulb that hung from somewhere in the rafters. I was able to see that the actual bar area took up little space of the factory. I could barely make out the assembly line machinery that lurked on the outskirts of the bar. There were three round tables with an assortment of chairs, some plastic, others wood and a couple of folding beach chairs. The bar consisted of a plank straddling two ancient oil drums. Behind the bar was a massive plastic container that looked like some sort of industrial vat.

Ali whispered, 'All they serve is *alua*; it is our version of moonshine. It is better than the rotgut you might get in other places, but if I were you I would drink nothing from this establishment.'

The bartender was, I would guess, a twelve-year-old boy who looked utterly uninterested in the fact that a *gringa* and a giant had entered his establishment. Ali said. 'Look up, to your left.' I looked and saw the outline of a man with a rifle standing outside an office area high above the floor. I imagined it was for foremen who once oversaw the labourers, ensuring they were canning the catch with efficiency and precision. Now it acted as a sentinel guarding the proprietors from thieves and the police. I could not see the man's face even when he took a drag from his cigarette and the embers briefly added colour to the dank and dark warehouse.

There were four men sitting at one of the tables. They, like the boy, showed little interest in us. They drank their *alua* out of plastic glasses and were playing Truco, a Brazilian card game. At first I thought these men were the only patrons and was just about to turn around when I saw a shadow lurking on the edge of light. I squinted and realized it was a man hunched over the table cupping his plastic glass as if it was the Holy Grail filled with the blood of Christ. I walked toward the figure and soon realized it was Luiz. I took a few steps toward him and quietly called his name. There was no response. I reached out and touched his shoulder. He put his hand on top of mine and gave it a gentle squeeze. I said, 'Come Luiz. It is time. You have prayed to Yemanja long enough. She has protected you, but now it is time to return to your one true love.'

He slowly shook his head and whispered. 'I cannot do that. I am broken.'

I replied, 'No, you are old. You are perhaps drunk, but you are far from broken. You are Cardoso the Kid. You are a sailor of renown. You are a gentleman who lives by a code of honour and chivalry. Most importantly, you are the one man who can bring happiness to the woman he loves; a woman who has suffered without her true love long enough. Come my friend.' I reached under his upper arm and helped him to his feet. He let me guide him toward the door but then stopped abruptly and shook free of my hand. He returned to the table and I thought he was going to plunk himself into the chair. Instead he grabbed the glass and threw back the *alua*. He walked toward Ali and myself. His back was a little straighter and his shoulders a little broader. He walked past us and pushed his way through the doors.

He waited for us with head downcast. I noticed him brush his forearm across his face. This did little to disguise the streaks of tears that tracked down his dusty cheeks. I pretended not to notice. I think he appreciated that.

***

I quietly introduced Luiz to Ali and Gretchen and guided him into the van. I sat beside him and attempted to put my arm around him. He sat up on the van's bench seat and made it clear that he did not appreciate such effeminate affection in a public setting. We rode in awkward silence; it was Gretchen who finally broke the quiet. She said, 'Luiz, Maddy tells us you are a fisherman.'

Luiz replied, 'That I am.'

I'm certain Gretchen had wanted more of a response, and to her credit she tried again, 'So how long have you been fishing?'

'I was born on the sea and for most of my life I have been wise enough to stay on it. There was a brief time when I dabbled on dry land, but I found little satisfaction in the results.' He looked at me as he said the last part of the sentence.

Gretchen, seemingly encouraged by the response asked, 'Maddy tells us you have a connection to our Dona Aurora. How do you know the wise lady?'

'My history with her is complicated,' was the only response forthcoming.

Ali interjected and said, 'Luiz, I am a lover of fish; I am a terrible catcher of them, though I am renowned as a master consumer of them. I rarely get to talk to true fishermen, could you indulge me and share your expertise on when the best time to buy a certain catch is and what is the best way to prepare and cook it?'

The rest of the van ride was spent with Luiz giving us recipes on how to prepare the different local fish. I think we were all grateful for the opportunity to fill the silence as we made our way back to Luiza's.

18

As we drove up to Luiza's front door she was entertaining the local children with one of her infamous sing-alongs. She was bellowing out a tune and I pointed to her through the van window and said to Luiz, 'That is Dona Aurora's only child, her name is Luiza.'

'Luiza,' was all he said.

'Would you like to wait here for a moment? I will get Dona Aurora.'

He nodded. When I opened the van door Luiza's singing infiltrated the cabin. I noticed Luiz wince and I quickly closed the door behind me.

When the children saw Ali they ran toward him. Luiza put down her guitar and walked toward Gretchen. She had yet to acknowledge my presence. I must admit, being a person with a healthy ego I suppose I was expecting more of a 'the return of the prodigal daughter' response, but Luiza was having none of that. She was playing it so cool I think her pee would have come out ice cubes. After her small talk with Gretchen she finally looked my way and gave a slight nod. I smiled at her and nodded back. A faint smile crossed her lips; she tried her best to erase it but realized it was too late. I ran toward her and practically leapt into her arms.

She welcomed my embrace and hugged me tightly, she said, 'You are such a brat, a true monster! We were worried sick.' She pushed me away from her and said, 'You must promise never to pull a stunt like that again.

We all had you dead in a …' She started to cry. I almost did but remembered my vow and quickly squashed the tears I felt rising.

Out of the corner of my eye I noticed the old woman come out of her house. My eyes darted to the van and I saw Luiz grip the seat in front of him. It was clear she had not noticed him. She pretended to not notice me and walked away from her house. I broke free from Luiza and called her name. She feigned deafness and continued to walk, to where I'm not sure. I was convinced she had no clue as well. I quickly caught up to her and tapped her shoulder.

She sighed. Then she grumbled and stopped. 'Can I help you?' It was clear her stoicism would be much tougher to break than her daughter's. She looked at me with dark, fierce eyes and said, 'You live. I am sure Luiza is relieved.'

I said, 'You have lived a hard life. Lost much. You know this land and its people. I have proven myself to be disrespectful to you and the history you have lived. I am the female version of the fool Icarus and have flown too close to the sun. Unlike him, and only because of people like you, I may be saved from plummeting to my death. My arrogance and naiveté has led me down a road that women wiser than me say I am not ready to travel. I did not listen and now find myself in a bind that is dangerous, but being who I am and where I'm from I am blind to the danger. I don't deserve your forgiveness, but I'm begging for it anyway.'

Behind me I heard a voice say, 'Forgive her, Lorinha, and while you are at it, forgive me as well.'

Her eyes widened as she reached her hand out and clasped onto my shirt in order to remain upright. She gasped and let out an almost inaudible wail. Her eyes teared up and she began to tremble. All pretenses of stoicism were erased, and for a moment I thought she was going to have a massive heart attack right there and then. Her knees were buckling and I grabbed her forearms; for a second I was able to prop her up. The only word she said before fainting was, 'Luiz.'

Luiz said, 'Dear God, I have killed her.'

Luiza, Ali and Gretchen came running from the front of Luiza's house. It was Gretchen who leapt into action. She found and checked the old woman's heartbeat and said, 'Her ticker is working fine. Strong and as steady as an ox, actually. Ali be a dear and run to the van and get my water bottle and the first aid kit.'

Luiza said shrilly, 'First aid kit?'

'Nothing to worry about Luiza,' replied Gretchen. 'Just a precautionary measure. I think the excitement was too much for her.'

Luiz said, 'I knew this was a bad idea. I should go.'

Luiza seemed to notice him for the first time. 'Who are you?'

'I am an old acquaintance of your mother's. I am afraid that it is my presence that has caused her such anxiety. I shall go before she wakes up. Perhaps she will think me being here was some sort of illusion. Good day.' He gave a small, quick bow and walked away.

Luiza said, 'Wait. Hold on a minute. What is your name?'

He stopped, then turned to her and said, 'I am Luiz, a fisherman by trade.' There was a brief silence. I looked at Luiza and saw she was busy processing this information. Luiz stood there awkwardly and when the silence got too uncomfortable, he nodded and turned on his heels.

'Your last name, sir?' Luiza asked quietly.

He once again turned to face her and said, 'Cardoso.'

I thought Luiza would soon join her mother in a fainting spell. She momentarily lost her colour but quickly regained her composure. She half-whispered, 'Cardoso the Kid.' She looked at Luiz and said, 'You are real.'

'Perhaps I once was. Now, I am just Luiz the fisherman, a lover of the sea, mangoes and *alua*.'

Ali, Gretchen and I were so engrossed by the interaction between Luiza and Luiz that none of us had noticed Dona Aurora get to her feet. She said, 'Stay Luiz. We need to talk.'

We all turned to face Dona Aurora. The frailness and vulnerability that I saw before she fainted was gone. The gritty, foul-mouthed matriarch stood before us. She said, 'Come Luiz. We shall retire to my humble abode.' She looked at Luiza and said, 'Get that idiot husband of yours to bring us over some rum. I, for one, will not drink that piss they call *alua*.' She walked to Luiz and tenderly touched his face, 'Remember the days of good rum, my old friend?'

He nodded and smiled. The couple made their way back to Dona Aurora's shack. They looked like any old couple anywhere in the world. Anyone seeing them that moment would believe they had been together forever and had never spent a day apart.

We watched them until they made their way through the threshold of the shack. Ali said, 'Gretchen we must get going.'

Gretchen replied, 'Agreed.' She looked at me. 'We have not had time to fully discuss your encounter tomorrow with the Pelanchhis. Whatever advice you were given by Maryanne I highly recommend you take it. Remember Maddy, these people can be very dangerous.'

'I heard Maryanne loud and clear and will do my utmost to follow her instructions to a tee. I am sorry, Gretchen, in no way did I mean to jeopardize all the work you are doing.'

Gretchen said, 'I know, and I never thought you did. If the truth were to be told, and if I was to pick a volunteer to go on this mission it would be you.' She then said sternly, 'But if I had my druthers, no volunteers would be walking into that hornet's nest.'

Ali gave me a hug and a kiss on the crown of my head. They made their way to the van. Luiza and I stood on the street until we heard the engine turn. We then headed back to her house. Before we got to the door I heard my name being called from down the road. I turned and saw Lievan running toward me.

Luiza said, 'I will leave you two. I need to get mother her rum before she gets too cranky.' She entered the house and I could hear Carlos yell about the injustice of sharing his well-earned rum with some old hag and her drunkard friend.

When Lievan caught up to me his face was red and he was out of breath. Through his panting he said, 'Maddy, are you okay? I have been worried sick and have been searching these godforsaken streets all day.'

I replied, 'I'm fine, Lievan. For heaven's sake, can't a person just have some down time?'

He looked at me as if he was about to scold me, but perhaps because of the look I threw back he thought better of it. Instead he smiled, touched my upper arm and said, 'I get the sense you are not in need of another lecture. Let's just say the circumstances of your leaving made others a tad edgy. Nonetheless, you are safe and that is the main thing – thanks be to God.'

'I apologize if I worried you. I went fishing with a friend I met at Itapua,' I said.

'Maddy, there is no need to apologize.' He looked at me with those mesmerizing blue eyes. 'You are right, it is none of my business, or anyone else's for that matter, what you do with your time off. Perhaps next time, however, you will invite me and I will take you to a bingo game or something less exciting than sailing the seven seas with a man you hardly know.'

I laughed.

He said, 'However, there may be more sharks in a church bingo hall than there are in the local waters, and from what I hear the local waters have their fair share of sharks.'

I laughed more and leaned in to give him a hug. He embraced and whispered in my ear, 'I can sleep well knowing you are home.' I pressed my body into his like the day I did in the Archbishop's palace. He did not retreat and I was certain I felt a stir in the nether regions.

We held our hug longer than we should have, but in the fading light of dusk I did not care. The streets were empty and quiet only to be interrupted by the cacophonous sound of an obnoxious Harley-Davidson being turned over. We both jumped and disentangled from our embrace. Neither of us had noticed Andres Pelanchhi sitting on his bike kitty corner to where we held each other. For once the howler monkey was quiet. He made his way slowly toward us, keeping the bike in first gear and walking it like a child straddling a bike without pedals.

When he got to us he turned off the engine. He looked at me and said, 'Madeline, so glad you are home safe and sound. I heard you went on a bit of an unannounced excursion today.'

It amazed me how fast news traveled in a neighbourhood void of phones. I replied, 'Yes. I had a wonderful day but unfortunately I unintentionally upset a few people.'

He said, 'Really? Sometimes I think the people of our own country do not give its people enough credit. Sure, there are a few rotten eggs, but for the most part we are hardworking people who look out for each other. Besides you are a friend of the Pelanchhis and that means you are safe in Dona Aurora, in fact you are safe in all of Bahia. Friends of my father's rarely, if ever, come to any harm. Is that not right, Father?'

Lievan said, 'Never have truer words been spoken Andres. You father is revered in these parts.'

'Revered, yes,' said Andres, 'but also feared by the cutthroats and rapists.' He smirked, and still looking at Lievan, continued, 'Ah, but such talk of sin and sinners in front of a holy man seems sacrilegious.'

Lievan nodded and shrugged.

I said, 'Andres, shame on you. Father Lievan is a priest of the people and he knows exactly who the cutthroats and rapists are.' I said this while looking directly into Andres's eyes.

Andres replied, 'Of course. How silly of me to think otherwise.' He looked at Lievan and smirked once again, 'I hope I have not offended you Father. It is just the priests I grew up with had a different approach on how to deal with the members of their flock who had strayed from the path of righteousness. They lacked the subtleness and the …' He looked at Lievan and then at me and then back to Lievan before finding his words, 'The affection of a modern priest.'

Lievan said, 'Yes, we young priests are perhaps more liberal in our views, but the Gospel and our vows are still what motivate us to do God's work.' There was a slight quaver in his voice as he said this.

Andres said, 'Well, the light has faded and these mean streets will soon be alive with the unrepentant.' He did little to disguise the sarcasm in his voice. 'Unless I am interrupting an impromptu confession or a meaningful meditation, I was wondering if I could offer you a ride back to town, Father?'

Lievan said, 'Oh, thanks, but I can bus back. I would not want to put you out of your way.'

'No worries, Father. I have all the time in the world. Come, hop on, I insist.'

Lievan stood, looking indecisive. I thought of saying something, but then recalled Maryanne's words and decided to keep my nose out of it. I was thinking about how I should not have made the cutthroats and rapists' rebuttal when, after what seemed a long, awkward silence, Lievan said, 'Sure, I guess if it is not putting you out of your way.'

'Okay, then,' said Andres. 'As the Angels of another kind say, hop on my bitch pad.' His laughter bellowed almost as loud as the bike had. 'It is nice to know there are... how did you say it Madeline? Priests of the people, regular guys one can joke with and not take seriously all the time. C'mon Father, straddle this hog and let's let Madeline get to her bed. It will be a busy day tomorrow.'

Leivan apprehensively put his delicate hand on Andres's meaty shoulder and hoisted his leg over the bike. He tried to smile at me, but I could tell he felt humiliated. I had hoped he would have told Andres to go fuck himself after he made the 'bitch pad' comment but didn't blame him. I had just witnessed a small dose of Pelanchhi bullying.

Before cranking the engine, Andres said, 'We will see you tomorrow Madeline, my father is very much looking forward to making your acquaintance.' He pressed a button and the engine roared to life. He yelled, 'Hang on tight, Father. If you are scared put your hands around my waist.'

For a second I thought Lievan was going to but he grabbed the seat instead. The bike popped into first and roared down the street. As the tail light faded into the approaching darkness, I couldn't help but think that Lievan would have seemed more masculine if he was wearing his frock and waving incense in the air. I wondered if a priest felt like other men when he was being emasculated.

I made my way toward Luiza and noticed Carlos dart back from the window. Before entering the house I noted Dona Aurora still had a candle flickering in her shack. I wondered what she and Luiz were talking about. Oh, to be a fly on the wall in that humble home.

19

I woke to the smell of tobacco smoke. Dona Aurora was sitting on the retaining wall that made up the open area of my penthouse loft. Through the gauze-like material of my mosquito netting, her silhouette appeared ghostly. She was staring into the distance, looking like she was in deep contemplation. I feigned sleep and watched her. She was beautiful.

She said, 'He killed my father.'

I wasn't sure if she was talking out loud or talking to me.

'I know you are awake, child.' She took a drag of her cigarette and motioned for me to join her on the wall.

I got out of bed and made my way to her. I sat on the floor and leaned against the wall. She looked down at me and said, 'You sure stirred up some ghosts for me last night.'

I opened my mouth to apologize, but she silenced me with the universal 'talk to the hand' gesture. She whispered, 'Sometimes ghosts are good; they remind us of the past, of our youth and the choices we have made.' She left her perch on the wall and slowly lowered herself to the floor and sat beside me. She said, 'I must speak softly.'

She rolled another cigarette, lit it, and began, 'He shot my father, got him right above the eye. It was his trademark shot. I knew he was not the shot he used to be, but on that day his aim was true.'

There was a pause and then she said, 'Are you not going to ask why?'

'Sorry.' I shrugged. 'I thought you would tell me.'

'Do you want to know?' she asked.

'Of course.'

'Then don't be so insolent, and ask questions once in a while,' she quietly scolded.

I thought I cannot win for losing but bit my tongue. I said, 'Sorry, Dona Aurora, if I don't appear interested. I am very interested, intrigued actually. Please continue and don't mistake my silence for disinterest, think of it as awe.'

This seemed to placate her. She continued.

'I first met him in the early 1940s. Both of us were just kids. I was a whore and he was an assassin for the Pelanchhis. The first time I met him he threatened to kill me because I had embarrassed him in front of his thuggish friends. However, let's just say it became obvious he had never tried to kill anyone from a horse. Instead of executing an insolent whore he ended up being dragged down the street by a large, frightened horse. His boss, Americo Pelanchhi, paid me to mend Luiz's broken crown and bruised ego. I gladly did as the pay was good and I would not have to deal with sweaty overweight middle-aged men salivating over and then smothering my beautiful seventeen-year-old body with their massive bellies and their flaccid cocks. Besides, he was not hard on the eyes.'

I shook my head. 'Oh my God, the life you've lived.'

She continued, 'The boy mended quickly and that week we became lovers. Americo had paid me to look after him for seven days – for four of those days we lay in bed fucking our brains out. The boy could fuck and fuck and fuck. I had quite the repertoire of tricks having hooked since I was thirteen and had used them all up on him. Between the fucking, we talked and we dreamed. He had big plans, plans that now included me. After making his fortune working for the Pelanchhis he was going to take me to Rio, where he would buy a nightclub and I would run it for him while he made cash as a freelance assassin, demanding big bucks from wealthy gangsters to do their dirty work.'

She took a drag of her smoke and said, 'It has become clear to me now that neither of us gave much thought to the value of life. It's hard to imagine that the old man who held me in his arms last night was once cavalier about life and death; both his own and those who crossed his path.'

I was thinking similar thoughts, and then thought of the look I saw in Luiz's eyes when he handed me the knife and how a shadow seemed to cross his face when he spoke of Dona Aurora's father.

As if on cue she said, 'The last night we spent together my father barged into my room. He was a massive man. Luiz reached for his gun, but my father kicked it off the bedside table and grabbed both of us by the hair. Luiz thought he was going to kill us because he had found us in bed together before being married. He did not know that my daddy was my pimp.'

'Jesus,' I whispered under my breath. 'Your very own father? How could he?'

Dona Aurora sighed and continued nonchalantly, 'My father said to no one in particular, "I go to Salvador for a week and come back to this? My prize whore sleeping with some douchebag of a kid for free? Sonny, you have made a big mistake." His hand moved to Luiz's throat and he let go of my hair and pulled his switchblade out of his back pocket. I had heard the click of that spring multiple times as he had threatened to scar my and my sisters' faces on many a drunk occasion. I am certain he would have slit Luiz's throat right there and then. I remember Luiz staring at him defiantly, not willing to plead his case or ask for a boon on his life. I screamed "Americo Pelanchhi has paid me to look after him for a week." My father hesitated and said something to the effect that "you better not be lying to me, you stupid little bitch." I said, "He is Cardoso the Kid."

'My father looked at Luiz and Luiz nodded. My father let go of his death grip and Luiz gasped for air. Wretched and quicker than a jaguar, he rolled off the bed and retrieved his gun. He had it cocked and pointed at my father's head in seconds. I should have told him then and there to pull the trigger.'

I found myself nodding in agreement.

'Instead,' she said, 'I begged for my old man's life. Terrible as he was, he was my flesh and blood and in Brazil that means something.' She paused and slowly nodded her head. 'Without him my younger sisters would be fatherless and there would be no one protecting them.'

I thought, *protecting them from what?* The man was their pimp.

As if reading my thoughts she said, 'To his credit he did give us a fair cut from the family business. Most pimps kept the money and gave the girls just enough to keep them from looking emaciated. He was also an intimidating figure and a few of our clients would get too rough with us. When he was in that stage between sobriety and inebriation he could be somewhat pleasant.'

She had a pensive look, then said, 'I digress. Luiz told him to get to his knees. My father wisely obliged. My father, like a whimpering woman, begged for his life. Luiz walked up to him and told him two things. He said that if my father ever laid another hand on me he would kill him. He also said that I was to be used by Luiz and Luiz alone. Luiz asked my father how much I made him a month. I can't remember what my father said, but I am certain he told Luiz more than I actually brought in. Luiz said he would match the monthly fee as long as I got half. My father nodded in agreement.'

Dona Aurora laughed. She said, 'I suppose he was in no position to argue.'

I laughed too.

'For me,' she said, 'the next few years were wonderful. I was considered a bit of a hoity-toity hooker, not like the paramours, mind you, kept by men like the Pelancchis, the Colonels, the Archbishops, and the land barons but not like my sisters either, who were nothing more than streetwalkers and casino whores. I was for all intents and purposes a kept woman. Sure, I lived just above squalor, but I only had one man and he loved me. Luiz paid my father faithfully every month and my father remembered his side of the bargain and kept his big mitts off me. He looked at it as a win-win. Not only was he getting steady income from me, he could also name drop. He got it out in the street that he had the services of Cardoso the Kid at his disposal. I am sure that Luiz would have never helped my father out in a pickle, but he gambled that when his rivals saw Luiz enter our home they would assume the kid was his muscle. My father began to prance around the neighbourhood like a regular cock-of-the-walk. He even muscled in on some girls, eleven-year-old twins, a real find for a pimp, even though they were ugly as sin.'

She vigorously scratched her knee and said, 'The perversions of some men are hard to fathom.'

I don't think I will ever get over or understand how women such as Dona Aurora are able to talk so unflappably about how they and other women were treated. She spoke of the eleven-year-old twins like they were chattel. There was no trace of horror or disgust in her voice. I asked, 'What became of the twins?'

'Can't recall,' she said. 'I think they ended up marrying some farmhands and then moved to Sao Paulo in '59 to work for Volkswagen. Last I heard they all got jobs there and did pretty good for themselves. But who gives a flying fuck? You are getting me off track. Where was I?'

'Luiz was keeping you as his concubine.'

'What the hell is a concubine?' she asked.

'A woman who, for whatever reason, can't marry a man but has a husband-wife relationship with the man.'

She stared at me. She said, 'What the hell are you talking about? I was his whore. Stop trying to sugarcoat it. I am not ashamed of what I did. I would have fucked him for free, no question, but the fact is my father needed to be compensated. He understood this. You make it sound so dirty. Jesus, child, we do what we need to do to survive.'

'Okay,' I said, 'but remember where I come from. You need to understand that I lived like a nun compared to you. The notion of children being used in prostitution, of fathers being pimps, is incredibly disturbing. I'm sorry, but I can't wrap my head around how matter-of-fact you are about this.'

She reached out and patted my head. She said, 'Sometimes I forget you are not one of us. Take it as a compliment.'

I did.

She continued, 'Luiz was busy. He was constantly fighting with the men from rival plantation owners alongside Americo and the Englishman. Estefan Pelanchhi, Andres's grandfather, was the brains of the operation and the other three were the field officers. Luiz told me that there was friction between the brothers. Americo lived by a code and only killed when necessary while Estefan enjoyed torturing his enemies when they were captured and would not hesitate to kill women and children. Luiz told me that he feared few men but that Estefan Pelanchhi was the spawn of the devil and was evil incarnate. However, even Americo, who was as bullheaded as they come and a ruthless killer in his own right would have to agree that his brother's tactics were effective. Nobody wanted to fuck with the Pelanchhis, and Estefan ensured he had secured massive land holdings and great wealth for Maximo to inherit. He also taught his son that instilling fear in men was far more profitable than trying to gain their respect through love.

'Again I digress. Luiz visited me regularly until disaster struck.

Americo was here in Salvador trying to pay off some state politicians and the Englishman had gone with him. Luiz was summoned by Estefan to the great mansion he had built himself in the outskirts of Ilheus. From information given to him by a spy, Estefan learned than Roman Sandusky, his number-one rival, was transporting his family from the coast to his compound in the jungle. The family consisted of a young and beautiful wife and her three- and five-year-old daughters. Luiz's orders were to intercept the convoy and kill all three. Luiz told me later he knew then and there he could not do it. He also told me that if he refused he would be unceremoniously shot. He cursed his luck that Americo was not there to intervene on his behalf and left Estefan Pelanchhi's mansion with his orders.'

Dona Aurora put her hand on the retaining wall and hoisted herself up. She said, 'Give me a second, child, I need to stretch.' She placed her palms on the small of her back and arched backward. She took a small walk around the rooftop and then plunked herself down beside me. She said, 'You should smoke; it is simply a good thing to do so that when someone is need of a cigarette you can offer them one.' She cackled and said, 'Being such a goody-goody has its drawbacks, no?'

I laughed and said, 'I suppose, or maybe you could quit, then you would not have to put hosts such as me in such awkward positions of not being able to offer their guests foul-tasting cancer sticks.'

She smiled and said, 'Cancer my ass. I have been hacking butts since I was ten and I am no worse the wear. Fuck cancer. Let me get back to my story and stop distracting me with your sermons.'

I said, 'Please do.'

'So,' she said, 'Luiz arrived in Ilheus and told me of his dilemma. He said he did not sign up to kill women and children and that he wouldn't do it. I was thinking he should just kill the bitch and her brats and get it over with. If he didn't someone else would and I was sure his enemies would do the same to him if he had kids and a wife, but I said nothing. He went on to explain why he couldn't kill them; of how they were not willing combatants in the cocoa wars and how children deserved a mother and deserved the luxury of being kids.'

Dona Aurora paused and looked skyward. It seemed like she was fighting back tears. She said, 'His words and the beautiful way he spoke them made me realize for the first time that there was more to life than protecting your own skin. He made me see beyond myself. It was then and there that I had truly experienced love. I knew I could no longer be the proficient whore I once was.'

I put my arm around her shoulder, half-expecting her to shrug it off. Instead she nestled into me and continued, 'He decided to botch the job and let fate run its course. I knew that it would mean he would be struck down by his enemy's men and I begged him to reconsider. I told him to just leave, to go to another region, another country. To establish himself and send for me. I begged and begged but there was no changing his mind until I played what I have come to think of as my hooker card. I told him that without his protection my father would have me back on the streets and that my sisters, who had become jealous of me – this was a lie as I shared my money with them – would be setting me up with the most vile and heinous clients and that I would rather kill myself than succumb to such degradation.

'The way he looked at me when I said this I thought he was considering some sort of suicide pact where we would both end it right there and then. He paced around my small room smoking smoke after smoke for what seemed an eternity. He then said he would agree to leave town and one day return for me. We made love that night like we had never done before. When I woke in the morning he was gone. Later that day one of his cronies dropped by with a large sealed envelope. Inside the envelope was enough money to pay my father off for a year. He wrote that he would send me money when he could and begged me never to return to the streets.'

'I thought he killed your father?' I asked.

She said, 'Yes, yes he did. For heaven's sake girl, can't you let me tell you the whole story?'

I patted her on the shoulder and said, 'When you're ready.'

She continued, 'So he left and within a few days Americo and the Englishman showed up asking for his whereabouts. I decided to tell them the truth. I said he had skipped town because he refused to do Estefan's dirty work and murder women and children and that he would not tell me where he was going because he did not know himself, and that even if he did know he would not share it with me because he was afraid that Estefan would get his hired sadists to try to torture the truth from me. I recall defiantly telling Americo that the sons-of-bitches would kill me before I would give up Cardoso the Kid.

'Americo shook his head and the Englishman gave me a beautiful leather holster all the way from Austin, Texas. He told me that he had bought it for the Kid because he had saved him from sure death by picking off one of Sandusky's snipers who had a bead on him. They left and made it clear they would miss their young accomplice, but as far as they were concerned he was shot dead on a riverboat by a jealous whore.'

'So your secret was safe with them. Nice to see there was some honour in the hearts of these ruthless killers,' I said.

Dona Aurora nodded, 'I don't have much time for that "brothers in arms" crap, but I must admit while they lived, Americo and the Englishman looked out for me.'

'While they lived?' I asked.

Dona Aurora said, 'Yes, while they lived. The lifespan of a thieving, gambling, murdering, whoremonger is generally a short one. Americo died in a gambling house, shot in the back; rumour has it he was set up by his very own brother.' The old lady spat and continued, 'Man turn his back on his family, well he just ain't no good.'

I thought of the knife given to me by Luiz and asked, 'And the Englishman?'

'Rumour has it,' she said, 'he went deep into the jungle and ended up living with savages, completely abandoning the civilized world. People say he taught them tactics to keep their land impenetrable from progress. Madness if you ask me. He must be dead by now or else he would be over a hundred. The savages probably ate his heart and fed his flesh to the piranhas.'

She shuddered, crossed herself and once again spat. I thought about the Englishman and wondered if it was penance that drove him into the forests; atonement for the indigenous peoples who were the brunt of the genocidal practices of the European empires and greedy land barons he had made himself a hired gun for. I thought of the depletion of the rainforest and how the world could use a few more men seeking redemption by saving the natural habitat and the people who called it home for eons. My thoughts were interrupted by Dona Aurora.

'For the next few years,' she said, 'I received envelopes full of cash from places I could only dream of visiting. Money came from Bolivia, Argentina, Mexico, the USA and even Canada. It was sporadic and although there was no rhyme and reason to when the packages would arrive, when they did, there was always enough money to ensure my father was paid his share and that I had more than enough to live on.

'However, after about eighteen months of no Luiz, my father became greedy. He figured Luiz would never return because of Estefan Pelanchhi and he forced me to work the streets. He knew that if he beat me I would just defy him, so instead he beat my sisters, going as far as threatening to rape my younger one with a broom handle. Before I knew it I was back on the stroll.

When the rubber trade started to slow down he moved us back to Salvador. He rented out our small apartment in Ilheus and had one of his lackeys collect the envelopes and send them to him. In Salvador I got none of Luiz's money.'

She paused and sat, silently drawing her knees into her ancient chest. I said, 'My God, forgive me, Dona Aurora, but your father, he was despicable.'

She chortled and replied, 'Despicable? The man was a monster and the older he got the more monstrous he became.'

I shook my head.

Dona Aurora said, 'It was a few years after we moved back to San Salvador before I saw Luiz again. He showed up during Carnival. I remember my father had me working just off the plaza when Luiz found me. He was wearing a mask and it was not until he spoke that I realized who he was. At first, I thought he was just another John and treated him as such. I think it took him a minute or two to comprehend I was working the streets. I will never forget the first words he uttered to me, he said, 'You fucking whore, you fucking cunt."

Tears streamed down the old woman's cheeks. She said, 'He turned and walked away. I was in shock. When it dawned on me that it was him, I ran after him and fell at his feet. I begged him to stop and to listen to what I had to say. He tried to walk around me but I grabbed onto his leg. Tears were streaming down my face and I was blubbering like a fool. He grabbed me by the arms and picked me up. The force of his grip hurt like hell, but when he looked into my eyes I realized his hurt was twice that of mine. He grabbed me by the wrist and hustled me through the crowded streets full of revelers to his hotel room. When we got inside I tried to explain my circumstances but he told me to shut up. He kissed me hard and pressed me against the wall. Our tongues entwined and I pulled upon his long dark hair. He threw me onto his bed and I whispered to him "Take away my pain." I have never before or since made such beautiful, violent love.'

I am sure the look on my face was one of embarrassment and awkwardness. Through her tears Dona Aurora said, 'I have shocked your prissy sensibilities; for this I do not apologize for you need to learn that life is terribly messy and full of shit, but from the shit sometimes grows the roses.'

Dona Aurora looked around and then very quietly said, 'Then and there I knew I was with child.'

'Luiza?' I asked.

'Luiza.'

'So does Luiz know?' I asked.

'He does now,' she replied.

She sighed and continued, 'We fell asleep in each other's arms. He stirred before dawn and made love to me for the last time. It was slow and gentle this time. I fell back to sleep and did not hear him get up. When I woke I found a letter.'

She reached into her brassiere and pulled out a worn piece of paper with *Convento do Carmo* stamped onto the bottom of the page. The note read, *Dearest Lorinha, Follow my instructions. Marry the man I will send your way, he will provide for you and honour you. You must treat him with love and respect. Do not look for me or contact me, ever. If what I do today pains you let me apologize in advance but know I do it because I love you. Be strong. Whore no more. Your Love eternal, Luiz.*

When I finished reading it, she said, 'I did not know he could write. I could barely read. Thank god he did not use big words. I returned home later that morning to find the police with my sisters. They were in shocked disbelief. On the veranda of his apartment sat our father. The police had not removed his body yet. I did not even realize he was dead until I saw the neat, bullet hole that punctured his right eyebrow.

'Two days later Manuel De Sousa arrived at my doorstep. I believe I told you a bit about him and his crazy first wife whose father ran off to Cuba?'

I nodded, recalling the incomplete story of Luiza's 'father' and the exploits of his father-in-law in Africa.

'Well, I suppose,' said Dona Aurora, 'I was not completely honest with you. Manuel showed up with a suitcase full of money. He told me it was Luiz's fortune and that he had given it to him if he promised to marry and look after me. Manuel said he would have married me if I was penniless but that the money was just icing on the cake. Hah! A real charmer, that one.

'I told him we would shack up, but I would not marry him. He agreed but was fearful that "Cardoso the Kid" would exact revenge on him if he did not honour the agreement. It was not until Luiza was three that I officially married the man. I held on to the hope that Luiz would return for as long as I could, but when I saw that my little girl had taken to who she believed was her father and that I was convinced he thought she was his child, I agreed to the marriage, knowing she would be cared for if I should die.'

I said, 'My God. What a story.'

Dona Aurora said, 'Manuel was no angel, but he was a good enough father and husband. He saw what happened to my father and did not want to tempt the same fate. We had enough money to live on for a long time. A lot of it went to looking after my older sister. She got syphilis and went nuts. We tried all kinds of treatment including that *candomblé* bullshit Luiz seems so enamored with. It was a waste of good cash; she offed herself with our father's old shotgun. She ate both barrels right in front of Luiza and me. Luiza was only one and a half; I don't think she remembers. There were brains and blood everywhere.

'I paid good money to send my younger sister to a secretarial school. She fucked and then married the instructor. She lives way up in Fortaleza. She is a good woman. She was able to put the streets behind her and make a good life for herself.

'The rest of the money was put into making sure Luiza got an education. You know she can read and write like nobody's business? I think a day will come when she will be able to put her talents to use. When Fabricio is older she will go back to her books and learning. She would be a wonderful teacher.' She paused, wiped her nose with the back of her hand and said, 'That is, if we ever get that damned school built.'

The mention of the school jolted me into the present, 'Shit,' I said, 'the Pelanchhi party! What time is it? I've got to get going.'

I went to stand up but she put her hand on my forearm and said, 'Slow down my child. You have plenty of time.' She looked into my eyes and touched my face. 'Thank you for bringing him back. If I die I can now do so knowing all those I love are in my life. You are an angel.'

I almost cried but I did not. No more tears for Maddy Saunders. I hugged her and said, 'Thank you for telling me your tale. Thank you for forgiving me.'

With that she let me up and I helped her to her feet. As she was walking away she said, 'Now I must find Luiza. God knows I have a lot of explaining to do.'

20

I went down the ladder and into the kitchen. Luiza was smoothing the wrinkles out of my only frock using an ancient flat iron she had borrowed from a neighbor. She heated it on the stove and when it was good and hot pressed the fine cotton, returning the iron to be re-heated when necessary. Carlos was preening himself and chattering away to no one in particular. He reminded me of a high school girl getting ready for the big prom. Fabricio sat at the table eating a mango, seeming oblivious of the nervous energy that crackled between his parents.

I said, 'Luiza, please, you don't have to do that.'

'Oh, she does not mind,' said Carlos. 'She is more than happy to help you out. Luiza enjoys ironing. Look at the masterful job she did on my slacks.'

Before I could scowl and scold him, he did a dainty pirouette showing off his far-too-tight black slacks and satiny red shirt. Though I despised the man, I could not help but laugh. Encouraged by my jovial reaction he picked up the broom and began to samba while humming 'La Bamba.' Fabricio picked up spoons and started drumming on the table while humming along. Carlos tossed me the broom and with a grace I would not have believed if I did not witness it, floated across the small kitchen and grabbed his wife, twirling her into the middle of the floor. They transformed the tiny kitchen into a ballroom, gyrating, taunting each other with seductive moves while keeping perfect time to their son's rhythm. Luiza and Carlos were no longer an overworked and under-appreciated wife and her ne'er-do-well husband; they were lovers bent on devouring each other with an all-consuming passion. I was riveted. Once again I was reminded of that contradiction named Brazil.

The dance lasted maybe two minutes, three tops, but it seemed to be able to tell a tale of love, lust and loss. It ended with him dipping her so low her head almost hit the floor while her back was arched on an angle that no woman her age and build should be able to achieve. In perfect synchronization they snapped their heads towards me and shot euphoric smiles my way. I dropped the broom and clapped, vociferously yelling, 'Bravo. Bravo.'

Carlos kissed his wife on the forehead and pulled her up. He gave her a pinch on the behind as she stood beside her man. She giggled and mockingly scolded him saying, 'Carlos, not in front of our company, and look, you are embarrassing your son.'

Luiza did a curtsy and, beaming, returned to the flat iron. She finished the last bit of my frock and handed it to me. She said, 'You will look radiant.'

I gave her a hug and made my way to the bathroom. When I returned to the kitchen Luiza fussed over me while Carlos sat at the table annoyingly tapping his fingers. From outside we heard the timid 'beep beep' of a car horn. Carlos darted to the door and returned. 'Our ride is here, Maddy. Come, we don't want to be late.'

Luiza pulled me aside and said, 'I know a lot of people have given you grief about going to this party and for good reason. The Pelanchhis are a bad bunch. But now, to hell with it, there is nothing you can do, so just enjoy yourself, have a good time. Pretend you are there for no other reason than to attend a la-di-da party, pretend you are part of high society and that you fit right in. Savour the food, the wine and the elegance and look at the experience as a snapshot into what it means to live in Brazil, for you will be coming into contact with the part of our nation that only a few Brazilians experience. You will see wealth and opulence hard to imagine. In light of what most of us have to live with, this might make you ill to your stomach, but Maddy this party is not a place for you to pontificate on the injustices of it all. I know you and I know you will want to shed light on the fact that the glass you will be drinking your champagne from costs more than what most of us here in Dona Aurora make in a month. Don't!'

Her eyes pierced into me with more intensity than the day she chastised me for meandering into the beating of poor Inacio. When I began to apologize, she said, 'Stop with the apologies already. What's done is done. Besides, your actions have revealed to me who my real father is.'

Again I began to speak only to be interrupted, she said, 'You look shocked. What? You think I am an imbecile? The moment he said her name I knew who he was. I cannot wait to hear how the old lady explains this one away.'

Her smile was diminished when from behind us Carlos snapped, 'Luiza, let the girl go. We can't be late.'

She whispered, 'Be the wise woman I know you can be.' She gave me a hug and sent me on my way.

21

Carlos sat in the front seat of his friend's cab while I, gladly, remained in the back by myself. His friend's name was Filipe. As we drove through the shanty town in order to make our way into the country he continued to gawk at me in the rearview mirror while tapping his fingers to what was becoming irritating Brazilian pop music. I tried my best to ignore his lecherous looks, but the man was relentless.

I barked, 'Take a picture, it lasts longer.' As far as keeping my big mouth shut, this was not exactly the start I was looking for.

Carlos seemed torn between defending the honour of his hurt friend, insulted by an insolent *gringa,* and keeping up the façade of finding any sort of value in my existence other than to stare at my rather modest breasts. The sycophant in him won out and he said, 'Keep your eyes on the fucking road. She is way out of your league.' Such chivalry.

I decided to concentrate on the changing landscape. As we wound our way out of the ravine that Dona Aurora was nestled in, we traveled through parts of the city I had not seen. There seemed to be little rhyme or reason to the directions we were going, nor to the beginning and endings of neighbourhoods. We passed by other slums, business centres, high-rise apartments and industrial areas, reminding me that the city of Salvador was approximately the same size as Toronto, Canada's largest city. By the time we left the urban areas in our dust I had no clue as to where I was.

All I knew was that I was in lush and green country. We turned left off a main highway and entered an unmarked private road. Filipe said to Carlos, 'Notice the surveillance cameras in the trees? The spider has his lair well protected.'

Carlos replied, 'I hear there are trip wires and even land mines in the jungle outside the main walls.'

Filipe, taking on the air of an expert in such matters replied, 'Trip wires and other sensory devices, yes, but no mines. He has men and his beloved dogs patrolling the perimeter, and though it is said he could not care less for human life, he dotes on his dogs like they were his grandchildren.'

'Did you know that his helicopter is the exact same as the Americans use?' asked Carlos.

'Everyone knows that,' replied Filipe. 'It is exactly like the ones used by the CIA. It stands for the Central Intel—'

'I know what the C fucking IA stands for,' countered Carlos, obviously not amused by being trumped by his friend. In order to rub it in a bit more he slyly said, 'I will be able to add to your trivial obsession when I return from the compound.' He might as well have said inner sanctum instead of compound for he spoke with a reverence usually held for holy places. Nevertheless his words had the desired effect and Filipe was squarely put in his place. He pouted silently for the rest of the drive up the private road. A thing I was grateful for.

The old cab rounded a long, gentle curb as it left the forest and entered a five hundred yard straightaway that ran through well-manicured lawns. I notice there were no trees, no shrubbery of any sort on the grass; it was as if it was acting as a giant moat protecting the villa ahead from the gnarled and ancient trees of the jungle. The villa was built on top of a slight rise. I could only glimpse the red clay slates of the roof for it was surrounded by a twelve-foot wall and a wrought iron gate. The gate opened slowly as we approached. Carlos and Filipe let out oohs and ahhs at this marvel. Filipe turned down his radio and I began to notice the ping of the diesel engine. The noise, along with the smell, seemed out of place in this country haven.

I was expecting to see men with machine guns manning turrets and sentries at the gate. I expected to see gaudy architecture, characterized by Corinthian columns and opulent gilded statues of lions, eagles and perhaps a centaur or two thrown in to spice things up. There was not a hint that we had just entered the home of a notorious crime boss. The gardens in the inner wall were refined, immaculate and dotted with strategically placed foliage, giving a sense of symmetry but in a very natural way. The house itself was low to the ground with understated windows and a rustic-looking door. I imagined if a refined renaissance Florentine duke was to build himself a home in the twentieth century it would look something like the Pelanchhi residence. The grounds and the façade of the home conveyed a message of refinement, elegance, subdued wealth and grounded power.

As we came to the front door we had yet to see a person other than a few groundskeepers off in the distance. One of them came walking toward us. Filipe said, 'My God, it is him.'

Carlos whispered, 'What the hell?'

I said, 'Who is it?'

'Senhor Pelanchhi,' replied Carlos.

Don't get me wrong I am not into the whole older guy thing, but I do not believe I have ever seen a more handsome man than Maximillo Pelanchhi. He was wearing a simple blue-grey shirt and jeans over his lean, but not too lean, six foot, two inch frame. His wavy hair was silver with hints of jet black as was the well-cropped beard and mustache. He had defined cheekbones, a nose that seemed to fit his face perfectly and eyes that, because of their smoldering darkness and vibrancy, mesmerized. As he approached the diesel, I wanted to scream to Filipe to turn the goddamn engine off. For reasons I can't quite explain, I felt embarrassed sitting in the pathetic cab in the company of a man of such wealth and taste. To this day I find it hard to come to terms with my initial feelings for a man who I knew was very, very bad. He reminded me of the way Count Dracula is sometimes portrayed: Though his female prey sense his danger, they cannot help but be drawn to him eventually offering their necks, their blood and their souls in exchange for a taste of his dark pleasures. Never before or since has a man had such an effect on me. Somewhere in the recesses of my mind I was cursing Gretchen and Luiza for not warning me about how hot the spider was.

As he got closer to the car he took a quick look at his watch. He then took out a kerchief and wiped his brow. He put his hands on the roof of the cab and leaned in. He said, 'Hello, you must be Andres's guests for this afternoon's soirée. Carlos, is it not?'

Carlos looked awestruck; he nodded.

Maximo leaned his head in more and turned to me. He smiled. His teeth were perfect. He said, 'And if my deductive skills are correct you must be Madeline from the true north, strong and free.'

Honest to god it was like being in the company of a rock star, it might as well have been Mick Jagger or David Bowie looking me in the eye; the man oozed charisma. I gathered myself enough to reply, 'Yes.'

He chuckled and then, while still looking at me – looking through me – asked, 'May I ask what time did Andres say the festivities would begin?'

I shrugged and said, 'I am not sure. He made the arrangements with Carlos.'

Maximo looked at Carlos and said, 'Carlos, what time did Andres tell you to arrive by?'

Carlos said, 'Four o'clock.'

'Oh dear,' said Pelanchhi, 'it is only quarter to three. My apologies. Perhaps my son told you it would take you longer to get here than it did.'

I was staring daggers in Carlos's back. How embarrassing.

Maximo said, 'Oh well, you are here now. I will have my assistant Vicente look after you.' He then held the back door for me to get out. When I did he said, 'Again, my apologies. Where are my manners? I have not formally introduced myself. I am Maximo Pelanchhi.' He offered me his hand and I took it. It was powerful and gentle at the same time. He said, 'Welcome to my home.'

Carlos got out of the front seat. He no longer looked like the beautiful dancer who hours ago was twirling his wife around their kitchen. He looked ridiculous in his red shirt and threadbare slacks. He looked like a clown.

Maximo closed both doors of the cab and said to Filipe through the open window, 'Wait here for a few minutes. I will have one of my people bring you some refreshments for the road as well as a token of my appreciation for bringing my son's guests to our home. There will be no need to pick them up as I will have a driver drop them off.' He then reached behind him and grabbed a small walkie-talkie that was clipped to his belt. He said, 'Vicente could you meet at the front of the house. Andres's guests have arrived a tad early. Could you please look after them until I am ready? I still have some bushes to work on and then must freshen up before the rest of the party arrives. Also could you have one of the guys grab some grub and a drink for the cabbie and also make sure he is well compensated for the long drive.'

Carlos said, 'You don't have to pay him. He owed me a lot from our last poker game and this is how he is repaying me. He did not drive here solely out of the goodness of his heart, Senhor.'

Maximo gave Carlos a smile that was tempered with an icy stare, he said, 'Forgive the man his debt, Carlos. I will still pay him. Do you know why?'

Carlos shook his head. Maximo said, 'Because I said I would.' He turned back toward me and said, 'Please forgive me, I do hope you do not think I am rude but every Saturday I trim that rose bush, it is planted in memory of my late wife.'

I replied, 'Please forgive us. I am sorry we have intruded upon your home so early.'

He said, 'Not a worry. Oh, here comes Vicente. I will leave you in his capable hands. Believe me, you will be well looked after.' With that he returned to his shearers and his rose bush.

After watching him stroll away my attention was drawn to the high-pitched voice of Vicente as he said, 'Welcome my friends, welcome.'

Vicente looked like a snowman. He wore a white suit over a round body. He had round legs and a round head with beady black eyes and a sharp nose that almost protruded as far as the wide-brimmed white fedora that was perched on his head. I had never seen such a pale, white-skinned Brazilian. He told Filipe to wait and shooed us into the foyer of the home. I was taken aback by the décor. Like the outside it resonated class and good taste. The floor was a subdued marble and the walls were painted in a brownish-red hue that matched the local soil. There was beautiful, original art done in a traditional Afro-Brazilian style. One painting depicted a mother and her child in a market; the mother had her baby in one hand and a basket full of goods in other. On the opposite wall a painting showed a mother cutting sugar cane with a child strapped to her back on a cradleboard. Below each canvas was an artifact from the painting; there was a reed basket similar to the one named *Mother at the Market* and a cradleboard that looked identical to the one entitled *Mother in the Cane.*

Vicente's walkie-talkie beeped and he said, 'Excuse me for a minute.' He walked down the hallway and into another room. I could not hear what he was saying. When he returned he said, 'Carlos could you wait here in the foyer? One of Andres's assistants would like to have a word with you.'

Carlos replied, 'Of course, no problem.'

'Good.' Vicente turned to me. 'Madeline, why don't I give you a tour of some of the more interesting rooms of the house? I can tell you have a keen eye for art and artifacts. I hope you will be impressed by some of Senhor Pelanchhi's collection.'

I nodded enthusiastically and said, 'If these paintings are an indicator, I'm in for a treat. Did you know my area of study was anthropology with a dabbling in archeology?'

His eyes lit up. 'I was never afforded the luxury of a university degree but since being under the employ of Senhor Pelanchhi I have become quite the dabbler in local artifacts. I believe you will find the collection very interesting.'

As we were walking down the hallway the front door opened and a man who looked every part the thug made his way toward Carlos. Like Andres, he wore aviator glasses. He sported a tight, black dress shirt that was unbuttoned to show gold chains half-buried in thick, black chest hair. A thin, six-inch scar ran down his left cheek. He put his hand on Carlos's shoulder and whispered something in his ear. Carlos nodded and left with the man.

Vicente said, 'There are two rooms I would like to show you. One is what I call the artifact room, which has handcrafted tools and artistries from this region going back to pre-contact. Let's start there. Then we will visit the photography room. It is an exhibit in the works put together by Senhor Pelanchhi of his family and their history in this region. He went to great expense to have the photos restored and re-imaged into large posters. The effort, I hope you will agree, was well worth it.'

The artifact room was set up like a museum area using track lighting and showcase boxes to highlight the relics. The only difference being there was nothing preventing anyone from picking up and holding the objects. I was in my glory as there was an array of artifacts ranging from poison dart blowguns and lethal-looking spears to silver coins, crucifixes and ceramics. Vicente said, 'I can tell you little about the pre-Columbian artifacts. By the way, I hate the term pre-Columbian as you and I both know the Scandinavians made contact well before Columbus. However, it is the term that has dominated academia for some time, no?'

I said, 'Yes, even in Canada we use the term in spite of the fact that the first euro-indigenous contact more than likely happened in Newfoundland.'

He nodded thoughtfully and said, 'Anyway, all I or the local curators could tell you about these pre-Columbian treasures are that they originated with one of the tribes in the area – either the Baenã, Pataxó Hãhãhãe, Kamakã, Tupinambá, Kariri-Sapuyá or Gueren. These groups traded and fought with each other. With settlement came diaspora and many were enslaved by the Europeans and were often bred with the African slaves. That is why you see such variety in the shades of our brown-skinned Brazilians. Others were continuously being pushed further and further into the jungle. It seems most were either wiped out or assimilated, most likely through slavery, into the interior tribes.'

I thought of the Englishman and his attempts to fight alongside the indigenous people against European expansion into the jungle. As if reading my thoughts Vicente said, 'Senhor Pelanchhi is part of a consortium of influential Bahians who have bought vast stretches of jungle land to be preserved for the indigenous groups that currently occupy them. The object is to have as little contact with these peoples as possible so they may continue to live like they have for thousands of years.'

I said, 'Sounds like a wonderful idea.'

After I had experienced every piece tactilely we moved to the other side of the room that was dominated by a European collection. Vicente explained, 'All of these gems were recovered from a Portuguese galleon, the *Santissima Sacramento* that had sunk just outside Salvador's harbour. It was 1668 and she was carrying seven, perhaps eight hundred people from Portugal and was the *Capitania* for a fifty or so vessel convoy.'

There were few Portuguese words I was unfamiliar with and with the ones I was uncertain about I could usually make an accurate educated guess and was typically spot on, but every once in a while I just had to ask. 'Vicente, what is a *Capitania*?'

He thought for a while, looking like he was trying to find the correct English word and finally said, 'A flagship.'

I nodded but must have had a look of puzzlement on my face.

He reverted back to Portuguese saying, 'In naval terms it is often the largest, fastest and most heavily armed ship that flies the admiral's flag. In most cases it is the ship that fronts the convoy.' He paused for a moment and continued, 'I do not know what exactly happened on that ship the fateful day she went down, but I, like many amateur historians, have created my own story.'

I asked, 'I would love to hear it.'

He smiled and took off his fedora, revealing a few strands of wispy hair covering an almost bald head in what looked liked a desperate comb-over. He said, 'Perhaps on another occasion.' He pointed out the coins and explained they were from the Don Joao IV era and he informed me that the broken ceramic bowls bore the seal of the da Silver's, a very influential colonial family.

Among many other things, I inspected musket and cannonballs. I held a piece of lumber that had the faded letters *sacre* etched into the wood. I wished I could have spent hours in that room. As we were leaving Vicente turned to me and said, 'Out of the eight hundred only seventy survived.'

I said, 'That is horrible.'

'They could see the shore, the harbour was right there. But they hit a shoal and that was it. No one knows what was going on in the captain's head. Was it arrogance, impatience, laziness, stupidity? Was there a woman waiting for him? Who knows? This, however, is a given. If he had set sail out to sea and waited for the storm to pass, then all would have been well. There is a lot to be said for patience and prudence.'

He paused for a moment and then said, 'Ah, forgive me. I always become sad and a tad dramatic when I think of these things. Shame on me, with this being a day for a party. Let me show you the photographic display in the next room. There are not many on large posters yet, but those that are there I think you will find very interesting.'

There were ten large photos hanging on thin guy-wires attached to the ceiling. They were all black-and-white and had little pedestals under each one with a brief description and date. The first one was a formal picture of Estefan Pelanchhi and his wife on their wedding day. She was a beauty and he was a rather nondescript-looking man. She was smiling up at him; he looked straight into the lens of the camera with a face free of emotion. The next seven photos showed the family homestead in Ilheus, the clearing of the jungle for cocoa plantations with men and animals doing burdensome labour, the ninth photo taken was of Estefan from the inside of what I assumed was a casino. He was at a table with a few other well-dressed men; they were surrounded by Afro-Brazilian servers and what I guessed were whores. I searched for Dona Aurora, but to no avail, and wondered if the younger-looking women were her sisters. My eyes settled on twins and I speculated if they were the ones owned by Dona Aurora's father.

The last photo was hidden around an enclave. At first I walked right by it and was ready to leave before Vicente pointed out I had missed it. I gasped when I saw it. Staring back at me was Luiz. He was sitting on the ground with his back propped up against a giant stump. Two men sat on the stump. All three were holding rifles. Luiz had his pointing down and had a knife in his hand; it looked like he was putting a notch into the butt of the rifle. The other man wore what looked like a worn-and-tattered military coat and the third looked like the spitting image of Maximo Pelanchhi. Goddamn he was handsome. I looked at the pedestal and it said, '*Americo Pelanchhi, Captain Bartholomew Dunn and a hired hand. Back country, Ilheus, 1944.*'

I was mesmerized. I barely heard Vicente say, 'Ah yes, this one is a prize. It captures my attention too. On behalf of Senhor Pelanchhi I have done some research.' He pointed to the Englishman and said, 'This grizzled old soldier remained a mystery for a long time. However, on a hunch I sent the picture to a military archivist in London who was able to give me lots of information. From what he can gather the man was a deserter and a soldier of fortune. He fought in the Boer War and was court martialed for beating a colonel senseless. He escaped from the stockade and was never heard from again. The coat in the picture is from his Regiment, The Royal Irish Fusiliers.'

I tried to contain my excitement and said, 'Fascinating.'

He pointed to Americo and said, 'That is Senhor Pelanchhi's uncle. He was known as a bit of a playboy and a swashbuckler I am afraid. Nevertheless, he was instrumental in building the Pelanchhi fortune. He died young.'

I said, 'I can see a family resemblance.'

Vicente pointed at Luiz and said, 'The boy whittling into the butt of that gun is a mystery. I have looked through hundreds of other pictures and he shows up in a few. There is only one where he is smiling. He is on a massive horse that makes him look like a dwarf and the Captain is holding the reigns. He seems so out of place, a boy in a man's world. I thought perhaps he was the child of the Captain or perhaps even the bastard son of Americo, but there are no records and then he just seems to disappear.'

Vicente then grabbed me by the arm and said excitedly, 'However, I do have something to link him to.' He guided me to another hidden enclave and pointed to a rifle hung on the wall. He said, 'This is the rifle from the pictures.' He took it down from the display case saying, 'See the notches? I have no idea what they represent, but they are the same pattern as the one in the picture. There are thirty-seven notches. At first I thought they meant kills, but from one so young?

'Furthermore, the rifle is a Mauser Grewehr 98, with the original scope, silencer and one hundred rounds of the finest German bullets fully intact. Perhaps the most deadly sniping rifle used by the Germans during World War One. Why would a boy have such a tool?'

I shook my head.

He said, 'Here's my theory. The boy is the captain's manservant and he looks after his weapons, including putting the notches in them.'

I nodded my head and feigned a smile. I said, 'It sounds like you have given this lots of thought, and you are probably right.'

I casually put my hand on the small of my back and faked a stretch. I slipped my hand down to my underwear and felt for the knife I had tied around my hips with the Afrikaan woman's home-made concealed belt, knowing full well it was the blade that was used to put the thirty-something notches on Cardoso the Kid's Mauser.

Vicente looked at his watch and said, 'Oh my God, it's half past four. Senhor Pelanchhi will be wondering where we are. Let me get you to the party.'

22

Vicente led me down a hallway and through a large kitchen and dining area, which had a rustic-feeling décor, and through beautifully designed French doors onto the backyard. The backyard was massive. There was acre upon acre of manicured lawns dimpled with oases of pools, flowers, shrubs and trees. On the perimeter lay the jungle, wild and untamed. I could barely see a trail off in the distance that seemed to cut through the jungle – to where, I was not sure.

I could see that there was a large canopy off to the right where Maximo Pelanchhi was standing and his guests were sitting down with their backs to me. He was wearing a resplendent off-white suit and a light pink shirt. Though I was positive it was one hundred-plus degrees it looked like there was not a drop of perspiration on the man. As we approached he said, 'Ah, Vicente, you have finally decided to give us back our guest. I thought you had kidnapped her and kept her for yourself.'

With this the four people sitting down turned to look at Vicente and me. I felt my heart jump when I made eye contact with Lievan who was sitting next to Archbishop Matos. The other two, I assumed, were the senator and his wife. Vicente said, 'The idea of abducting this young woman was tempting, it is rare to find someone with as keen an interest in the past as I have, at least not one who is as charming as this young lady.'

Maximo laughed. 'My apologies, Madeline, if my good friend bored you with our rather sparse collection of relics and old photographs.' He nodded to Vicente and Vicente, without another word, returned the nod and headed back to the house.

I said, 'I was hardly bored. I was fascinated. I think you are most fortunate to have such a knowledgeable curator.' I was hoping Vicente heard my words as he marched back to house.

Maximo replied, 'Yes, Vicente is wonderful. I am not sure how I would manage around here without him. With no further ado, let me introduce you to my guests.' The Archbishop, the senator, and Lievan stood up. Maximo said, 'I believe you are already acquainted with Archbishop Matos and his assistant Father Van den Broeck.' Lievan, wearing a light orange Lacoste golf shirt and khaki pants walked toward me and shook my hand. 'Wonderful to see you again, Maddy.'

The Archbishop, dressed in a purple shirt and wearing his clerical collar nodded and said, 'Hello, Madeline.'

Maximo said, 'Now let me introduce you to a good friend of mine, and though we do not always see things eye-to-eye on the political realm, I cannot deny he is a skilled politician. Madeline say hello to Senator Alberto de Moraes.'

The senator looked me up and down and said, 'Welcome to my good friend's humble abode.' He was a tall man, bald on top with a thick, black mustache. He looked athletic with the exception of a modest but noticeable paunch. Maximo said, 'Our senator is almost as nimble in the political arena as he was on the soccer field, not many Bahians can boast to play for the Verde-amarela.'

I must have looked confused. Lievan said, 'The green and yellow; it is a reference to the national football, or should I say, soccer team.'

I looked at the senator in what must have been awe. The other men, even Matos, were smiling at me. I said, 'Did you know –'

Matos and Maximo continued to smile and Lievan and the senator laughed as the senator said, 'Yes, I knew and still know Pele.'

'How did you know I was going to ask that question?' I inquired.

At that moment the senator's wife stood up and faced me for the first time, she said with a dry smile, 'Because regardless of my husband's accomplishments as an athlete and politician it is always the first question asked by people introduced to him once they know he played for the National team. For some reason he and the other men find this incredibly amusing. I believe you just earned Maximo a wager, as my husband thought, you being Canadian, would not know who Pele is.'

While she was saying this I tried to keep my eyes locked on hers as she had the roundest, firmest, and fakest breasts I had ever encountered and they were staring right back at my tiny little mandarins. I said, 'I wonder if Doctor Randy Gregg gets it the same way.'

They looked at me inquisitively. I said, 'Randy Gregg was a teammate of Gretzky's and now a practicing doctor.'

The inquisitiveness continued. Lievan rescued me: 'Gretzky is an ice hockey player; many would argue he is the Pele of his sport.'

This produced some ohhs and ahhs and the senator mumbled, 'Yes, I think I have heard of him.'

Maximo said, 'Please, out of the sun and into the shade.'

We made our way back to the canopy. Under it was a large oak table with a smorgasbord of treats ranging from sushi to smoked salmon, a plethora of fruit and cheese. A smaller table housed the alcohol. It was stocked with hard liquor, red and white wine and Brahma, a popular Brazilian beer. My mouth watered. Maximo said, 'I am not sure where Andres has gotten to, but I think we should fill our plates before the ice melts. Come, ladies first.'

The senator's wife walked toward me and said, 'My name is Vania; my friends call me Nia, so please call me Nia.' She reached out her hand and I shook it. She motioned me toward the table and said, 'After you.'

'No Nia, I insist, birthday girl goes first, and please call me Maddy.'

Nia smiled and said, 'Thank you, Maddy.'

I was proud of myself for thinking it would be good to follow her lead just in case I screwed up on the proportions of food or took things out of order. What a mistake that was. Here in front of me was the most delectable spread I had seen in months and I was following behind a woman who had the tiniest waist one could imagine supporting such voluptuous breasts, and she was eating like an anorexic. I swear to God the woman could not have put less on her plate. The bitch! When we got to the alcohol she poured some soda water into a wine glass and filled the rest with, I think it was safe to assume, excellent white wine.

I thought of my father who considered himself a connoisseur of vintage wines and imagined he would have a conniption if he witnessed such a crime against the vine. I thought to myself 'fuck that' and grabbed a Brahma.

The men followed, and to make things worse, plied mountainous heaps of food onto their plates. My mouth watered watching them. I looked over at miss sparrow legs as she daintily picked at the few morsels of cheese, cucumber and honey dew melon that barely made a dent on her plate and then looked down at my own meager pickings and felt very sorry for myself. I took a swig of the ice-cooled beer and felt somewhat better. I had not had a beer in a long time and it felt good.

The men joined us, and Lievan sat beside me. His plate was stacked more than anyone else's. I thought he was cruel sitting beside me with so much food, but then he whispered, 'Sometimes my eyes are bigger than my stomach, plus I feel a need to keep up with the big boys as far as learning the art of strategically placing as much food on a small plate as possible therefore I often overindulge. Would you mind if every once in a while I sneak some of this delicious grub your way.' I smiled and nodded. He said, 'It is good to see you smile, Maddy.' I swear I ate half the food on his plate. I particularly savoured a giant prawn that he had already bitten into. I chased the delicious food with another beer and began to feel rather good about myself and the world in which I lived.

During the meal, which I later found out was only a precursor to the formal dinner we would be enjoying in the house, the talk centered around Maximo and the Archbishop. In many ways they were very similar. It was clear they were not friends, but there was a mutual respect between them. At first I thought they were sparring with each other, telling tales of one-upmanship, the Archbishop recounting his carpentry exploits while Pelanchhi told tales about horticulture and agriculture. It became apparent neither was bragging but both were passionate about their chosen fields of interest.

In many ways both men reminded me of my father; I could envision him joining the conversation and adding his two-bits about his cattle or his helicopter piloting. Having said that, the men who sat in front of me exhibited a hardness that my father did not possess; it was something intangible, but they lacked warmth toward others.

The only thing I was enjoying more than the conversation was having Lievan sit so close to me. Our chairs were positioned together, meaning our forearms often touched. I felt every brush of his skin when he moved his arm. It gave me tingles in my spine. Maximo broke off his conversation with the Archbishop by saying, 'Forgive me and my good friend Thiago, we could talk like amateur tradesmen and farmers for hours about what real labourers would find to be the epitome of the mundane. Let's change the subject. Madeline, tell us a little about yourself and Canada.'

'Yes,' said the senator's wife, 'enthrall us with tales of bears and red Indians.' It was said with a hint of sarcasm I am certain only another woman would pick up on.

I replied, 'Well, I hate to disappoint you but the only native people I know have beautiful brown skin and my encounters with bears are few and far between. I grew up in a densely populated area by Canadian standards. Although I did spend a summer in a place called Hartley Bay, which is very remote and the home of the spirit bear, while doing a field study for my anthropology degree.'

The senator said, 'A spirit bear; sounds interesting.'

'Well, the official name is a Kermode bear,' I said. 'They are very rare and are identified by their white fur.'

This seemed to get the attention of everyone. I swear the faces of the Archbishop and Pelanchhi told the same story – both men were thinking about how a Kermode bear pelt would look in their respective studies.

Lievan asked, 'So were you studying the local people's connection to the spirit bear?'

I took a swig of my third beer and said, 'Nope. The nation that resides in Hartley Bay is called the Haisla. The people are matriarchal and I was studying the influence modern media was having on their traditional, matrilineal ways.'

At this point the senator's wife stifled a subtle yawn. Again, I am certain none of the males noticed, but I received her message loud and clear.

I continued, 'While there I ran into a Japanese film crew doing a documentary on the Spirit Bear. Unfortunately, their angle was not about the threats the forest industry could have on the bear's habitat; it was about the uniqueness of the bear itself.' I giggled and continued, 'I remember sitting around the docks with the guides from Hartley Bay conjuring all kinds of myths about the bear. The guides were good guys, they did not share their made-up myths with the documentarians, because, in all seriousness, the people of Hartley Bay and other native communities along the coast wanted to ensure the protection of the land from forestry and mining and publicity in Asia and Europe about the plight of the bear and other animals would be beneficial to the environmental cause. I spent more time trying to influence the angle of the documentarian than I did on my own project.'

Maximo said, 'Fascinating. Here in Brazil there are similar concerns with our forest. We are seen as incorrigible industrialists bent on destroying the land and causing the extinction of many species for doing what Europeans, North Americans and Asians have been doing for centuries.'

The senator said, 'Yet we have people of influence like you, Maximo, who have committed their resources to protecting vast tracts of land.'

'True,' said Maximo, 'and as you are aware by my constant badgering of yourself, it is my belief the government must take the lead in protecting the rainforest, not just for Brazilians but for the planet. I agree with the scientists and the environmentalists. That is not what bothers me. What irks me is the hypocrisy of those who have raped the earth like no other, wagging their fingers at us.'

'Here, here,' said the Archbishop. 'It is the same with our poor and indigenous people.' He looked directly at me and said, 'Would you not agree, Madeline, that there is much to be said about how poorly you Canadians have treated your natives? Yet, North Americans seem willing and ready to turn a patronizing and often judgmental eye toward us in Brazil?'

The Archbishop's eyes looked at me with an intensity I had never noticed before. A quick scan of the guests showed me that all eyes were on me; even Nia seemed engaged. I felt panic take over and thought that this is exactly the kind of conversation I was to avoid. The beer buzz was not helping. I was trying to think of a response beyond the fuck you Thiago that was on the tip of my tongue. To delay I took the last swig of my beer.

'Hah,' said Lievan. 'Canadians, Brazilians they have nothing on us Belgians. What we did in Africa ... I don't even want to think about. I would go on, but it is not good birthday party conversation.'

While Lievan rescued me I looked at the Archbishop and saw a slight twitch on his face. For Lievan's sake I hoped his boss did not believe the commentary on Belgian colonial sin was intentionally made to deflect attention from me.

Nia said, 'Father Lievan, please, I am intrigued by this conversation. Please, Maddy, feel free to express your opinion.' She gave me a smile and her teeth were daggers.

Before I had a chance to respond, our attention was diverted by loud music coming from the edge of the forested area. Through the trail that led into the forest came what can be best described as a souped-up golf cart. It had green-and-yellow tiger stripes with customized mirrors and tires that were placed on customized rims. The golf club storage area was taken over by a massive sound system. I am sure there must have been extra batteries added just to power the stereo. I later learned that the back seats lifted up and were used as coolers. The cart came racing toward us, blasting the Scorpions' 'Rock You Like a Hurricane'. As the cart got closer the occupants became identifiable. Andres was driving and a blond woman sat beside him.

I glanced at Maximo Pelanchhi and could tell he was not impressed by his son's entrance. His poker face was cracked ever so slightly and for a brief moment disdain seeped out. Andres had the cart floored and it whirred past us, circling the canopy before coming to a complete stop. He dismounted and took off his aviators. He was wearing black leather pants, black cowboy boots and a black Bon Jovi *Slippery When Wet* t-shirt with the sleeves removed.

He moved under the canopy, ignoring the girl who remained in the cart, and made his way toward the senator's wife. As he hugged her he said, 'Nia, my love, I can't believe someone who looks so young and beautiful as you is still with that old politico Alberto de Morales.' Andres then made his way to the senator and gave him a fake jab, 'Just kidding, you lucky old dog.' He whirled around and yelled at the woman in the golf cart, 'Caprice get your ass out of the cart and let me introduce you to our guests.'

Caprice was close to six feet. She wore the shortest shorts and the tightest of tank tops. Her breasts made Nia's look modest. Her skin was golden brown and her hair was blond. She wore slightly too much makeup but underneath it I could tell she was beautiful.

She joined us and for the second time in less than an hour I felt like I was out of my league with another female. She giggled coyly when she was introduced to the senator and curtsied to the Archbishop, showing him her ample cleavage as she bent down. She nodded to me and Lievan and offered her hand to Maximo saying, 'Pleasure to see you again.'

When introduced to the birthday girl she gave her a hug and a kiss on each cheek saying, 'You are so beautiful.' It was evident Nia was not impressed.

I had another beer and silently toasted Caprice as she had inadvertently taken the heat off me and had given Nia something else to worry about.

Andres grabbed two beers and kept both for himself. He chugged the first one and said, 'Damn hot out here; thank God for air conditioning.'

Maximo said, 'Caprice, forgive my son his manners. Would you like a beer or perhaps a glass of wine?'

'Wine would be nice.'

Andres said, 'Sorry. Caprice usually bolts right for the wine before I have a chance to offer her anything. That is, if there is no hard stuff to be had.' He cut off his father, who was heading for the wine, and roughly poured a glass of red. He handed it to Caprice without even looking at her and turned his attention toward Lievan. 'So Lievan, did you enjoy our bike ride last night. What a sight, eh? A priest on the back of a hog. I bet the kids at the orphanage were impressed. Maybe the Archbishop should consider buying you one, as I am sure it would make you look even cooler than you already are.'

Looking at Archbishop Matos, Andres said, 'You know, Thiago, these young priests need to be more like Lievan here; less stuffy and more able to connect with the youth. If not, I think the church will lose a generation. And then how are you going to pay the bills for your fancy palace?'

Andres looked back at Lievan and said, 'Liev, have you ever thought about a tattoo?' Andres turned his flabby bicep toward Lievan and showed off a tattoo of a woman's face; she had dark hair and dark eyes with a halo behind her head. Above the portrait was the word 'Mother' and underneath was inscribed with, '*R.I.P. 1950 – 1976*'. He then turned his back to us and lifted up his Bon Jovi shirt. The massive tattoo of a blue angel holding a fiery sword almost distracted me from the flab that poured over the leather pants. He pulled his shirt down and said, 'Pretty cool huh? That angel hurt like a son-of-a-bitch but it was worth it. Imagine if priests were to get tatted up. The kids would dig it. And there are so many religious tattoos out there, I am surprised nobody has thought of it yet.'

Archbishop Matos said, 'Interesting proposal.'

He was about to say something else, when Andres said, 'Plus getting inked is painful. Aren't some of you guys into that kind of shit?'

The Archbishop said, 'Not really. Self-flagellation went out with the middle ages.' There was a definite hint of annoyance in his voice.

As Andres spoke I noticed Maximo glance at Caprice. As he did so Caprice quickly tapped her index finger to her nose. Maximo nodded and looked blankly at his son. He said, 'Andres, I am certain Archbishop Matos has heard worse language than what you just used.' He smiled and continued, 'I would not be surprised if even he used such language when accidentally striking his thumb with a hammer.' This got a laugh from the crowd. Maximo continued, 'Nevertheless, I would appreciate it if you could refrain from using common language in front of our guests.'

Andres shrugged and said, 'I am sorry, but I am also confused. Why just last night I happened upon Father Lievan and Maddy, and was scolded for assuming priests were above the common folk. So here I am talking like a regular Joe, in my own home nonetheless, and I am hearing it from the other side about how boorish and vulgar my words are when said in front of the holy men.'

Archbishop Matos said, 'I am not offended by your words, son, and I know you mean no offence. I am sure Father Lievan is right in his belief that we in the church need to be more like the people if we wish to be accepted by the people. I guess your father is concerned that an old fuddy-duddy like me is not used to being spoken to with such frank and common language. He is right; I am not used to it. There is another point of view to consider. The church has been around for a long time and has held tight to its traditions through times that seemed more desperate than what we are in right now. Let us remember the church, at one time, was reduced to little more than a few sanctuaries in outposts such as Ireland and Scotland. Yet here we are, still vibrant, still growing. Making massive inroads in Africa and places like the Philippines. Imagine what we will be like when Russia and even China is ready for us. Sometimes I feel it is best to stay the course and not be swayed by fad or fancy. Therefore, I do appreciate it when gentlemen use respectful language in front of me and my clergy, for as immodest and old-fashioned as some might think, we are, after all, Christ's representatives here on earth.'

I thought *what a fucking killjoy and an arrogant prick to boot*. I wonder if he had considered that the church's gains were in countries with low literacy rates and extreme poverty and that in developed countries its power was dwindling with each generation. I was thinking of adding my two-bits when Andres said, 'My apologies father, you are right of course. I ask your forgiveness.'

The Archbishop replied, 'There is no need to ask. I have already done so.'

'Well then,' said Andres, 'perhaps I can take the younger folks for a bit of a tour of my neck of the woods. Maddy and Lievan would you like to join me for a ride to my pad? I would love to show you my side of the property.'

Lievan looked at me and shrugged. I said, 'Sounds great. Dibs on the front seat.'

The entire party looked at me strangely. It took a moment, but I realized I had used the English word 'dibs' and did not know of a Portuguese translation. I explained, 'Dibs means I claim the front seat.'

'Oh,' said Caprice, 'by all means.'

Andres said, 'Caprice, you stay here and keep Nia company.' He walked toward the golf cart. Lievan and I followed. The electric engine kicked in and he cranked the stereo. Ratt's lead vocalist attacked their big hit 'Round and Round' singing with bravado and gusto about knockin' the shit out of anything that got in his way. As we headed down the pathway to the forest and whatever lay on the other side, I smiled and took a sip of my beer, and reminisced of partying on the Chilliwack River with my high school friends, buzzed on beer and weed and getting our hair whirling like dervishes to our favourite hair bands. Andres and I sang along with the boys from Ratt when they hit the chorus. We were off-key and got most of the words wrong, but I was thinking 'that's rock 'n roll.' I could hear Lievan laughing from the back, he was standing on the plastic bumper and holding onto the poles that supported the canopy.

We went through the woods and came out on an expanse of lawn as big as the one we had left. Smack in the middle was a large house. It stood in direct contradiction to Maximo's house. It was gaudy, opulent and massive. It looked like a cross between an English manor house on steroids and a medieval castle. There was a faux moat surrounding it, and a drawbridge leading to the main entrance. The driveway was lined with teak trees, their thin, tall trunks acting as a processional guard for guests arriving at the house. I noticed cameras perched on several of them. The house itself was made of stone and was dominated by two features: a copper roof that flared out at the bottom and a large, round tower perched on the west side of the house. The tower had a turret on the top and was built with narrow slits included. Halfway across the drawbridge Andres stopped the cart and turned off the engine. He said, 'I designed her myself. She's inspired by the Zvikov Castle in Czechoslovakia. I worked very closely with several architects until I found one who was able to share my vision.' He paused. I assumed he was waiting for the deluge of compliments his guests would usually bestow on him.

I said, 'Looks very European.'

Lievan whistled and said, 'Impressive.'

Andres shrugged and said, 'It's nothing, really. It's been hinted that I might be an architectural visionary, but I like to think of it as a hobby; an expensive one, but just a hobby. Besides, wait until you see the back.'

He turned the cart back on and we crossed the drawbridge and made a right on a lane that circumnavigated the house. About halfway round we hung another right across another draw bridge and passed a covered parking lot that housed several motorbikes and cars. Andres explained he was starting a collection of Harley-Davidsons that would be the most extensive in all of Brazil. The cars were all American muscle cars from the 1960s and 1970s.

On our right was a massive pool and pool house. I spied Carlos and the man with the scar hanging out poolside with several other men and a bevy of buxom beauties. We dipped down into a slight valley and came back up the other side. When we got to the top of the rise I thought, *you got to be fucking kidding me.* In front of us stood a zoo. There were compounds for two gorillas, lions, tigers, a grizzly bear, jaguars, a rhino, an elephant, a small herd of warthogs and several cages for exotic birds and monkeys. There was also what looked like a petting zoo stocked with goats and chickens. We parked by the petting zoo. The animals paid us no heed. They continued to lie in their cages or stand at docile attention, with the exception of the elephant. She came trudging over to the fence closest to us. Andres grabbed some hay and gave it to me. He said, 'Would you like to feed Marilyn?'

I asked, 'Marilyn?'

'Marilyn, my elephant. I name all my pets and they are named after American movie stars.'

I said, 'I would love to.' I took the hay and walked toward Marilyn. I hesitated. She nodded her head and gently waved her trunk.

Andres said, 'Don't be afraid. She's harmless. Got her from a circus when it went bankrupt. She is used to people. Just reach out your hand.'

I followed his instructions and Marilyn's massive trunk swung down and grabbed the hay from my hand, her moist nostrils making contact with my open palm. I felt giddy. I squealed in delight. Lievan laughed and asked if he could try. Andres said, 'By all means, and then we will feed Arnie and Sly.'

Lievan was a little more hesitant than I; clearly he did not consume as many beers. He pulled back his hand too quickly and dropped half the hay. He asked for a do-over and Andres granted him one. This time he stood in there and Marilyn tickled his palm as well. He, too, squealed in delight. He asked, 'Can I also feed Sly and Arnie?' Andres smiled back and said by all means.

We made our way to the petting zoo and I wondered which of the goats were Sly and Arnie. Andres told us to wait outside the chicken coop. He opened the gate, went inside and with a quickness I did not expect from him, grabbed two chickens and expertly held them by the feet, ignoring their squawks and fluttering wings. He left the coop and showed Lievan how to hold the chickens and we headed back to the zoo.

Lievan asked, 'Where are we going?'

Andres said, 'To feed Arnie and Sly.'

'Who are Arnie and Sly?' I asked.

'My tigers,' replied Andres. 'We will be just giving them a pre-dinner appetizer.'

Lievan stopped in his tracks. He said, 'You can't be serious.'

Andres asked. 'What do you mean?'

'You want me to feed these poor chickens to your tigers?'

'Of course,' said Andres. 'Forgive me, but did you not ask if you could feed them?'

'Yes, but...' Lievan mumbled. 'I did not think you meant feeding them live animals. It seems so cruel.'

'I try to make life as real as I can for my animals. What's the difference if I break the chickens' necks and toss them in or give the tigers some semblance of their natural world and let them do the deed? Believe me, the terror the chickens experience will only last a second or two. Now you said you wanted to do it so man up and do it. If you can't handle it perhaps Maddy would give it a try. She grew up on a farm and knows how it is.'

Lievan looked at me in desperation. I said, 'We had dairy cattle and that was about it. This does not appeal to me.'

By the time I had finished speaking we had arrived outside the sixteen-foot fence that housed the tigers. Both cats were lazing in the grass, seemingly oblivious to our presence. Andres said, 'Okay, Liev, either you do it or I do it. Chances are the tigers will do nothing and we will leave. It will not be until later that they will become a snack for my big boys. If you can't handle it just say.'

Lievan looked at me and then at Andres and then down at the chickens. Andres said, 'All you got to do is climb that ladder and toss them over the fence.' He pointed to a stepladder a few feet way.

Lievan said, 'I hate heights,' and passed the chickens back to Andres. Andres sighed and looked at me, 'You got the guts, Maddy?'

I looked at him and said, 'It ain't about guts, Andres.'

'If you say so.'

Perhaps it was the beers, perhaps it was the fact that I had been told to be a good girl and keep my pretty mouth shut, or perhaps it was the peer pressure – I have always believed that peer pressure does not leave when you get a high school diploma – it just takes on other forms. I said, 'Tell you what. I will go into their pen with you if you want to release the chickens that way.'

Lievan said, 'Maddy that is insane. I won't allow it.'

I ignored him and stared down Andres. Andres licked his lips and said, 'Let's do it.'

I nodded. Andres said, 'I hope you can outrun a tiger.'

I said, 'I doubt it, but I might be able to outrun you.'

Andres laughed. 'I am faster than I look, especially when chased by a four-hundred-pound cat.'

We headed toward the locked gate. I tried my best to swagger and hoped my legs wouldn't give out.

Lievan said, 'Stop! Both of you cut it out. I will throw the bloody birds over the fence. Give them to me, please.'

Andres looked at me and said, 'You okay with that, Maddy?'

I shrugged and said, 'Whatever.'

Andres handed the chickens back to Lievan and we made our way back to the ladder. Lievan climbed the ladder and when he got to the top, Andres said, 'Say a prayer for them, Liev, and then toss them.'

Lievan did as we he was told. It seemed that no sooner had the chickens left his hand than the tigers were on top of them. I swear one did not even touch the ground before it was pounced upon. The other made two maybe three steps before a massive claw crushed every bone in the chicken's body. Within seconds there was nothing but feathers and dust. I shuddered. Andres said, 'Well, I guess they were hungrier than I thought. Perhaps we will have to give them four goats tonight.'

Lievan descended the ladder. He was ashen. Andres put his big hand on Lievan's shoulder and said, 'They are just chickens, buddy, and they have served their purpose.'

We walked in silence back to the golf cart.

While heading back to his house, Andres said, 'I want to show you one room in my house. It is my tribute to the greatest priest of all time.' I guess he took the silence from Lievan and me as a yes. I looked to the pool and spied Carlos dancing with some floozy on the deck. He was wearing nothing but his underwear; they were a leopard print.

Andres parked the cart on the west side of his home, underneath the tower. He opened a compartment at the front of the cart and fished out a large set of keys. One of the keys was massive, the kind in old movies to open up jail cells or castle doors. We walked to the door. He showed us the key and said, 'This key and door come from an actual castle in Romania.' He beckoned for us to gather closer and said softly, 'It was smuggled out from under the noses of the Commies; it is a door from Hunyad Castle.' He paused. Lievan and I stared at him blankly. 'Hunyad Castle, where they held Vlad III prisoner for seven years.' Our blank stares seemed to irritate him. 'Vlad III, aka Vlad the Impaler aka Dracula.'

Lievan said, 'Oh, wow, that is fascinating.'

I nodded and said, 'Interesting.'

Andres put the key in the hole and turned it, it was evident it took some effort. He pushed the thick, wooden door open and a whoosh of cool air escaped. He said, 'I tried to build this tower as authentic as possible, but I did add an air-conditioning unit. It gets too damn hot otherwise, besides I figure it was always cold in the old castles.

C'mon.' We crossed the threshold and found ourselves in a small rotunda, almost too small for three bodies. Stone stairs spiraled skyward and Andres started up them, signaling us to follow. There were medieval weapons bolted to the wall: maces, crossbows, shields, swords and some other torturous instruments I could not name if I tried. They were illuminated by dim lights that were designed to look like torches. They were far more interesting to look at than the leather-clad fat ass that was only inches from my face as we ascended the steep, narrow stairway.

When we got near the top, Andres suddenly stopped and I almost found my face implanted in his buttocks. Lievan bumped into me and put his hands on my hips. In a momentary lapse of reason I reached back and held his hands against me. He did not recoil. Andres opened a trap door and a small stepladder lowered itself to the stairs. He said, 'Watch your step and be careful; it's pitch black.'

He went up the ladder and I followed, holding the railing to guide me. It was not quite pitch black as there was a little light coming from below. Lievan held my hand as we made our way off the stepladder and into the room.

Andres said, 'Watch this.' He flicked a switch and black light lit up the room. Lievan immediately let go of my hand. My jaw dropped. The circular wall was a black velvet homage to Judas Priest. The velvet tapestry began with the iconic Judas Priest logo and progressed into a massive portrait of the band in full leather-clad metal regalia posing with their assorted instruments in classic rock n' roll stances, with lead singer Rob Halford arching back and pushing his crotch toward the viewer while belting into the microphone. The tapestry ended with a chronological black velvet discography of their S&M-infused albums covers.

Andres flicked another switch. I swear I jumped a foot, as did Lievan, as an incredibly loud stereo blasted Judas Priest's song 'Sinner,' and multi-coloured strobe lights abounded. I could barely hear Andres's laughter over the deafening music. He let the song play for a minute or so and then turned it off and flicked another switch that turned on regular fluorescent lighting. He said, 'Welcome to my lair' and grinned. Below the tapestry there was a circular leather couch and in the middle of the room was a round bar. There was a metal ladder behind the bar that led to another trap door. The carpet was black and had the Judas Priest logo emblazoned upon it. The room was laden with Judas Priest concert memorabilia, including a signed flying V guitar that once belonged to K.K. Downing.

I found the whole place creepy to say the least. Andres looked at me and asked, 'Well, what do you think? A little more interesting than my dad's collection of old photos and relics?'

'Definitely more modern and colourful,' I responded.

His smile disappeared. 'And more expensive. That guitar alone costs more than his whole collection. Anyway, sit, relax, let's have a drink.'

I said, 'Should we not be getting back. I hope your father won't be offended. We've been gone quite some time.'

Andres said, 'I said relax. It's a party for fucks sake and this is Brazil, baby, we take things slow here.' He reached below the bar and grabbed three beers. He opened them quickly and motioned for us to sit down. We had no choice but to do so.

'Hey,' said Andres, 'are you two interested in making this shindig a little more interesting?' He went back behind the bar and returned with a razor blade, three cut straws and a bag of coke.

Lievan said, 'Andres, please put that stuff away. Have you forgotten I am a priest?'

Andres laughed and said, 'C'mon Father, you're not as pure as you want us to think. I think it is fair to say you have a wandering eye and are tempted by the flesh and perhaps other things.' He looked at me when he said the word flesh.

Lievan said, 'Excuse me, but I am true to my vows. I think we should leave.'

Andres said, 'Relax. Fuck. Sorry if I offended you, Liev, but seriously, take it as a compliment. I just mean you don't walk around with a pole shoved up your ass like that pompous Archbishop "fuck face" Matos. Did you see the look on that dumb cunt's face when I called him Thiago?'

'Enough,' said Lievan. 'I will not permit you to talk that way about the Archbishop; he is a good man and is not deserving of such derogations.' Lievan remained calm but I could tell he was upset.

I said, 'Andres, perhaps we should go.'

Andres laughed. 'Okay, okay just drink your beer and let me do a line and then I want to show you one more thing and then we can go back to the party and celebrate that phony bitch's birthday. I am sure by the time we get back the old man, the senator and his royal Archbishopness will have made whatever backroom deal they have construed.'

Lievan looked at me and I shrugged. We drank our beers and watched Andres expertly prepare a line of coke. He bent over the low-slung coffee table and snorted. Every speck of white was vacuumed up his pudgy nose. He leaned back and said, 'Ahh, that's better.' He looked at us and said, 'Drink up.'

I guzzled the rest of my beer, but Lievan said, 'I've had enough.'

'Suit yourself,' Andres said. 'Follow me.'

He walked behind the bar and proceeded to climb up the metal ladder. He opened a trap door and sunlight poured in. He called for us to follow. I looked at Lievan and whispered, 'Sorry about this, Lievan. He's a total asshole and a bully.'

Lievan said, 'It's not your fault; let's just humour him so we can get back.'

We ascended the ladder and stepped onto the turret of the tower. I must admit the view was spectacular. For miles in three directions was jungle with glimpses of rivers. To the east was the ocean and the distant skyline of San Salvador. One could also appreciate the vastness of the Pelanchhi property as you could see bits and pieces of the perimeter road that surrounded their land. I caught site of at least two jeeps that seemed to be constantly patrolling the road. I also saw several armed men on foot with dogs.

Lievan seemed intentional on distancing himself from me while on the tower. Andres said, 'Not bad, eh?'

I replied, 'This is an amazing view.'

'Truly spectacular,' chimed Lievan.

'Thanks,' said Andres. 'Well, I guess we should head back. But before we do let me say I am fuckin' sorry for being such a dick, especially to you, Lievan. I think you are pretty cool, but that Matos just rubs me the wrong way. It's like he thinks he's better than everyone else or something. He is no angel, regardless of his title.'

'Thanks for apologizing, Andres. Please, though, can we not say anything else negative about the Archbishop,' Lievan said.

Andres walked over to him, put his arm around him and mussed his hair. 'I hear you bro. Let's go, we're burning daylight.'

We returned to the cart and as we drove back I thought three things: Andres was a dangerous man, Andres was a complete asshole, and Andres spoke nothing but the truth when we were at the tower.

23

The rest of the party went by with little controversy. We had an incredible meal and I got my drinking under control. With the exception of one minor foray with the senator in which I argued the Cuban revolution could have worked if the Americans had not have been so obtuse about the whole affair – I let him win – otherwise I kept my big mouth shut and hung out with Caprice. She confided in me she was a very expensive escort who was supposed to keep Andres happy and out of trouble. The senator, Nia and the priests were staying the night, so I bid them all a good night and Maximo Pelanchhi escorted me to a Range Rover. One of his men was behind the wheel. Maximo opened the back door for me and said, 'Madeline, it was very nice making your acquaintance. It is assuring to know that young people such as you are interested in helping the poor of our country.' He looked toward the driver and said, 'This is Paulo; he will get you home safe and sound.' I looked in the rearview mirror and Paulo looked back, nodded and smiled. Maximo said, 'He will swing by Andres's place and pick up your escort. Forgive me, I cannot recall his name.'

'Carlos.'

'Carlos, of course. Married to that fine woman, Luiza, who is the daughter of one of our town's most colourful characters, that stubborn beauty Dona Aurora.'

I smiled, as did he. I said, 'Thank you so much for a wonderful evening.' I decided to make one pitch. 'I know you are very busy, but if you ever have the time it would be truly appreciated if you could at some point contact my boss Gretchen Levi-Meyer. She would love to hear from you.'

His smile disappeared momentarily and he said, 'Perhaps someday that will happen. For now the bulk of my philanthropy will be directed through the church. It is what my late wife would have wanted.'

I said, 'Of course. I understand. I hope my forwardness caused you no offense.'

'None whatsoever,' he said. 'Now you should be on your way before old Dona Aurora has my hide for keeping you out so late.' We both laughed.

He closed the door and stood in the driveway watching us drive away. We navigated a dirt road that took us to Andres's home. Carlos was waiting. One arm was slung over the shoulder of the man with the scar, the other over a skanky-looking whore. His hand dangled over her breast and just before we came to a stop he copped a feel. She giggled and let him have a good squeeze. Paulo got out of the SUV, opened the back door and unceremoniously threw him in the back.

He was plastered. About halfway back to his home he grabbed my hand and started kissing it, slurring, 'Thank you, Maddy, thank you, thank you. I am in; I am part of the posse. That's what we, Andres's men, call ourselves. I will show that wife of mine and her old bitch of a mother that I am a somebody, and you were my lucky break, you scrumptious little Yankee.'

'I am a Canadian, and quit slobbering over my hand.'

'Oh, my apologies,' Carlos said. 'My little Canadian Eskimo. I bet you are not as cold as your country huh? I saw you watching me dance.' He reached his hand between my legs, and I slapped his face. He said, 'Fuck you, bitch.' He grabbed my wrists with one hand while the other lifted my skirt and tugged at my panties. I kicked and screamed. Neither of us noticed that the Range Rover had stopped until Paulo's hand grabbed a handful of Carlos's hair and pulled him off me. In a second Carlos was on the ground being pummeled by Paulo's fists and then feet. Paulo pulled Carlos up, opened the front passenger door, and shoved him onto the seat. Paulo said, 'The boss told me to get this young lady home safe and sound, and that is what I plan on doing. Another stunt like that and you will be found dead on the side of this road. Fucking posse, you boys are nothing but a bunch of amateurs, a bunch of psychopathic clowns. Maximo's men would cut you boys to ribbons if you ever defied the spider. Now sit down and shut up.'

I sat in the back and was surprised at how I was not surprised by the violence I just saw. Paulo looked back, 'I apologize for my outburst.'

I smiled at him. 'Apology accepted, though not necessary. He had it coming. Thank you for interfering.'

He nodded and we drove back to the ghetto in silence.

24

The next several weeks of my time in Brazil were, by far, the best. I was back in everybody's good books. Dona Aurora had forgiven me, Luiz had made himself a fixture at her door just about every night, Luiza and I worked tirelessly organizing the women and real progress was being made in the building of the school. Although he said he would not be able to help, I sensed that the spider was behind the shredding of the red tape that had caused next-to-impenetrable roadblocks in the past.

We had a building permit, the go ahead to interview teachers and the promise of government resources if we got the school opened. Building codes in the shanty towns were non-existent so we had a basic schoolhouse up and running in no time. I was amazed at how ingenious and hardworking the volunteers were. Men, taut muscles glistening in the sun, would toss buckets full of cement to compatriots on the roof, who would pour while women spread with makeshift trowels. Framers framed with discarded wood found at the dump. One night two blackboards showed up. From where, no one knew.

Gretchen fussed about the legalities of the endeavor and was calmly reassured by Ali that all would be okay and that one of the few good things about being in a place like Dona Aurora was that once you got the go-ahead, the authorities were more than happy to leave you alone as long as you greased their palm. Gretchen looked as happy as I think Gretchen could look.

Ali was like a machine, one day helping pour cement, the next framing and the next driving around scrounging up material.

Andres came around once in a while. He was driving a new Harley; it had a customized Judas Priest logo painted on the gas tank. He spent his time with Carlos and would come into the kitchen to collect something in a paper bag, more than likely money. Carlos was taking on the air of a hard man, strutting around the neighbourhood like he owned the place. People laughed behind his back, although they did so discreetly. Carlos was usually in the company of the man with the scar. One day the man showed up in a cop uniform and it was then that I realized he was the sadist who had beaten young Inacio to within an inch of his life. I decided then and there to stay clear away from Carlos and his accomplice.

I saw Lievan on a regular basis. We would meet at the beach and would spend our time discussing our projects and plotting ways to get the church and organizations such as Saints for Sanctuary working on the same page with the same goals in mind. We would also talk about our homelands, our families and our dreams of the future. I would usually get to the beach first and sit on our favourite log. My heart would skip a beat when I saw him walking toward me. We would hug when we departed. It was clear to me he was attracted to me but he resisted his urges. A few days before Mardis Gras Carnival I kissed his neck as we hugged. He said nothing and did not return the kiss, but he held me tighter. My body ached for him.

Things were good, then came Carnival.

25

Carnival in Bahia San Salvador is almost indescribable. There is no party like it. Take the most hedonistic elements of African, European and South American cultures, blend in the most corporeal rhythms you can imagine danced by men and women who ooze sensuality and who are fueled by alcohol. Now imagine tens of thousands of these people throwing off the shackles of Catholic restraint under hot skies from which the chthonian-like deities of Candomble have descended and consumed the revelers. The only form of exorcism is epicurean exhaustion. In other words the party ends when everyone has either drunk or fucked themselves silly. Achieving both seems to be the ultimate goal.

The party starts on the Thursday before Ash Wednesday and peaks on Shrove or Fat Tuesday. I was in the right frame of mind for a party and apparently the rest of the city was as well. I went into the city the first night with the younger women from Dona Aurora and took it relatively easy, feeling out the vibe of the shindig. I crashed at Gretchen's the first night and stayed with her the rest of the time. Gretchen and Ali and I partied the next night with Gretchen's husband, a man who brought the devil out in his wife. I would not have believed it if I had not seen it, but there was Gretchen, a sexy ball of fire shaking her thing like a local yokel.

Ali was practically mauled by women who were less than subtle about looking for an anaconda. I danced the night away with steely torsoed local boys who copped feels at will and rubbed their semi-hard dicks against my rump and legs. Before I knew it I was on some guy's shoulders dancing down the street. I came against his neck. I felt no shame, only an inexplicable joy and a desire for more lasciviousness.

On Sunday we took a break from the city and partied on the beach. On our way we passed some Protestant missionaries; I recognized the man who was handing out the comic-style bookmarks and Bibles. They were holding the usual "repent, the end is nigh" signs. I was already half-baked on some weed and decided I was going to flash them some Canadian titties. I went to pull up my t-shirt, only to feel someone tug it down from behind. It was Ali, he said, 'Now, now Madeline, the only time that should happen is if it is a gesture of love and is asked for. You little brat.' He smiled and I smiled back.

Monday was another night of partying in the city. I was living on little sleep, followed by lots of water and aspirin in the afternoon to prepare my swollen brain for more debauchery. Then came Shrove Tuesday, a night that would change everything.

I couldn't believe the city could ramp it up any more but it did. The processions and floats were spectacular and the music seemed louder, more intense. Many people donned the traditional masks and the crowds became almost immovable. It was around ten o'clock when I felt a familiar hand on my wrist. I looked around and saw a blonde-haired man wearing a mask. I knew it was Lievan. He signaled for me to follow him. I did not hesitate. We went down an alley and away from the main square. He led me down several more alleys. I was completely lost. There were still partiers all around but the crowd had thinned. We came to a door. He looked both ways and then opened it. We entered and he shut it behind us. He ripped off his mask and I lunged at him. My lips found his. I pressed him against the wall and kissed his neck. My hands found his cock and I rubbed vigorously. He pushed me away and said, 'This is insane, we need to stop.' I ignored him and grabbed his belt, pulling him toward me. I whispered in his ear, 'I want you, you want me.'

He kissed me, took my hand, and led me up the stairs. We went into a bedroom and he started to undress. I watched as he nervously took off his jeans and tried to undo the buttons of his shirt. I said, 'Let me help.' I calmly undid each button with my right hand while I rubbed him with my left. He stood before me, pale-skinned and vulnerable in his underwear. I looked him in the eye and unzipped my jeans, and then took off my t-shirt. We gazed at each other, like two innocent virgins staring, unsure of what to do next. However, looks can be deceiving as I was neither innocent nor a virgin. Fact was, I had never felt so horny.

I decided to take charge, I said, 'Take your underwear off. I am going to give you the best of me. I have wanted to do this since Rio.' For a second I thought he was going to bolt. I started caressing my breasts. He got under the covers, raised his hips and threw his underwear on the floor. I took off my panties and joined him, straddling his thin, lithe body. My tongue and lips caressed his mouth, nipples, belly, and finally found his cock. I pulled him into my mouth and felt him harden. I licked and sucked as his body began to gyrate. I could hear him moan softly. I got up on my knees and rubbed his tip between my legs and then impaled him into my wet self. He groaned as did I. Our bodies rocked back and forth. I was just starting to feel the rhythm, feel the beginning of what would have been a great orgasm when he moaned and tried to stop my hips from moving, but it was too late. I could feel his hot ejaculate inside of me. He pulled me down toward himself and rolled us over. He withdrew from me and sat on the side of the bed. He began to cry. I put my hands on his shoulders and said, 'Come back to bed, this can't be wrong.'

He obeyed.

26

I woke with first light and found myself alone in the room. I realized I had no clue where I was. I heard a noise from downstairs and threw on my jeans and t-shirt and made my way to the landing. Lievan was in the kitchen reading a Bible and drinking a coffee. When I entered he stood up and backed away from me like I was a leper. I smiled and said, 'Good morning. Is there a cup for me?'

'Of course,' he said, 'please sit down.' He motioned for me to sit, but I walked toward him. He turned briskly and made his way to the cupboard saying, 'How do you like your coffee?'

'This morning I will have it black.' As he reached for a cup I made my way to him and put my arms around his waist. I hugged him tight. He whispered, 'Please Maddy not now. We need to talk. Go. Sit. I will pour you a coffee.'

My stomach churned. I let go of his slender waist and sat at the table. While he poured my coffee I looked at the Bible and a piece of paper beside it. Corinthians 6:18-20 was written down. He sat opposite me. I said, 'Thank you Lievan.' He nodded and took a sip of his coffee. I said, 'So can you tell me where we are?'

He said, 'We are close to the old town. I am housesitting for a prominent member of the Cathedral's congregation. He and his wife get out of town every year to escape the madness of the carnival.'

'It's a very nice home.'

'Indeed,' he said.

I took another sip of my coffee.

'I love you, Maddy. I truly do. Last night was not about lust, it was about love.'

'I love you too. I have loved you for a long time.'

He put his head in his hands, 'That is why this is so hard. So confusing. I can't do this, Maddy. I have taken sacred vows. Last night made me realize that I can't be part of the physical world. I am fated to a life of service and celibacy. I can only love you as a sister of Christ.'

'Oh, God,' I said. 'I am sorry. I should not have pursued this. I didn't mean to cause you pain. I know you made sacred vows and I have compromised you in ways I never should have. Please forgive me Lievan.'

'The sitting too close together, the looking in each other's eyes for longer than necessary, the intense hugs – we participated equally, but I am the one to blame, I am the one who took the vows, I am the one who is supposed to set an example, I am the one who needs to resist temptation.' He looked at me and said, 'All you did was fall in love with a man. The day we met, I should have told you I was a priest. I am a fool.' He went back to burying his head in his hands. He sobbed.

I got up from my chair and walked behind him. I put my hands on his shoulders and rubbed gently. I said, 'Lievan, we could leave this place. You could come home to Canada with me. We could start over.'

He stood up and turned to me. For a moment I thought he was going to push me away, but instead he grabbed me and held me tight. I pressed myself against him and found his lips. We kissed, our hands groping each other. I tore off his shirt and he lifted up my t-shirt and feasted on my nipples. While he did so I undid my jeans, and let them and my panties fall to the ground. His hands found my ass and he pulled me closer. I unbuckled his jeans and found he was hard, harder than he had been the night before. We stepped out of our jeans. While kissing he guided me over to the kitchen counter, my back was pressed against the sink. He grabbed my shoulders and turned me around, and then pulled my hips back away from the sink. I held onto the counter as he spread my legs and entered me from behind. I took one hand off the counter and rubbed myself while he pumped harder and faster. It took him less time to come than it had the night before. His body seemed spent. I continued to rub myself and finally came while I felt him go limp inside me.

He pulled out of me and left the room without saying a word. I could hear him weeping in the bathroom. I gathered up my clothes and noticed my knife had fallen out of the secret pocket I had sewn into the back of my jeans. I wondered if Lievan had noticed. I knocked on the bathroom door. At first he ignored me. Finally, he said, 'Please Maddy, just leave.'

I left but not before reading the Bible verse that he had written down, it read: [18]*Flee fornication. Every sin that a man doeth is without the body; but he that committeth fornication sinneth against his own body.* [19]*What? know ye not that your body is the temple of the Holy Ghost which is in you, which ye have of God, and ye are not your own?* [20]*For ye are bought with a price: therefore glorify God in your body, and in your spirit, which are God's.*

27

In the daylight it was not difficult to find my way back to Gretchen's. I left Lievan around 7:00 a.m. and walked by a few hardcore revelers determined to make the most of the street party. The streets were littered with garbage and empty bottles. I cried as I walked, until I was a block from her apartment. I sat at a bus stop and focused hard on controlling my emotions, remembering my vow that I would not let them see me cry.

When I had pulled myself together, I buzzed Gretchen's place. She answered almost immediately. I prepared myself for a scolding as the elevator whisked me to her floor. Her door was open and she was waiting for me, smiling, holding a flute full of champagne and orange juice. She said, 'Have you been a naughty girl? I hope so, because now it's forty days and forty nights of repentance in your crazy religion.'

I smiled and took the flute from her. I downed it like a trooper.

28

Although things were happening fast around me, the next three weeks went at a turtle's pace. The finishing touches were put on the school, the teachers were hired and the students were enrolled. Around the neighbourhood there was a sense of joy and a feeling that we had accomplished something that would forever change the destiny of the children.

Luiza headed up the community hiring team; she was an integral part of the interviews and had hired teachers she believed had the best qualifications to teach shanty town students. Andres donated more money and we were able to buy books. His two stipulations were that there be a plaque in the school honouring his mother and that I meet with him for a progress report. Carlos was to drive me to his place once a month for updates. I agreed.

I spent my days painting the school, recruiting more students during the evening and helping the teachers, Luiza and Gretchen selected the best books with the money we got from Andres. Gretchen wondered what the cost would be for dealing with Andres. I explained my theory, telling her I thought he was doing it for two reasons: one he wanted to fill his giant ego, and two, he saw it as an act of getting back at his father as his father clearly supported the church. I believed the plaque he was having placed in the school would anger his father, especially since it was being done, from what I could tell, without his consent.

I tried my best to be in good spirits for the opening day of the school. We had worked extremely hard and the fortitude and resilience of the Brazilian people was paying dividends. I was proud to be part of such an occasion; however, the absence of Lievan left a void in me that not even the opening of the school could completely close. The days after our tryst I kept looking for him, half-expecting him to show up, unshaven and shaggy haired wearing a t-shirt, jeans and sandals, ready to renounce the church for the love of a woman. He was nowhere to be seen. I even snuck into a Cathedral mass and sat at the back. I could not spy him and had to sit and listen to the blowhard Matos rant about how we must turn back to our traditional roots.

After the service I made some inquiries about Lievan's whereabouts and was told he had gone on a retreat and would not be back for at least a fortnight. Gretchen noticed his absence and espoused her own theory. She believed he had disappeared because we had won. Winning in her mind meant establishing a community school without church support. She believed his service to the Archbishop as a spy was no longer needed because we had won the battle, but that Lievan would be around at some point, because the battle may have been lost but the war continued. I had come to see Gretchen as a friend and respected her intelligence, but I was amazed that such a bright woman could honestly think that the Catholic Church felt a need to go to war with organizations like ours.

Don't get me wrong, I am not suggesting there was no feeling of pride, satisfaction and joy as I watched Dona Aurora cut the ribbon. There was a sense of euphoria as I witnessed the children march into the school, holding each other's hands as local musicians played their guitars, trumpets and drums. My heart swelled when I saw the tears of joy flow from their mothers. I looked around and saw before me the people whom I had come to respect and love: my protector, the gentle giant Ali; my wise Luiz, the yoda-like gunslinger; my industrious and no-bullshit friend Gretchen; my feisty Dona Aurora whose spirit could not be quashed; and my Luiza, a person who held more capacity for love than any other. She had become my sister. They were there that fine day and I reveled in their happiness. To me they were Brazil: its beauty, its complexity and its enduring strength, warts and all.

However, my joy was dulled. My true love, my man, the beautiful blue-eyed owner of my soul was not there. I sorely missed my lover, my Lievan.

That day also made me realize that my time in Dona Aurora was drawing to a close and that I would soon be whisked off to Rio for my debrief and then return home to my family and friends in Canada. I felt a sense of panic. I realized that these people would no longer be part of my life and chances were I would never lay eyes on them again. I also realized that returning home would mean I would have to answer the question I was sure my parents and siblings were asking: So what are you going to be when you grow up?

After the ceremonies I walked to the beach. I walked to Luiz's *Baby Rain* and lay down on her weather-worn hull. I looked up at the darkening sky and watched the first stars make their appearance. I remained there and listened to the surf, felt the Atlantic breeze blow over me and smelt the ocean. I said a prayer to Luiz's favourite deity, Yemanja – the protector of women and children. I prayed for my soul and that she protect me and all her children.

29

About a week after the school opened I woke up feeling sick. I cursed my laziness and inattentiveness as I had stopped using my iodine pills in the water weeks ago. I thought that through some sort of osmosis I had become immune to the local bacteria. I found it odd, though, that it was not diarrhea but instead nausea. Dona Aurora saw me and looked at me funny, she said, 'Come here, Maddy.' When I got to her she studied my face and then gently pinched my breast.

I squealed in pain and said, 'What the hell Dona Aurora!' She grabbed my hand and took me into her shack.

She said, 'Sit on the bed and take off your shirt and bra.' I mumbled a protest and she snapped, 'Do it child!'

I was startled by the urgency in her voice and did what she asked. She brought me a piece of a mirror perhaps two by three inches and said, 'Look at your nipples, especially the round circlely part.'

I looked at her in disbelief. She said, 'Do it.'

I said, 'You want me to look at my areolas?'

She gently circled her finger around my left areola and said, 'If this is what you call these bits, then yes, inspect them.'

I held the mirror to them and said, 'Look fine to me. Sexy as ever.'

She ignored my sarcasm and said, 'Do they look any different, especially the colour?'

I looked again. For the second time in one morning I felt nauseous, I said, 'Oh my God, they're way darker. What the fuck? Does this mean I'm dying?'

Dona Aurora cackled and said, 'No my dear princess, you are not dying.'

'Then why are you inspecting me like this? You are freaking me out.'

The old woman asked, 'Do you remember the last time you were on the rag?'

'Jesus Christ,' I said, 'you think I'm pregnant. I can't be preg – . Oh my God! No, no, no, no, no. Wait, I had my last period.' I counted back on my fingers and realized I was at least a week past my usual visit from who my mother called Aunt Flow. I began to laugh. Dona Aurora looked at me like I had lost my mind. I said, 'I was just thinking about a silly thing my mother used to say.'

'This is very common around these parts,' said Dona Aurora. 'I call it Carnival fever. You and hundreds like you are probably coming to the conclusion that your shenanigans during Carnival have left you with a bun in the oven. Who is he?'

I looked her in the eye and said, 'I don't know.'

She said, 'Typical. I thought you and your big-shot ideas about birth control and the spread of AIDS would mean you would have used common sense! What is it about us women? You would think we were the randy dogs!'

She said, 'Let's get rid of it, child.'

I looked at her and saw she was prepared then and there to end the life that was growing inside of me. I looked into her eyes and saw nothing but love. I shook my head. She rested her hand on my knee and said, 'Madeline, you yourself are a believer in legalized abortion, you have argued passionately for the cause. You are young, you are in a foreign country, you don't know who the father is, no one but us will ever know and I can assure you there will be no pain to that tiny thing inside of you. You will feel sick for three or four days and then life will go on.'

I thought *life will not go on*. I had never felt more Catholic. I looked the old woman in the eye and said, 'I am keeping my child.'

She said, 'Very well, then I insist you let me take care of you at least until you get home. If I am good at one thing it is looking after wayward children.'

30

Dona Aurora and I decided to keep my pregnancy secret. I was not even certain if I was with child, although Dona Aurora assured me she knew when a woman was knocked up. Still, I woke every morning half-expecting my period to start. A week later there was still nothing. On my day off I made my way into the city and went to a pharmacy in a part of town where I was confident nobody knew me. I purchased a pregnancy test and found a café. After eating some lunch and drinking water I made my way to the bathroom. I peed on the stick and followed the instructions. My eyes flitted back and forth between the urine-soaked stick and the second hand of my watch. After two minutes, the stick turned blue. I was, indeed, with child; the bastard offspring of a Roman Catholic priest.

I sat in the cubicle and thought about the ramifications of my actions. I realized I would be back in Canada before I began to show. I thought about my parents and how they would take the news that their little girl was knocked up. I thought about the conversation regarding who the father was. Should I tell the truth or just lie and tell them it was a one-night stand? Either way they would be, to say the least, extremely disappointed. I knew one thing for certain. They would love the child regardless of what they thought of me.

Should I tell Lievan? Why burden him with the guilt and the shame? Perhaps he would want to know; perhaps he would leave the priesthood and be a father to my child. We could get married and flee to Canada together and he could reinvent himself for my family. My parents would be furious with me, but once they met him and knew we were starting a family they would be thrilled. I was certain he would win them over as long as they did not know what the circumstances were when our child was conceived. I decided to go to the Cathedral and pay the father of my child a visit.

I arrived at the Cathedral twenty minutes later. I asked if Father Lievan was around and was told he was in the confessional. I turned to leave and thought otherwise. I went to the confessional. It was a traditional booth where the priest and penitent sit side by side and are divided by a screen.

I made the sign of the cross. I spoke in English: 'In the name of the Father, and of the Son, and of the Holy Spirit. My last confession was over twelve months ago.'

There was a pause, a long pause. Lievan spoke softly in English, saying, 'In him we have redemption through his blood, the forgiveness of our trespasses, according to the riches of his grace, tell me of your sins, my child.'

'I have slept with a man Father. I had sex with him twice in less than twenty-four hours.'

He said, 'Have you any other sins my child?'

'Yes father, during Carnival I drank, tried illicit drugs, flaunted my body. I have also defied my elders and lied several times. I have fallen in love with a man who is unobtainable to me and, although I know it is wrong, I have lusted for him day in and day out.'

He said, 'You need to do penance, my child. If you are still seeing this man you must see him no more. You must pray every day to the Heavenly Father for the strength to stay away from him. You must do five Hail Mary's daily until this man is clear out of your conscience. Now say a prayer of contrition.'

I prayed the Canadian version I was most comfortable with:

My God, I am sorry for my sins with all my heart.
In choosing to do wrong and failing to do good,
I have sinned against You whom I should love above all things.
I firmly intend, with Your help, to do penance, to sin no more, and to avoid whatever leads me to sin.

Our Saviour Jesus Christ, suffered and died for us.
In His name, my God, have mercy.

Lievan said, 'Now child you are forgiven. Sin no more.'

I said, 'Father, forgive me but there is one more thing I need to share with you.'

There was another pause. 'The Sacrament of Penance must follow the prescribed order my child.'

I said, 'Sorry Father, I am not much of a traditionalist. I briefly contemplated ending the life of another.'

Lievan asked, 'Whose life would that be?'

'The life of the child that is growing in my womb,' I said.

'*Mijn God heeft genade*,' said Lievan. I assumed he was saying something about God in his native Flemish.

I was trembling. The silence and the heavy air that seemed to be pushing down on the confessional stall was making me feel claustrophobic. I waited and still there was nothing. I reached for the door and began to open it.

The voice from the other side was quaking, 'Meet me at the beach at six. Our usual place.'

I left without saying a word. I did not know what to think or what to feel.

I arrived at the beach at quarter-to-six and found Lievan was already there. He was wearing casual clothes and sunglasses. He never wore sunglasses. I sat down beside him on what I thought had become our log. He said nothing until I said hello.

He replied, 'Hello, Maddy.' I reached for his hand but he withdrew it from me and crossed his arms. He said, 'Is it mine?'

Stunned, I replied, 'Of course, who else –'

'In your confession you said you did a lot of carousing during Carnival. Perhaps you did what you did with more than one person.'

'Oh, my God, what *I* did? You mean what *we* did. I did a lot of drinking, flirting, but there was only one person I had sex with.'

He asked, 'Did you not use some sort of birth control? I thought women such as yourself were prepared for such encounters?'

'I am not going to lie to you, Lievan. I am not a virgin, but I have used no contraceptives since arriving in Brazil. I had no intention of having sex here. I came to work and to try to improve the lives of others. Did I fall in love with you? Yes, yes I did. It wasn't planned, Lievan. I did a terrible job of respecting the fact you were a priest, because I am so in love with you. For that I do not apologize.'

'So you got yourself pregnant in order to force me out of the priesthood?'

I gasped. I wrapped my arms tightly around my body and said, 'Are you serious? Are you fucking serious?'

He shrugged. He said nothing, he just shrugged.

'Was it I who found you and hauled you back to some stranger's house? Was it I who led you up to a bedroom? I suppose I forced myself upon you and demanded you to be hard and then…' I stopped talking. He was sobbing. I put my hand on his back and rubbed.

He said, 'What am I to do? I have ruined everything. I have abused the sacred trust of my flock, the Archbishop and most importantly our Lord. Oh Maddy, this is bad, this is very bad.'

I said, 'Lievan, what do you see as your options right now?'

He continued sobbing and finally said, 'I don't know, Maddy. I have no idea what to do!'

I said, 'I think there are three things you can do. Confess what you have done to whoever it is you need to confess to and suffer the consequences. Do nothing. I will never reveal you as the father and I will be long gone from Brazil before anyone knows I am pregnant, besides I have already lied to Dona Aurora and told her I have no clue who the father is. Your other choice is to leave the priesthood and come back to Canada with me where we could raise our child together.'

He took off his glasses and wiped his eyes. He looked toward the sea and said, 'There is another option.'

I said, 'I would go back to Belgium with you if that is what you want. I thought about that, too, but Lievan, I must tell you it would break my parents' hearts.'

He guffawed and said, 'No, Maddy, that is not an option. Mother – oh my god she would hate you, and the baby would be a daily reminder of the shame you brought to the good name Van den Broeck. How old are you Maddy?'

'I will be twenty-two in May,' I replied.

'And I am twenty-nine. We are both young. I have started my career, or should I say my vocation, and you, Maddy, are clearly full of potential and will do wonderful things with your life. This potential child that you say you are pregnant with will change all that. If the pregnancy was terminated you could get on with your life and I mine.'

In my short time in Brazil many people had said many things that had dazed and confused me. Yet they all paled in comparison to the words uttered by the man I loved dearly. A priest, a man who was the father of the child that was growing inside me was advising me to abort. The same man who only weeks before testified that although he was a modern priest he was still a servant of Rome and a man who lived by his vows. I recalled the first time I saw his face and the first words I heard him say to Gretchen; he had told her he was not like the rest. The man I had fallen in love with was not like the rest of the priests I knew; I was beginning to wonder if that was a good thing.

I recalled the first conversation I had about him. It was Gretchen who said, 'He is a fairly smart guy, although I think he could use some backbone.' Sitting on that beach I questioned Gretchen's assessment. Was he really a fairly smart guy? I said not a word. I got up and walked away.

He called out for me to stop. I continued walking. I could hear him running in the sand. He stood in front of me. He said, 'Maddy, please listen to me. You do not think I have struggled with this? Besides it was the likes of you that made me see that there may be a time and a place for an abortion. Can't you see that? I am asking you to do this because it will make your life easier. The burden of this sin is something I will carry forever, but I can offer you absolution, I can offer you forgiveness.'

I looked at him coldly and said, 'Would that not be a conflict of interest?'

'Maddy please,' he whined, 'this is not the time for sarcasm. We need to be rational and look at the big picture. There are two ways we can do this. You can either claim to be raped and they will allow a legal abortion for that. I will testify on your behalf and tell them I found you beaten. If not we can go the illegal route. In the past, the Archbishop had me find out which doctors provided abortions. Some of them are still in business. I know of a doctor who will do it in a safe, private clinic. I'll pick up most of the cost if you like. There would be none of this backroom, risky, amateurish stuff that common whores have to use.'

I slapped him in the face, knocking his ridiculous aviator sunglasses into the sand. I walked away.

He said, 'I will pay for the whole thing Maddy, the whole thing. Please Maddy come back.'

I walked back to the sanctuary of my ghetto.

31

For the next few days I meandered around the neighbourhood like I was in a fog. I could tell that Dona Aurora was keeping a close eye me. The others seemed oblivious even though I was sick in the morning and felt tired all the time.

Luiza was focused on the school. She had made herself the unofficial headmistress and spent her time ensuring the teachers were well-prepared. Although she had no experience with formal education, it became clear that she was the most intelligent and talented educator of us all. Her Zen-like patience with the children and the inexperienced teachers had a calming effect on everyone. Although she had always seemed so content with her lot in life, the establishment of the school had created within her a sense of joy I doubt she had ever experienced.

A week after my encounter with Lievan, I was summoned into the city for a teleconference with Maryanne Lucas. Ali picked me up and drove me to the office. On the way he said, 'Maddy, are you okay?'

'I'm fine, Ali. Just feeling very tired these days.'

'Well,' he responded, 'no wonder. The work you have been doing is exhausting. I still cannot believe we have a school up and running. You must be so proud.'

'It was a total team effort,' I said. 'And I feel proud to be part of such an awesome team.'

He said, 'True enough, but you were a catalyst. None of your predecessors were able to accomplish so much.'

'Thanks Ali. But I like to think I built on what they started and just happened to be here when the final pieces were put in place.'

He smiled. 'Well said.'

During the rest of the drive I encouraged Ali to tell me about the newest restaurants he had tried and about the cross-cultural gourmet dishes he was contemplating. He was particularly intrigued by the idea of cross pollinating Italian and Thai cuisine. I knew if I got him talking about food I wouldn't have to say too much, and I didn't feel like talking. However, as he described his delectable dishes I began to feel like I was going to puke. I wondered if there would come a day when I would see the humour in all this.

We walked into Gretchen's office. She was on the phone. She looked at us and said, 'She just walked in the door, Maryanne.' She put her hand over the receiver and whispered to me, 'Maddy, are you okay? Your skin is almost grey.'

I replied, 'Just feeling a little carsick; it happens to me once in a while. I'll be fine.'

Gretchen spoke back into the phone, 'Would you like to speak to her?'

I went to grab the receiver from her but she said, 'Oh, okay, no problem.' She hit a button on the phone and hung up the receiver. She said, 'We're on speakerphone.'

Maryanne said, 'Hello everybody, can you hear me?'

We all said we could. She said, 'Okay, first things first. Ali be a dear and go to the fridge. I believe Gretchen has some wine there. Pour yourselves a drink. We are going to have ourselves a little toast to the fine work you folks are doing.'

As Ali went to fridge I said, 'Just some water for me, Ali.'

Gretchen said, 'Well, this is a first. I never thought I would see the day Maddy Saunders would pass up some wine.'

Maryanne cackled, 'That's not the Maddy I met at Richard what's-his-face's party for his undergraduate students.'

I said, 'It's my lent thing.'

Maryanne said, 'My, my, aren't you becoming the good little Catholic.'

I thought, *you don't know the half of it sister.*

Maryanne continued, 'Have you got the glasses yet, Ali?'

He was handing them to us as she spoke. 'Yes,' he replied.

She said, 'Well here's to a job very well done. Cheers.'

We clinked glasses.

Maryanne continued, 'I didn't call just to congratulate you guys. I wanted to let you know that our organization has now got the support of a major philanthropist who wishes to remain anonymous. However, his funds are to be used in Haiti. I'm not sure what you know about Haiti but it is the poorest country in the western hemisphere. The women and children there could use our help. I'm hoping we'll be able to set up shop there in the next eighteen months, and I'm hoping that all three of you would consider helping out. My idea is pretty straightforward. Gretchen, you and Ali would go to Port-au-Prince with Maddy and train her to do what you do in Bahia. What do you think?'

At first none of us said anything, each signaling for the other to go first. Finally, Gretchen said, 'I would certainly consider once there are more details.'

Ali said, 'Me too. It sounds like a real challenge.'

Maryanne said, 'Maddy?'

'I am honoured you would ask me, Maryanne, I truly am, and of course I will think about it, but right now I need to focus on the immediate future and bring closure to my time here. Can we talk about it when I get home?'

I knew she wanted, expected, more of a commitment, so I was not surprised that there was terseness to her, 'Of course we can.' She continued, 'Okay you guys enjoy the wine, and Maddy, I look forward to seeing you when you get back to Vancouver.'

We all said our obligatory goodbyes. I sipped my water. I was beginning to realize the restrictions my life would have now that I was going to be a single mom.

32

Two days after my conversation with Maryanne, Andres requested I visit him to discuss further funding for the school. I was picked up by Carlos and the man with the scar. He introduced himself as Matheus. For a moment I felt numb as I remembered he was the cop who took part in the beating of Inacio on the morning of my first full day in Dona Aurora. I nodded to him but did not introduce myself. He chewed on a toothpick and he and Carlos talked quietly up front while I faked sleeping in the back so that I wouldn't have to talk to them.

A few miles from the Pelanchhi compound the skies opened up and the rain poured down. It was incredibly hard and drummed a deafening tattoo on the roof of the car. The wipers were on high gear and still Carlos could barely make out the road. Matheus told him to pull over. We waited for five, maybe ten minutes for the rain to subside to at least something relatively safe to drive in. Carlos drove at a snail's pace. We arrived at least forty-five minutes late. The skies were still dark and the rain still emptied in a deluge as we pulled up to Andres's monstrosity of a house. Matheus said, 'Wait here,' and got out of the car. He ran to the front door and knocked. He stood for a few minutes and knocked again. Nothing. Then he went over to the tower. The massive door was ajar. He pushed it open, and then returned with Andres in tow.

Andres was wearing a Slayer *Hell Awaits* T-shirt and camouflaged army pants. He came storming out to the car and motioned for Carlos to roll down his window. When he got to the car he said, 'What took you so long, you fucking idiot? You were supposed to be here an hour ago.'

Carlos recoiled from the window and said, 'Sorry boss, the weather was terrible. I couldn't see a foot in front of me.'

Andres grabbed the front of his shirt, 'I don't give a shit about your excuses; when a guest of mine is expected to be here at a certain time you need to make sure it happens.'

I said, 'Andres please, settle down. I asked him to pull over when the weather was really bad. I don't think he wanted to but I insisted. I am sorry.'

Andres looked at Carlos and then said, 'Okay, fine. Help the lady out of the fuckin' car and then wait in the house for us. Don't touch a thing, eat a thing or drink a thing.'

He said, 'No problem boss.' He scurried out of the front seat and ran to the back and held the door for me. He didn't even try to thank me for getting him out of a jam.

Andres motioned for me to come to the tower. We entered the big door and he shut it behind me. I walked up the stairs in front of him. I could feel his breath as we ascended the stairs. He reeked of rum. When I got to the top I noticed there were a couple of lines of coke on the coffee table. There was also residue from two freshly snorted lines.

He motioned for me to sit down. He then asked, 'Snort?'

I replied, 'No thanks.'

He said, 'Suit yourself, it's your funeral.' He sucked up the cocaine and let out a loud sigh. He said, 'So how are things with you?'

'Very good. Thanks in part to you, Andres. The school, as you know, is up and running and the children seem eager to learn. The teachers we've hired are working out really well and we're already thinking of adding another grade next year.'

He said, 'Huh. Well, I hope it's worth it. Y'know I had my doubts about helping out. These fucking kids, they are ghetto rats like Carlos and unless they luck out and get in a crew like mine chances are they will be nothing but slum dogs the rest of their lives, scrounging a living by selling trinkets and exotic birds to tourists from the States or even Canada. The girls will more than likely be whored out to pimps who work for my old man. One good thing, though, at least some of the boys will escape the quasi-orphanage run by the fine Archbishop Matos. He likes his boys poor and pretty.'

I felt my heart plummet. I said, 'Andres, how much have you been drinking.'

He laughed and said, 'Quite a bit actually, but I find the coke acts as a stabilizer.'

'I should go.' I got up to leave but felt his hand on my shoulder. He pushed me back down on the couch.

'No. Stay. I insist. After all, you made the deal right?'

'I would like to leave. Please let Carlos know I am ready to go,' I said in as calm a voice as I could muster.

Again, I tried to get up. This time he grabbed my wrist and pulled me down on the couch. He mimicked my voice repeating what I just said. Then he grabbed my head and pulled my ear to his mouth. He whispered, 'You will leave when I tell you you can leave. Be patient, listen to all I have to say and then you will walk out that door. Understand?'

I began to tremble and nodded.

He said, 'Am I scaring our little Canadian do-gooder? I am so sorry! I thought such a brave girl who came all the way from Canada to come help us poor ignorant Brazilians get our shit together would not be intimidated by a teddy bear like me.'

'Andres,' I said, 'please, you're scaring me. I just want to help.'

'You should be scared,' he said. 'I have found out a few things about you I do not like and, as they say, you will have to pay the piper.'

'What? What are you talking about? I've done nothing wrong, nothing to offend you,' I said.

He said, 'Oh, we will get to that in a minute, but first let me tell you things your naïve little, actually not-so-little ass, does not know.

'Let me start with Archbishop Thiago Matos. Did you know he has his own little stable of boys? I bet you didn't. Not many do. My father knows because he makes sure nobody does anything about it. Do you know why? Because the church has massive political power in this region. Matos tells the priests who tell their congregation who they should vote for. That way my dad gets the men he wants in power. Men he knows will do his bidding. In return Matos is allowed to keep his collection of boy toys. Of course, my father also makes financial contributions to the church even though he does not have to any more for he could expose Matos at any fucking time he pleased, but the old man is conservative and he likes the status quo. And guess who negotiates with the families to get the boys to the Archbishop's palace?'

I shook my head.

'Oh, I am sure you can guess, and your guess would be right. Yes, it is that little pussy Lievan. He goes into the homes of wayward whores and convinces them that their sons would be better off getting a good education and three squares while living at the palace.'

I slouched forward and put my head in my hands.

'Now, in his defense, he does no diddling himself and he may be stupid enough to actually think that when the Archbishop has one-on-one time with the kiddies that they are in there learning Latin, but c'mon ask anybody on the streets and they will tell you Matos likes 'em young.'

I said, 'There is no way Lievan would participate in something so ... heinous.'

'Like I said,' Andres replied, 'I have no proof, but he would have to be blind to not know what is going on. He seems like the kind of guy who could lie to himself and actually believe his lie.'

I tried to get up but wasn't quick enough. Andres grabbed my blouse and pulled me down. 'Where the fuck are you going?'

I said, 'I need to use the washroom; I feel sick.'

'Puke in the sink for all I care, but you are going nowhere until I say so.'

'Please let me go, Andres.'

He smiled. 'Are you scared?'

'Very much so. You are freaking me out.'

He laughed and said, 'You should be, for you are in a spot of trouble. Let me explain. I always thought that Lievan was a faggot. Just assumed so because of his demeanor. And as far as faggots go he would be a cute little piece of ass. Now here's a dirty little secret but you must promise not to tell anyone: I have an inclination toward faggotry every once in a while. Remember that night I gave little Liev a ride home on my bike? I won't lie to you, by the time I dropped him off I was rock hard, all I could think about was hoisting that frock of his up over his hips and dipping my unit in his honey pot.

'Did you know that fags have their own unspoken language? I looked at ol' blue eyes, stared him straight in the eye for longer than necessary, took a peek at his unit and then back to his eyes. Nothing! He gave me nothing. I thought maybe my gaydar was off, but I held out hope because honestly I did not want to rape the little fuck unless I had to; I much prefer it be consensual with my boys.

'Then the other night he came to me asking me to help him out of a jam. I was thinking, here it is, come home to daddy, little Liev. But instead of professing his lust for me – me who has been nothing but a friend to him, he asks for a favour. Can you guess what that favour might be Ms. Maddy?'

Although my clothes, soaked from the rain and the cold air-conditioned air should have made me shiver, I found that instead I was sweating profusely. I said, 'I have no idea.'

He grabbed the back of my hair and yanked my head up. He got in my face and screamed, 'Liar! You lying fucking bitch! You know exactly what he asked me. He asked me to find him a doctor who could perform an abortion on some fucking slut he had knocked up! My little Liev liked girls. Who the fuck would have thought?'

Andres's hand moved from the back of my head to my throat. He squeezed tightly and pulled me up. He grabbed his stereo remote with his other hand. He said, 'I got some music for you to listen to. You know there are few good Canadian metal bands and there is only one worth mentioning from Vancouver. The band is named Thor, and I picked this song just for you; it's called, "Let the Blood Run Red". I will play it loud so you can scream as much as you want.'

He pressed a button and the metal music blasted as the strobe lights kicked in and the black lights illuminated the Judas Priest shrine. With a quickness hard to fathom from such a fat pig, he ripped open my blouse and tore off my bra. He slapped my breast with the back of his hand and yelled, 'These belong on a twelve-year-old.'

I scratched at his face and pulled his hair. He laughed and threw me across the room. He picked me up by the hair and punched me. He meant to punch me in the stomach but I twisted my body to the right and felt his massive fist slam into my ribs. At this point I remember thinking about my baby and how I needed to protect it. He punched me in the face and then spun me around. He grabbed my left arm and pulled it up toward my shoulder blade. He walked me over to the couch and yelled, 'I am going to do to you what I wanted to do to Lievan.' He threw me on the couch and straddled me. He undid his camo pants while my arms flailed aimlessly on either side of him. He pulled out a knife and brought it to my throat. 'One fuckin' false move and I will slit your throat.'

I thought *my baby my baby my baby* and stayed still. The song ended. He yelled 'Fuck! Don't move bitch or I swear I will kill you.'

To my utter disbelief he got up. I looked back and saw he was searching for the remote. He spied it on the floor. As he went to pick it up, I bolted for the trap door. I didn't even make it halfway before he pushed me from behind. I sprawled into the couch.

He laughed and said, 'Aren't you the feisty little bitch?' He clicked the remote and said, 'Let's listen to a little Morbid Angel. This one is called, "Bleed for the Devil". I especially like the ending.'

As the song kicked in he stood over me and kicked me in the face, breaking my cheekbone. He grabbed me by the hips and threw me on the couch. He turned me over and lifted up my peasant skirt. He pulled my underwear to one side and delicately cut through the cotton with his knife. My underwear fell on the couch beside me. He spread my legs apart using his knee to kick out my inner thighs. He slapped his penis against my rear end and said, 'You have the titties of a twelve-year-old and the ass of an old lady.' He then spread my cheeks with his hands and forced himself inside of my anal cavity. The pain was almost as unbearable as the humiliation. I clenched my teeth and did all that I could to not cry out and beg for him to stop. He pumped four perhaps five times before I heard him groan and felt his semen inside of me. He collapsed on top of me. His rum-soaked breath assaulted my senses as he panted on the side of my face.

I threw up. My vomit spewed all over his couch. He got off me and laughed. He said, 'It wasn't that bad, was it?'

I thought I was going to pass out, and curled into a fetal ball on the couch. He kicked me off and I landed on the floor. He said, 'I don't want the blood from your asshole on my good furniture. Have you no manners?' He laughed.

He said, 'We have one more song to listen to...'

I passed out. I am not sure how long I was out but it was probably less than a minute. I woke when he threw cold water on me. He said, 'Am I boring you? I didn't mean to bore you. Now please sit up and pay attention.'

I sat on the floor with my back propped up against the couch. I couldn't open my mouth. He continued, 'Now as I was saying, we have one more song to listen to; goes along with today's theme. It's a new one from Brazil's own Sepultura. It's called "Dead Embryonic Cells". D'you know why we're listening to it, Maddy?'

I shook my head. He said, 'Because I am going to fulfill your boyfriend's wish and get rid of his bastard child for him. I am going to cut that baby right out of your cunt.'

A calmness came over me. I knew I was down to my last card. I spread my legs and raised the middle finger of my left hand and made the a-okay sign with my right. He said, 'Fuck you asshole. Must admit, you have more guts than your man.' While he snorted the last line of his cocaine and grabbed his eight-inch hunting knife I was able to reach for my underwear. He turned on the music and made his way between my legs. He said, 'No more fighting, eh? Kinda takes the fun out of it, but okay.' While he looked down I found my hidden knife tangled in my torn underwear. He said, 'Hmmmm, where to begin,' and ran the knife over my left thigh. I remained as calm as I could and was able to get my knife from its secret compartment while he inspected my thighs. He seemed to be enjoying the torture. He ran the knife over my pubis bone and said, 'Never did get the attraction of these things.'

He looked down again and drew the knife back. Just as he was about to thrust it into me, I sank my little knife into his back, right between the shoulder blades. He arched up and then squealed in pain. His knife moved toward me and caught me in the inner thigh. He dropped it and tried to grab the knife that was embedded in his back. I kicked him in the face with the heel of my foot. He fell backwards and impaled the knife deeper. As he rolled onto his stomach I picked up the K.K. Downing flying V guitar and smashed one of the pointed edges into his skull. He fell to his side. I struck him again with the guitar; this time I demolished his eyeball. The third blow crushed his cheek. He rolled back on his stomach and I bashed the back of his head. By the tenth blow the point of the guitar was smeared with blood and brain matter. I laughed hysterically as I looked at his one dead eye staring up at me; the other was pulp, ensconced somewhere behind his eye socket.

The room smelt of his shit. I threw up again and tried to figure out how to turn the fucking strobe lights off. I couldn't, so I escaped to the roof of the tower.

It was still raining, but it was only a drizzle. I looked over the edge and for a second thought of jumping. I swear to Christ I would have if it wasn't for my baby. I saw Matheus and Carlos waiting by the car. They saw me and looked at each other.

At that moment I knew Carlos had knowingly driven me to my funeral. I returned to the scene of my crime and grabbed my little knife, along with the eight-incher. When the men entered the room they had their guns drawn. They saw their boss bludgeoned and lying there with poopy pants.

Carlos yelled, 'What the fuck. You've ruined everything, you stupid bitch.' He raised his gun.

Matheus knocked his hand down and a shot went through the floor. Matheus yelled, 'Don't be a fucking idiot. Just keep your gun pointed at her.' He reached behind his back and pulled out a walkie-talkie. He said, 'Matheus to Vicente.' He then found the remote and turned off the strobe.

I heard Vicente. He sounded very uninterested. He said, 'Vicente.'

Matheus said, 'We have a situation here, an extremely bad situation.'

33

Within fifteen minutes Maximo Pelanchhi arrived at his son's lair. Vicente was the first up the stairs. He said, 'Oh dear, my white suit.'

Maximo was close behind, he looked at his son. He looked at the mess in the room and stared at the blood and brain-stained guitar. It was as if he was trying to piece together what had happened without asking any questions.

Finally he said to Carlos and Matheus, 'Put your guns away and don't move.'

He looked at me and said, 'Why?'

Through a clenched jaw, I replied, 'He raped me.'

'Fair enough,' he said. He looked at Vicente and said, 'Kill her.'

As Vicente reached for his gun, I said, 'He raped me and then wanted to abort my child.'

Maximo signaled for Vicente to stop. He said, 'You're pregnant? Who's the father?'

I pointed to Andres and said, 'He was.'

'My son?'

I nodded. 'It happened at Carnival. I said he could have me if he supported our school, which he did, you can check. He wanted to do it in an alley, so we did. I was very drunk.'

He said, 'Why would he rape you?'

'He told me that I had to stay here for the child was his. I told him to go to hell and that my baby would be raised in Canada. That's when he told me he preferred boys to girls and raped me anally. He then said if he could not have the baby, nobody could.'

Maximo said, 'Listen to me, I will give you one chance and one chance only. If you are telling the truth so be it, but I will have a doctor look at you. If you are not pregnant I will have you killed after you have been tortured to a degree that you could not possibly fathom. Before I kill you I will kill all the ones you are close to.' He pointed to Carlos and said, 'Including his entire family. So, if you are lying, admit it now. Vicente is an excellent shot; it will be quick and relatively painless.'

I said, 'If I am pregnant, then you must promise me no harm will come to Carlos's family.'

'Of course,' Maximo said.

'I have your word?' I asked.

'You have my word.'

I looked him in the eye and said, 'I am pregnant.'

He held my gaze for quite some time and then said for the second time, 'Fair enough.'

He looked at Vicente, nodded and then pointed at Carlos and his crony. Vicente raised his gun and shot Matheus in the heart twice. He then turned the gun on Carlos. Carlos fell to his knees and begged for his life. The bullet in his forehead silenced him instantly. I lost the feelings in my legs and collapsed to the floor.

Maximo said, 'I promised to spare his family, not him.' He looked at Vicente and said, 'Does Matheus have a family?'

Vicente shook his head. Maximo said, 'Very well. Make sure the widow Luiza is very generously compensated. Get her son a job with one of our legitimate outfits. Tell her her husband died in a car bombing. There are no remains. Feed these two to the warthogs; I want no trace of them being here. Blow up the car. We will bury Andres beside his mother in the family plot. The official word is he died in a car bombing, but I want a very discreet embalmer to make him presentable for a funeral and I want no one other than the Archbishop to be here when we bury him. We will have a public service first. Let's blame the car bombing on the communists; that should get us some good political traction.'

He turned to me, 'You, young lady, I am not sure what do with. I am usually very decisive. You have taken away my son. Granted, he was a complete failure and an embarrassment, but he was still flesh and blood. However, if you are being truthful, and I do believe you are, you have also given me a grandson. A second chance, if you will, to leave my estate to someone who won't squander it. I am going to be blunt. After the child is born there is a very good chance I will have you killed. It will sadden me to do so, but I won't have you sneaking my grandson out of the country. I liked you from the day we met.'

He walked over to me and offered his hand. I reached for it and he said. 'Come let's get you to a quiet place. My own personal physician will see you immediately.

'Vicente, make this place spotless. I want no one but you here until we need to remove Andres's body. I left the chainsaw in the shed by the pond.'

34

I passed out in the Range Rover and must have been carried into one of the guest rooms. I woke a few hours later to find myself surrounded by Vicente, a nurse and a doctor. The doctor was pressing his hands on my belly. I heard him say, 'She's with child. I will need to take her to my clinic to determine if there has been any trauma. Her vitals are fine so I imagine the fetus's is as well, but you never know. The cheekbone will heal itself as will the ribs, but she should rest as much as possible. I will give her some sedatives for the pain, ones that will not affect the pregnancy. Unfortunately, I can't prescribe stronger narcotics. She is lucky to come out of a car accident with the baby intact.'

His nurse noticed I had opened my eyes. She said, 'Good morning.' I looked at her blankly. I tried to speak. My face hurt. The doctor put his hand to his lips and signaled for me to hush. He and the nurse then gently lifted me up to a sitting position. I winced in pain. The nurse fluffed up my pillows while the doctor held me forward. He eased me back and the nurse grabbed a glass of water. She held it in front of me and I sipped on a straw. The cool water felt good on my throat but it hurt when I swallowed.

The doctor said, 'Hello Madeline, my name is Doctor Cabral and this is my nurse, Ms. Yaritza Mata. I know you have been through a lot, but I need to run a few more tests just to make sure you are okay. Okay?'

I nodded.

He took out a penlight and looked into my eyes. He then asked me to follow the light. He checked my temperature and took my blood pressure. He said, 'Here is the good news: Your baby seems fine and you, too, will be fine; for someone who was in a serious car accident you are in fairly good shape. The bad news is there is little we can do for broken ribs and cheekbones. I have not x-rayed it but the cheekbone seems to be a minor fracture and once the swelling goes down there should be no noticeable signs of disfigurement. Your ribs, however, are badly broken and will cause discomfort for some time. I have stitched up your lip; there may be some scarring but it will be very slight – hard to see if you wear a little lipstick. Unfortunately, the cut in your thigh was much deeper and I am afraid there will be scarring. Do you have any questions?'

I looked at Vicente, then the doctor and shook my head.

'Okay,' said the doctor. 'I want you to rest up. Yaritza will be staying here for the next little while. She is an excellent nurse and has a background in midwifery. When you feel like talking she will answer your questions, and if she can't she will call me. Okay?'

I nodded and tried to smile. It hurt.

35

I woke in the sitting position the doctor and nurse had left me in. Nurse Yaritza was reading a book. When she noticed I was awake she put it down and made her way toward me. For the first time I noticed her. She was beautiful. Her black hair curled around her oval face, accentuating her dark eyes. Her skin was gorgeous and her smile was warm and inviting. She wore a traditional nurse's uniform along with the little watch pinned just above her bosom. Under her uniform one could tell she had an athletic and well put-together body. She smelled like Gardenias in early spring. She was a younger version of my mother.

As she made her way toward me the door opened and Vicente walked in. He walked briskly to the chair beside my bed. Yaritza smiled at him and said, 'What a coincidence, she just woke up.'

He said, 'Just lucky I guess.'

Yaritza put her head on my forehead and looked into my eyes. 'You are looking better already. I am going to give you a couple of pills.'

I said, 'What about my baby?'

She said, 'Your baby seems to be fine. These pills will do it no harm. Trust me Doctor Carbal would have you suffer as much as you possibly could before he would administer anything that would harm your child. These pills are not the best for your pain control, but they are the best we can give a pregnant woman. You are in good hands.'

I took the pills and the nurse handed me a glass of water. It hurt a little less to swallow. Yaritza said to Vicente, 'I am going to get her some soup. She needs to eat.'

Vicente nodded and watched her leave. He looked at me and said, 'Listen, my child, you have been through hell, I know. Things in many ways are going to get much better. Senhor Pelanchhi will make certain you have the best of care. He will be coming to talk to you very soon. In the meantime, you must not say anything to the nurse that would tip her hand to the truth of your situation. As far as she knows you were walking toward a car and it exploded. The blast propelled you through the air. The good doctor used the euphemism of a car accident, because he thinks you might have suffered from amnesia and that is the way we will play it. You have no memory of the event. For God's sake don't try to tell her the truth or pass her notes or anything like that. There is more than one camera in this room and you are being observed all night and day. I hate to say it, but so is your bathroom. I can assure you I will watch as discreetly as possible but that is the reality of your situation.'

I looked at him in stunned disbelief. He continued, 'Trust me, child, if you play by the rules I will do everything in my power to try to get you out of this jam alive, but you need to reconcile an unequivocal truth: The baby will be staying here. You have some, very little, but some nonetheless, self-determination as to whether you live or die. And I give you my assurances I want you to live. Do you understand?'

I nodded.

He said, 'Good.' He reached into his pocket. 'I believe this belongs to you.' He handed me back my knife.

'Why are you giving me this?'

'Is it not yours? I hope a day will come when you will be able to tell me how you came into possession of such a curiosity.' I took it from him and put it on the side table.

He left when the nurse returned. She had brought me a huge bowl of chicken soup, apparently the universal cure-all of grandmothers and nurses worldwide. She softly sat on the bed and began to feed me. It smelled and tasted delicious but after three gulps of mostly broth I thought I was going to throw up. I gagged and she stopped. She took the bowl away and came and rested her hand on my shoulder. She said, 'I will bring it back to the kitchen. You can try some later, unless you do not care for chicken soup.'

'It's not the soup, it was delicious. I don't think I could keep anything down right now. What happened to me?'

'Did Mr. Smith not tell you?' she asked.

'Who is Mr. Smith?'

'The man who was just in here; the man who always wears the white suits. Quite eccentric if you ask me.'

'I didn't realize his last name was Smith. He doesn't seem like a Smith.'

She laughed. 'Not all of us Brazilians are Silvas, Sarmentos and Souzas. I am not sure of Mr. Smith's ancestry or where his father immigrated from, but I am guessing he's English.' She whispered, 'I hear they are quite eccentric, which is a polite way of saying crazy.'

In spite of myself I laughed, causing her to laugh along. My ribs hurt instantly. When the laughter subsided, she stroked my hair and said, 'You were in a car accident.'

I asked, 'With whom?'

She shrugged, 'I know none of the details, but I am sure Mr. Smith will tell you. The main thing is you need to rest up. It was good to see you smile.

'Now I am going to leave you be. Rest up and we will try some more soup in a few hours. The baby will need the nutrition, no?'

I said, 'Yes. Yes of course.'

She left and I drifted in and out of sleep. It was unsettling to know that my every move was being watched by god knew who. For the first time since my rape I dreamt. My dreams were horrific depictions of Lievan sodomizing me.

36

Maximo Pelanchhi was sitting in the chair by my bed when I woke. He looked at his watch and said, 'Good evening.'

I sat up and winced, drawing the sheets close to my body. He said, 'I need to fill you in on our plan of action.'

I said, '*Our* plan of action?'

He ignored me, 'I have been busy trying to figure things out. I called your parents and let them know you are okay, that you suffered a concussion and broken ribs in a car accident. I assured them there was nothing to be alarmed about and that you were in good hands. Of course I mentioned nothing about your pregnancy. I also told them that you would be calling them,' he looked down at his watch, 'in a half hour from now.

'I spoke first with your mother. She was rather frantic, but I calmed her down. Your father became accepting; he seems like a gentleman of fine character, although he did say some disparaging remarks about our drivers and our healthcare system. I attribute that to his lack of understanding and his anxiety over his child's well-being. When I explained I had the means to have my own private physician and had hired you a nurse, he seemed more at ease.

'It is my hope that when you speak to them you will echo my version and downplay the severity and circumstances of your injuries. It would be unfortunate for all if your parents showed up on my doorstep, and I doubt it would take much for both of them to be on the first plane out of Vancouver if they sensed their child was in danger. It goes without saying that your conversation with them will be monitored.'

'Naturally,' I replied.

'Your sarcasm is tiresome. I know it is an understatement to say you are in a situation you don't care to be in. Let us remember you are the one who consented to have unprotected sex with my son, and I find it hard to believe that you knew nothing of the reputation of the "howler monkey". It was you who killed him right here on my land. You can continue to be insolent; it makes little difference to me, for while you are carrying my grandchild you will be treated with the best of care. Nevertheless, continued disrespect toward me will not serve you well after the baby is delivered.'

He got up and walked away. With his back to me he said, 'I will return in twenty minutes. Please think carefully about what it is you wish to say to your parents, and unless you want them dead make sure they have no inclinations of coming here.'

I blurted out, 'Maybe I will tell them the truth. You know they will raise hell with the Canadian embassy.'

He stopped dead in his tracks but did not turn around. He said, 'Maybe you will.'

He continued walking and opened the door then shut it quietly behind him.

I thought about my options. If I blurted out that I was pregnant and being held against my will, they, along with a good chunk of the Saunders clan, would be on the first flight to Brazil and they would let the embassy and the press know. I wondered if even Pelanchhi would be able to weather the political shit storm that would develop. On the other hand, I imagined that the second I started to go off script the line would go dead before any full explanation was forthcoming.

Then I would be taken from the compound and hidden away in the jungle or God-knows-where until the baby was born, after which I would become a nutritious snack for wart hogs, alligators or the like.

I thought about the knife in my side table and wondered if it would be possible to hold myself ransom. I imagined myself walking out of the villa with the knife pressed to my belly saying 'one false move and the fetus gets it' while guns were trained on my head. Would he let me walk?

Perhaps. Perhaps not. Most likely he would call my bluff, wrestle the knife from me and I would be chow for the hogs after giving birth.

He returned with Vicente twenty minutes later. He said, 'After your call Vicente will fill you in on how we are dealing with the Saints for Sanctuary people.'

He handed me the phone and then pulled it back. 'We both want the same thing, Madeline. We both want the baby to be healthy. I know you will not put your child in harm's way. I know this because if you were fighting my son for yourself and yourself only, you would be dead right now.

'The only thing you have on your side right now is time. Use it wisely.'

He handed me back the phone and in spite of myself I automatically said, 'Thank you.' I took a deep breath, closed my eyes and envisioned myself giving the performance of a lifetime.

37

Vicente stayed in the room with me. Maximo left and then used the walkie-talkie to tell Vicente to tell me to phone. I began to dial home.

The phone rang less than once and I heard my mother's voice for the first time since I had left. She sounded frantic, 'Hello? Maddy?'

I said, 'Hi mom.'

My dad said, 'Hello Maddy.' My mother said something as well, but I couldn't tell as she was speaking at the same time my dad was. They started speaking again at the same time. I might as well have been connected to the tower of Babel.

I said, 'Mom, Dad, you need to stop speaking for a second and listen.' They paused. I said, 'We need to figure out a system here, obviously you are both on the phone and it is clear you want to talk to your favourite daughter, but if you continue to speak at the same time I will not be able to understand a word you are saying. So why don't we do this? Let's assume you both want to ask questions; why don't we let the ladies go first every time. Okay?'

There was a very long pause. They both said okay at the same time. I had not seen them in months, but within mere seconds they had me rolling my eyes and biting my tongue.

My mother said, 'Gus, I was supposed to go first.'

Dad said, 'So is that why you took until the cows came home to say something? For God's sake Cathy, get a move on.'

'Gus,' she said, 'you aren't being fair. I am so upset right now and you are not helping.'

I interjected, 'Mom, Dad. Let's try to focus. How about I speak for now?'

Again a long silence. I continued, 'Okay, first and foremost I am fine. Absolutely nothing but a few broken ribs and a very minor fracture on my cheekbone. My face is already returning to its beautiful self. I was a little annoyed at Mr. Pelanchhi for even calling you guys, because I knew it would just worry you, but he is very concerned for my well-being, and in my humble opinion a tad overprotective. If I was at Luiza's I would be told to suck it up and get on with my work, but because the accident happened to involve Mr. Pelanchhi's son and was close to his home, I have been receiving the best of care.'

Mom said, 'Please thank this Pelanchhi fellow and offer our condolences on losing his son and the two workers … the poor man.'

I didn't realize Pelanchhi had mentioned fatalities as part of the accident scenario. I said, 'Yes, by far the most disturbing part of this ordeal has been the death of the others. Andres Pelanchhi donated money to our cause and to think he died in such a violent manner is causing me nightmares. There is no question it will be harder for me to get over his death and the death of his two men than it will my physical injuries.'

My dad asked, 'Madeline, how did you suffer so little injury while these other three died?'

I felt panicked. I was unsure what Pelanchhi had said and knew if our stories did not corroborate my dad would become instantly suspicious. I said, 'I haven't a clue dad. I was unconscious when the ambulance arrived and have no recollection of the accident. The doctor said that with time, my memory might return.'

'I just thank God you are okay, Madeline,' said my mom.

Dad asked, 'Is this guy being good to you? Does he want something in return for his hospitality?'

I said, 'He's being very good to me, and no, Dad, he wants nothing other than a pound of flesh from me.'

My mother laughed and Dad said, 'I can pay him for the medical fees, but I wasn't talking about money, Maddy.'

'Oh my God, Dad,' I whined. 'Do you really think every Latin American is some sort of crook or perv? Mr. Pelanchhi is a good man; very tight with the Archbishop and he's a philanthropist. No Dad, he does not want to have sex with me, and I do not want to have sex with him.'

'Your dad is just being overprotective of his little girl,' Mom interposed. 'This man could be Norwegian, Australian or African, it wouldn't matter; your dad is just suspicious by nature. You know he wanted to get your Uncle Bufford to see if he could find information on this man, and he has spent hours tying up my phone on that bloody Internet thing of his trying to get information.'

Dad said, 'Enough Cathy, and as for you young lady, if you run off to a foreign country by yourself and don't expect us to be concerned when something like this happens, then you need to get your head examined. Your mother has been worried sick.'

'When he says your mother has been worried sick,' my mom cut in, 'he means both of us. One minute he's fretting around here like a skittish colt and the next minute he is angrier than a Protestant.'

I laughed. I wasn't acting. My mother continued, 'You know we support you, dear. I am so proud of you, as is your father. He's always bragging to his Knights of Columbus buddies about how his Maddy is building a school for kids. We've just been worried sick.'

I felt pangs of guilt thinking about the priest's baby growing; nesting in my tummy. I said, 'You two have nothing to worry about. I am fine.'

My father asked, 'Have you been going to church?'

'As a matter of fact, I have, Dad. This accident has really made me question my life and my faith. I think I will be spending a lot of time with a priest trying to sort out why I lived and others died.'

'I hope you are not feeling guilty about that,' my mom said. 'God's will is beyond our understanding, although I think you should seek providence.'

'I couldn't find anything on this Pelanchhi fellow on the Internet, but it sounds like we have some things in common. He's a good Catholic. In fact, he was saying he is on the Senatus for his region's Legion of Mary. Also, he says he has some cattle, mostly beef, but some dairy. If he's a Catholic and a cattleman, he must have some redeeming qualities.'

I laughed as I knew that was my father's attempt at humour, and that his way of saying sorry for jumping down my throat earlier. My parents seemed appeased and the rest of the conversation was me telling them a G-rated version of my adventures; stuff I had already told them through my letters home. They filled me in on local gossip, the goings-on of my siblings, and my dad informed me of what he thought were news stories that would pique my interest: the signing of NAFTA and the fact the army was allowing homos to serve. He said he did not get the big deal, he'd served with queers and they were as good at killing people as normal people.

Sometimes I find it hard to believe I am that man's child. We ended with heartfelt 'I love yous'.

38

Minutes after I hung up the phone Maximo joined Vicente and me in the room. Maximo said, 'Well done, a convincing performance. You are a natural liar.'

'It didn't come as naturally to me as it might to others.'

'Hmmm,' he said, 'I am not so sure about that.'

Vicente said, 'Are these your notes?'

Maximo nodded and handed a pad of paper to Vicente, then asked me, 'Who is this Uncle Bufford?'

I replied, 'An old army buddy of my dad's. Dad is convinced he has connections to spy groups or something. He is a retired old drunk.'

'I see,' he said. He turned to Vicente, 'I got a sense the father thought the call might have been tapped. Let's see if we can figure out who this Bufford fellow is. I am curious that when the mother mentioned it he shut her up pretty quick.'

Vicente nodded. 'He has Internet access. Thank goodness we got it at our offices in Rio.'

'I knew being connected to that Earth Summit would pay dividends,' Maximo said. 'I want you to get one of our computer guys to find out everything he possibly can about me and fax all information here right away.'

Vicente took out a small pad of paper from his white suit pocket and wrote down his boss's instructions. Maximo said, 'From the notes, does anything else jump out at you?'

Vicente studied the large notepad and said, 'No, not really. The father seems concerned for her safety, but that is a normal reaction I would imagine.' He hesitated and then continued, 'It does strike me kind of funny that there was no mention about the Saints for Sanctuary. That Maryanne woman said she would screen her calls and if he called she would not return his calls until Maddy talked to him. Just curious that he mentioned no frustration about not getting in contact with them.' He looked at me and said, 'What did your father do in the army?'

I said, 'It was before I was born. I think he was a pilot.'

Pelanchhi asked, 'He never talked about it?'

I thought for a few moments and said, 'No, not really. My sisters and I were not that interested. My cousin Ronald would pester him to see his uniform and badges or medals or whatever but that was about it, except every couple of years Uncle Bufford would come round and they would go to the Legion in Chilliwack and tie one on. They would be pretty giddy when they got home and would talk for hours. About what, I have no clue.'

'So he wasn't in Special Ops, or anything like that?' asked Vicente.

'Even if I knew what that meant I couldn't tell you. All I know for sure is he flew around and more than likely dropped bombs on people.'

Maximo said, 'I hope not all children have such insolent ideas about their fathers who serve to defend their countries.'

Maximo left. I thought he was right; I was a good little liar. My father served in Vietnam from 65-68. He flew a Huey for the 1st Cavalry Division's Company A, 229th Assault Helicopter Battalion and fought at Ia Drang. It was there that he met his lifelong friend, Captain Bufford Crane. My dad landed his bird a dozen times and rescued over sixty soldiers from certain death in a zone so hot that the medvacs wouldn't go in. He was so ballsy he performed vertical landings. In 1966, during Operation Masher he landed his chopper in the dark, in an area surrounded by trees on three sides with Charlie throwing lots of heat. Again medvacs would not go in, not even during the day. He didn't want to give Ho Chi Minh's boys a target, so he radioed Captain Crane to turn on his flashlight and to shine it skyward; that was his only landing light. Twelve men were saved by him that night, including Captain Crane.

My father never ever spoke a word of this to me or my sisters. It became an ingrained part of the family's oral history when Uncle Bufford came to town. Minus the cuss words and almost indecipherable southern colloquialisms, I have recounted it pretty much verbatim. A story almost told liturgically by Colonel Bufford Crane, Central Intelligence Agency Rt.

I prayed none of this information would show up on the Internet, a device I had never used. Thank God there was no Google in '92.

Vicente said, 'What are you thinking about, Maddy?'

'I can't believe I'm alive. Two days ago I would've thought I'd never hear my mother's voice again.'

He said, 'I need to fill you in on how we are dealing with Saints for Sanctuary. I will be back after the nurse comes in with some dinner.'

When he left I turned over on my side, guessing I was out of the camera's eye and allowed my face to show some emotion. I could not believe they were discussing their ideas in front of me until it dawned on me: I was a dead woman walking.

I also wondered what Maryanne's angle was in all this. I got the sense I would be treated like a pariah by the officials in Saints for Sanctuary.

Nurse Yaritza knocked softly on my door before entering with another bowl of chicken soup and a plate of *coxinha*, a fried dumpling snack. As she approached me she said, 'I am not sure if you are ready for *coxinha*. They are delicious and Mr. Pelanchhi had his cook make them up for the Archbishop who will be visiting tomorrow. I asked if I could steal a couple for you.'

I didn't feel like eating, but not because of the trauma my body and mind had suffered. It was dawning on me that the only time I would see my child was at its precious birth. The future, not the past, was making me ill.

I got out of bed and made my way gingerly to the small table located by a large window in my room. Yaritza said, 'Good for you. I think it is good to get out of your bed, just be careful of the stitches in your leg.'

My leg hurt; it was not excruciating pain but I could feel most of the bruises incurred by Andres' fists and feet. I felt soreness in my buttocks when I sat on the hard chair. Yaritza put the food down in front of me. In spite of my discomfort and my frame of mind I was overcome by the aromatic pleasantry of the *coxinha* and chicken soup. I took a timid sip of the soup and swallowed tentatively; it went down with much greater ease than it did earlier in the day. I took another, and then another and another sip, and before I knew it the entire bowl was devoured.

I then had a *coxinha*; a tiny nibble at first. It was delicious, enchanting really. The dumpling was stuffed with chicken, tomato, fried onions, garlic and several spices I could not identify. I suppose I was ravished and soon cleaned the plate. Yaritza clapped and said, 'Good for you! Baby will appreciate the nutrients.'

I said, 'Well, I guess if I have to eat for baby, then poor ol' me will have to eat. That was frickin' delicious. Is there more?'

She laughed and said, 'I'll be back in a while. The cook, I am sure, will make you some more.'

I truly don't understand why I don't weigh four hundred pounds; I love food. There is something about it that lifts my spirits and makes me think. While I was slurping up my soup and chowing down my *coxinhas*, I was thinking about my dad.

In particular, I was thinking about where he would have been when talking to me. Dollars to delicious donuts (although I would rather have the donuts) he was in his office sitting behind his desk. On the wall above him there were three quotes he got me and two of my sisters to needle point for him as part of an exercise in learning patience. My oldest sister was commissioned to write Henry Ford's '*Whether you believe you can, or whether you believe you can't, you're absolutely right*'; and the next oldest sister had to write James West's '*Fight hard when you are down; die hard – determine at least to do – and you won't die at all*'; and I was ordered to write '*Illegitimus non carborundum,*' which is Latin for 'don't let the bastards get you down'.

I decided my only way out of this jam was to believe I could survive, fight with everything I had and never let my adversaries know I was down. I waltzed into the bathroom, looked at the camera and took the most animated bowel movement I could imagine, even though the pain was almost unbearable from my recent run-in with Andres. I unrolled the toilet paper with panache and wiped my ass with a shit-eating grin plastered over my face. In my mind I was thinking *fuck you Pelanchhi.*

39

Vicente visited me soon after I had used the washroom. I felt like asking him if he enjoyed the show but decided it would be to my advantage to tone down the insolence and start looking for weaknesses in Fortress Pelanchhi.

I also decided I was no longer going to stay in bed. I realized I needed clothes. I am not sure who the long T-shirts that came down past my knees belonged to. The sleeves were intact and there were no band logos on them so I assumed they weren't Andres's. Me wearing his dead son's clothes may have even been too much for the ice-cold Maximo.

Before Vicente said a word I said, 'Vicente, could I trouble you for some clothes? I no longer see the point in lounging around in bed all day. I can give you my sizes if you would like.'

He replied, 'It has already been taken care of. Senhor Pelanchhi had me recruit two office girls from one of our businesses in San Salvador to go on a shopping spree for you. I asked the women selected be stylish yet practical in their choices. Your wardrobe will arrive sometime tomorrow. If you find their choices agreeable we will use them to purchase maternity clothes.'

'Another thing I would like to discuss is where and what I am allowed to do. I'll go stir crazy if I'm forced to stay in one room for nine months.'

'I can imagine,' he said. 'You will be able to leave the house for exercise, etcetera, but only when accompanied by either myself, Senhor Pelanchhi or your nurse. You will never be permitted to leave the compound. In order to maintain this privilege it is our understanding that you will not communicate with anyone else on the property. Our regular staff has been informed they are not to talk to you unless directed to do so by myself and, you guessed it, Senhor Pelanchhi; not even the nurse can give permission. If the occasion arises like it will tomorrow when you are to meet with a guest of Senhor Pelanchhi's, you must ensure you are never alone with that person. These visits will be very infrequent; in fact, tomorrow may very well be the only one.'

I replied. 'Under the circumstances, that sounds reasonable.'

'I am glad you think so. Now, we need to discuss how things have been explained to Carlos's family.'

'You've seen Luiza?'

He nodded.

'How is she? How's her mother? Fabricio?'

'You can imagine they were devastated by the news of Carlos's death. Well, the son and mother were, the old lady not so much. The son took it particularly hard and the wife, Luiza, is it?' I nodded. 'She cried and said something to the effect that she knew he would end up dying before his time. The old woman took over and tried negotiating the very generous compensation package Senhor Pelanchhi offered the family. She was ruthless in her doggedness to the point I emptied my own wallet right there and then to appease her. She seemed happy with the arrangements made for her grandson, as did the mother, but she was feeling the shock of the news and it was a little harder to gauge her reaction. The boy was a mess; I'm not sure he heard what I was saying.'

I asked, 'Did you find it difficult?'

'Delivering news of tragedy is always difficult.'

'That's not what I mean.'

'Then I am unclear as to your question. You need to be specific.'

'The fact you killed him. There you were, expressing your condolences, when all along you were the one that shot him right between the fucking eyes while he was begging for his life.'

'My dear, I felt no remorse for killing that piece of shit. It's men like him that give Brazil a bad name. Where was he when you were being tortured and sodomized? Don't think for a second he didn't know your fate. His family will be far better off without him. Hopefully he hasn't poisoned his boy with his macho bullshit too much; perhaps the boy will see merit in hard work and the pursuit of an education as opposed to hanging out with a bunch of louts and hangers-on. Maybe the widow will find a man who treats her with the respect she deserves.'

'I am sure all the men under Maximo Pelanchhi's employ are perfect gentlemen; law-abiding citizens who put family first and go to church on Sundays.'

He took off his fedora and wiped his brow with a white silk handkerchief and said, 'I am not sure about the church part, but yes, for the most part Senhor Pelanchhi's men are decent, law-abiding Brazilians just trying to make their way in the world.'

I said, 'You keep telling yourself that.'

'Of course,' he said, 'there are those of us who are involved in the relatively small part of his, what can best described as non-sanctioned business activities.'

'By non-sanctioned, you mean illegal. By illegal you mean selling drugs to kids and selling kids to pedophiles.'

'Among other things, yes, there is a vested interest in the drug trade and prostitution. Non-sanctioned businesses are lucrative, no question about that. They are also very difficult to get out of. To assume no responsibility for these enterprises would lead to carnage on the streets of Salvador and the towns of Bahia. The violence would be unprecedented; the most viscous days of the cocoa wars would pale in comparison. Senhor Pelanchhi tries his best to ensure as little bloodshed as possible occurs and makes sure people on both sides of the law are well-compensated for their involvement. If you were to ask the men and women who work in these initiatives I believe they would tell you they are fairly paid and that as long as they play within the rules they run little chance of getting themselves killed; however, if they go rogue or do things without Senhor Pelanchhi's consent, they will suffer extremely severe consequences.'

'With one exception,' I said.

He looked at me blankly. I said, 'The one exception would have been Andres. He got to do what he wanted. I imagine that in the non-sanctioned businesses loose cannons such as him must have been detrimental. In fact, I am sure he did more harm than good.'

He said, 'Such is the nature of youth. Unfortunately, that is no longer a concern. I don't want to talk about Andres. I knew him since his birth and will miss him. It is comforting to know that his legacy will live on. Hopefully his son or daughter will have a temperament better suited for the stresses and responsibilities of being a Pelanchhi. I would hate to think he or she would have the same fate of its father. I think, in part, Andres struggled because he did not have the luxury of a mother in his life. Hopefully, his child will not suffer the same circumstances.'

As he spoke I subconsciously rubbed my belly. He noticed and said, 'There's no point in fretting over the future. My hope would be that Senhor Pelanchhi will see merit in keeping you and your child together after its birth. You are a bright girl; I am confident you are thinking of an angle in which you become indispensable, and as long as you realize you can never leave Brazil there is hope.

'Now I hate to be so cut and dry about such delicate matters.'

I interrupted him, 'Delicate matters? You mean if I live or die.'

He ignored me. 'I need to tell you what we have told your Brazilian family and the Saints for Sanctuary woman.'

I shrugged and said, 'Continue.'

He replied. 'So we have told them there was an accident, but we have also let it leak out that it was actually a car bombing. It is our hope that as the lie disseminates people will come to the conclusion that the communists or at least the trade unionists were behind the bombing. They are a wonderful political scapegoat; similar to a bogeyman. I digress. The point is, they think you were in a coma-inducing accident and you have no recollection of it because of amnesia. That is the easy part. However, they want to see you, and frankly I do not see why they can't as long as you behave. But here's the rub. How do we explain to them why you'd stay here and not return to do your work? I'm stymied, any suggestions?'

I was quiet for a while and then started to laugh. 'You're serious?'

He said, 'I am not sure why you are laughing; of course I'm serious.'

'You want my input into concocting a cockamamie story that would for all intents and purposes be the narrative for my own imprisonment. I find that fucking hilarious.'

He leaned in close and said, 'I want to devise a story that might save your life. The hilarity of that escapes me.' He walked away and with his back to me said, 'Let me know if you have any epiphanies.'

He closed the door softly. I thought about how I was doing a lousy job of toning down the insolence. My thoughts were interrupted when Nurse Yaritza bounded through the door. 'God must be shining his light upon you today, Madeline. The chef made you *coxinhas* he claims are tastier than the ones prepared for the Archbishop. The braggart says they are divine!'

A light bulb went on and the genesis of a hair-brained story that could buy me some time entered my head.

40

In the fall of 1989 I went on a religious retreat just outside of the town of Squamish, British Columbia. I was invited by a woman in my religious studies class who came from, what seemed to a Fraser Valley farm girl like me, a very radical religious place. We went to hear a speaker who was considered a rogue priest. He maintained that the Catholic, and for that matter the Protestant churches, had gotten the entire original sin thing all wrong. His contention was that we are all born a blessing onto God and that the church at its reactionary, misogynistic best did everything to control its followers through fear and self-loathing. He believed the tenets of the church were put in place to suppress spiritual awareness with God and to make the church itself the only intermediary between the divine and the worldly. They succeeded. Holy fuck did they ever.

During the retreat I was introduced to female mystics; women whose ideas, whose genius, had been repressed by the mainstream church for centuries. Women such as Julian of Norwich and Hildegard of Bingen; medieval mystics who attempted to convey a message of hope and unconditional love in a time when the church used fear and punishment as methods to keep the flock docile and compliant. I also discovered the Beguines, Catholic women from the lowlands who lived a life of solitude and devoted themselves to prayer and good works. My idea was to combine the traditions of the Beguines and the experience of Julian of Norwich in order to justify my resignation from the Saints of Sanctuary and my newfound, or at the very least rekindled religiosity.

Julian of Norwich believed she was going to die and on her faux deathbed had a series of visions. Her return to good health led her to re-ev*alua*te her life and to devote herself to pursuing the meaning behind her visions. The Beguines lived in solitude and spent countless hours in meditation. Like Julian, I had a near-death experience, an experience that led me closer to God and questioned my unfettered relationship with the divine. I, like the Beguines, would need to isolate myself from the world and devote myself to prayer and meditation before re-entering the world and continue to do good works. Simply put, I would need a sabbatical to get my shit together before I could move on to helping others.

I wondered if people would buy it and supposed they would. Gretchen was well aware of my flighty side and my parents were used to me changing my course midstream. I would send Luisa a note of condolence explaining I was overwrought with guilt that I had lived and Carlos had died and that I could not face her until I had things sorted out in my head. She would be hurt, perhaps even angry, but I knew she would forgive me. She would also be focused on her work at the school.

Lievan, not that I gave a shit about what Lievan thought anymore, would accept any truth as long as he was not revealed as the father of the child. I was sickened to think what would happen if the true identity of my child was ever disclosed and hoped that Lievan in his pathetic weakness would not confess his sins to Matos or one of his priestly brothers. I doubted very much, as self-preservation seemed to trump guilt in the immoral hierarchy of the man I once loved. It was the old woman I worried about. She knew of my condition and would not buy my story for a second. Dona Aurora would study my situation from every angle. I could only hope she would trust I was construing this charade to protect my baby.

I started to write my letters. I wanted to sign them Madeline Saunders, the unwed pregnant foreigner who is carrying the child of a cowardly priest while being held captive by an extremely handsome but brutal crime boss who believes that his dead son – who was killed by me after he brutally raped and tried to murder me – is the father of the child that grows within me. For all involved I decided it would be best to opt for *love, Maddy*. Besides, I doubt my original would make it past Pelanchhi's censor.

41

After breakfast I met with Maximo and Vicente and explained my plan. They agreed that there was a feasibility to it, but asked why I would need to stay in the compound; would it not make more sense to go somewhere by myself. Vicente answered their question. I would stay on the compound because it was a place where I could be isolated from the goings on of daily life, but where I could also be in contact with my spiritual guide, Archbishop Matos himself.

I asked why Matos would take an interest in a twenty-one-year-old foreigner. Pelancchi replied because he was doing it at the request of a good friend who wanted to see something positive come out of the death of his only son. They then explained to me that the Archbishop would be let in on the fact that I was pregnant. They would not reveal the truth about me killing Andres, instead they would stick to the car accident angle. He would be told I was ashamed about being pregnant and did not want my family and friends to know. Therefore, I would stay isolated from everyone using my spiritual quest as a ruse and when the baby was born I would leave it a month or so afterwards and return to Canada knowing the child would be raised by a loving grandfather and that it would have the opportunities of the world at its disposal. We rehearsed our angle and made sure we were on the same page before Matos' arrival in the early afternoon. Matos would also act as a conduit between me and the Saints of Sanctuary people, keeping them in the loop as to how I was doing. I was forewarned to not allow myself any opportunity to be left alone with the Archbishop.

In the company of Vicente, I exited the house for the first time and made my way to the backfield and the canopy where only weeks ago I enjoyed a fine meal fed to me from the plate of the man I thought I loved. Only weeks ago it was from this place where I boarded a golf cart and sang along to eighties hair metal while being driven by the man who would rape me; the man I would kill. I looked at the cluster of trees that separated the home of the father from the home of the son and noticed something that did not catch my eye before. Above the tree line I could make out the silhouette of the turret perched on Andres's tower. In spite of the humid heat I shivered.

I sat under the shade of the canopy and scanned the rest of the property, trying to put together the information I knew of the compound. I recalled there were no fences or walls but there was a perimeter road that was constantly patrolled. According to Carlos and Matheus the woods were also inundated with sensors, cameras and dogs. The dense jungle forest, more than likely teaming with hostile fauna and poisonous flora would make infiltration or escape next to impossible. I suppose some super-secret agent guy trained in martial arts and espionage might be able to make his way out, but it would be a mission impossible for a pregnant woman who dropped out of Girl Guides when she found out there was no member's discount on the cookies. At that moment I accepted the fact escape on foot was too risky.

Acceptance was not as devastating as one might think. I sat down and enjoyed my quasi-solitude realizing it would be one of the few times in the next nine months, or perhaps the rest of my life depending on how long I was to live, where I would be more than a dozen metres away from another human being.

I heard voices coming from the house and turned to see Maximo, the Archbishop and Lievan approach me. I was glad that I was sitting down as I am certain my legs would have given out. The men approached, chatting and laughing like they were walking down a golf course. Matos and Lievan were wearing their formal black suits while Maximo wore predominantly white. I noticed Lievan had all but shaved his hair and that he was wearing a large crucifix over top of his black shirt. I assumed it was to protect him from the she-devil whore he was about to encounter. I remained sitting as they came under the canopy. The Archbishop came toward me and put his hand on my shoulder. He said, 'Madeline, my child, how are you?' There was little warmth in his words or his touch.

I subtly moved my shoulder and he withdrew his hand. I replied, 'I live, your Grace.'

'And thanks be to God,' he replied. 'The lord has spared you for a reason. May we sit?'

I nodded. As they sat I scanned their faces, all but Lievan made eye contact.

Maximo said, 'I would like to thank my good friend Thiago for coming here today to help us in this very trying time. He has been very supportive, as has Father Lievan in helping me deal with the loss of my son.'

Lievan crossed himself.

'He has also taken time from his very busy schedule,' Maximo continued, 'to assist me, us, in a very delicate and challenging time. I have explained to him that you, Madeline, are with child.'

I interrupted him, 'I am grateful for the Archbishop's support in this matter, but I am wondering why Father Lievan has to be here? I find what we will be talking about to be humiliating enough without another person having to know my dirty secrets.'

Matos said, 'My child, Lievan shared similar concerns. I insisted he accompany me, for often times an old man like me feels the need for understanding when dealing with younger people and the issues they find themselves embroiled in. Lievan will help me put your situation in a context I can understand. Secondly, it is always good to have someone witness conversations such as these to ensure there are no misunderstandings. Remember, he and I are part of the same holy body of Christ.'

I looked at the ground.

Maximo said, 'Let me get to the crux of the matter. Madeline is pregnant with Andres's child.'

I looked at Lievan. He was staring directly at Maximo. I sensed he could feel my eyes on him but knew he would not avert them toward me.

Maximo continued, 'Madeline and I have agreed that she should stay here until the child is born. Upon its birth she will leave for Canada and continue with her life. She is a young, intelligent and beautiful woman and I am certain she will find love and start another family knowing her illegitimate son will be raised by me and that the child will want for nothing and have the love of a doting grandfather. It is our hope, for everyone's sake, that her pregnancy remains a secret so there is no unnecessary shame brought to Madeline's family, and that the legalities of custody can be done expediently and privately as possible. My hope is that Madeline leaves Brazil unburdened.'

Matos said, 'How do you feel about all this Madeline?'

I replied, 'I will never leave Brazil completely unburdened. I will forever regret that I will not have the opportunity to fulfill my commitment to Saints of Sanctuary, and more importantly, I will always wonder about the well-being of my child. A mother, regardless of the situation, should stay with her child.'

'So stay,' said Matos.

'That, I'm afraid, does not seem to be an option,' I replied.

Vicente said, 'Getting citizenship would be next to impossible. However, Senhor Pelanchhi's influence could make it happen. Madeline knows she could stay here but that would mean little contact with her family. I believe she has chosen her family and life in Canada.'

Matos said, 'I see.'

I said, 'I have been asked by Maximo to lay my cards on the table during this conversation; well here goes. I realize that legally the child is mine and that I have the right to walk off this property and make my way back to Canada; I also know that will not happen. Maximo's power and influence will ensure I remain in Brazil under his care until the baby is born. If Brazil has made me one thing, it has made me a pragmatist. Accepting my child will not leave and that I can't stay means I must opt for the next best thing: The best care for me and my baby until I come to full term, and the knowledge my child will grow up in a situation full of opportunity. I do, however, have one dire reservation, one substantial request and one moral question.'

Matos said, 'Let's address them one at a time. What is your concern?'

I looked at Maximo. 'Again,' I said, 'I have been given carte blanche to speak frankly?' Maximo nodded. 'Okay. If Andres is an indication of how my son will turn out then I am extremely concerned. I know I have little room to stand on moral high ground and admit that I had sex with Andres on Shrove Tuesday if he promised to support our school. Having said that, the man was in many ways infantile, he was a bully and a blowhard and addicted to more than one substance. What assurances are there that my son will turn out differently?'

Even the stoic Matos could not hide his incredulity at my brashness. I swear I saw Vicente reach for the gun I knew was holstered under his white suit jacket. Lievan was shaking his head but could not bring himself to look at me. The only man who appeared unfazed was Maximo. He said, 'It is not often people talk so directly to me, Madeline. In most circumstances I would find it unforgivable, as unfortunately my own sense of self-importance gets the best of me. Nevertheless, I did ask that you voice your concerns and your concern is very legitimate. I failed as a father to my son. His mother, whom I loved more than I ever thought I would have the capacity to love, died while giving birth to him, and I suppose I never forgave him that. I see the raising of my grandchild as a second chance. I do not deserve a second chance, but I can give you my word that your son or daughter will grow up feeling loved and cared for. I will be the father to the child that I wasn't to Andres.'

Matos said, 'Does that satisfy your concern?'

I said, 'Yes, I suppose it will have to. One thing I am confident of is Maximo's word.'

Matos said, 'Now your substantial request.'

I said, 'I had sex with Andres for one reason, and that was funding for our school. I would like Maximo's word that he will fully fund the school's teaching staff in perpetuity in honour of the gift I am giving him.'

Maximo said, 'Of course.'

Matos said, 'Your moral question.'

I looked at Lievan and said, 'Perhaps I can ask this question to Father Lievan as he may be able to provide a modern theological answer.'

He could no longer avoid eye contact. When he looked at me I saw a scared little man. I felt nothing. I asked, 'Father Lievan, after discovering my pregnancy I debated abortion. I could have gone home to Canada early and had it performed within days of my return. Can you look me in the eye and suggest, considering the quandary I find myself in, that wouldn't have been at the very least, a viable option?'

He swallowed, looked at Matos and then back to me. He said, 'Maddy, we both know the sanctity of life will always take precedent over our own inconveniences.'

'Thank you, Father,' I said. 'It is good to know younger Catholics such as us are true to the faith in such vital and moral deliberations.'

I went on and on about the conjured epiphanies and revelations I had when I realized my life had been spared from what I was told was a terrible accident. I explained that I wanted to spend my time reflecting on what God had in store for me and how I would be able to find redemption through acts of charity. I told Matos I agreed with him; my life was indeed spared for a purpose and that I needed to embrace my faith in order to discover the path God wanted me to walk. I peppered my conversation with jabs and barbs directed at Lievan. In essence, I focused on manning up and taking responsibility for the sins I had committed, and that I was certain God did not like cowards who hid behind cloaks of denial and self-preservation.

I handed the Bishop two sealed envelopes, one was addressed to Gretchen and the other had Luiza's name on it. I said, 'Please, your grace, could you assure these letters get to their rightful owners. They are, in a nutshell, an explanation of what I have just said to you.'

He took them and said, 'They will be delivered tomorrow.' Without saying a word he handed them to his messenger boy.

42

The months passed and my belly grew as my scars faded. I tried to stop myself from lulling into a false sense of security but it was very hard to do. Yaritza turned out to be a wonderful doula, often giving advice and encouragement, calming not only me but the uptight Maximo and the nervous Vicente. She would do everything from holding my hair out of the toilet as I wretched and spewed, laughing and teasing my habit of running my finger up and down the dark line that ran from my belly button to my pubic bone, and massaging my tense and sore muscles. I was almost oblivious to the cameras and had become accustomed to the fine food and pampered lifestyle. Almost. Still, in the wee hours of the night I fretted over the fate of my child, a person I would never know unless I figured a way out of this jam.

During the day I had free range of the house. I got to know the staff, often joking with the kitchen and the grounds crew. Vicente ensnared me into helping with his museum and would often seek my advice before purchasing relics that had shaped Bahia's past. He also gave me access to the Pelanchhi archives. I spent hours upon hours reading letters and legal documents that explained how the family became wealthy and gave insight into the men who made the empire. To me, Maximo was a distant and stoic man, but compared to how his father wrote and what was written about him, Maximo was a barrel of laughs.

Maximo even allowed me to look after some of his gardens, but it was made clear I was to stay away from the one he had dedicated to his late wife. He spent an inordinate amount of time pruning and fussing over the plants and flowers. Often I would watch him work from the veranda. It was the only time he seemed content. He would sing while working away, at least that's what I thought. It wasn't until my third trimester when I ventured out for a walk that took me past the memorial garden that I realized what he was actually doing. He was intent on pruning some Gallica roses, oblivious of my nearby presence. He was not singing at all. He was talking to his dead wife. I heard him say, 'The girl is getting close. Our grandchild will be here soon, my love. If it is a girl, I shall name her directly after you, my beautiful Estefani. A boy you ask? We shall call him Estefan; kill two birds with one stone, eh? The little emperor will be named after you and father.' He laughed. It was real. I kept walking, knowing intrinsically that it would not be good to be caught eavesdropping. I realized the man did indeed possess a soul and that there was perhaps some chance the child would be nurtured and loved by a doting grandparent.

It was then and there that I began to hope for a girl. My reasoning was quite simple. A girl would remind him more of his wife and perhaps a girl would be less involved in the 'family business'.

As I hit week thirty things were going well. Then Yaritza came to work looking like she had seen a ghost.

43

I was in the bathroom and did not hear Yaritza enter my room. I was singing, very poorly I might add, Michelle Shocked's 'Anchorage'. Yaritza was standing in the corner of the room near the head of the bed. I jumped and let out a little yelp. She put her fingers to her lips and quietly shushed me. I think she was there because she thought she was out of sight of the cameras. I realized we never spoke of the cameras and wondered if she was aware of them. Evidently she was.

Yaritza motioned for me to come close. I tried to do so as casually as possible, fully aware that if we were being monitored those observing would be made highly suspicious of our behavior. She whispered, 'Let's go for a walk.'

I replied, 'Okay. Yaritza, I haven't a clue what's going on, but whatever it is you need to relax or you will draw attention to us.'

She took a deep breath and said, 'You're right, let's get out of here. We'll walk down to the orchid garden. I like the bench there.'

I nodded. We linked arms like we usually did when we went on our daily walks. Walks in which Yaritza would entertain me with the exploits of her four-year-old twins, a boy named Alarico and a girl named Claudia.

We walked in silence. The pace was brisk, too brisk for a waddling preggers like me. I said, 'Yaritza unless you want to deliver this baby right here, right now, I suggest we slow down.'

'Sorry,' she replied. 'I am so fucking out of sorts it is unbelievable.' I had never heard her utter a foul word during the time we spent together. Then she started to cry – massive tears streaking down her flushed cheeks. I looked around and was thankful to see no workers.

I squeezed her arm and said, 'It's okay, keep walking. Do you have sunglasses?'

She said, 'Yes, they are in my bra. I always take them out before leaving my purse with Vicente.'

She fished them out and handed them to me. I said, 'Not for me silly. You put them on in case anyone sees your eyes.'

She replied, 'Oh, of course, good idea.'

I said, 'Did you see Vicente this morning?'

'Yes,' I see him every day. I am instructed to wait in my car until he comes for me. He's always there. He escorts me into his office and has a female assistant pat me down. I am not allowed to bring in anything that is not related to work or can't be justified as something that might benefit you. Books, for example, are allowed, but they must be new and have absolutely no writing other than the text in them. I am also quizzed every day I leave. The man takes copious notes on everything we do.' She tried to stifle her tears but failed miserably and cried, 'That is why I am so terrified.'

Luckily, we were only feet away from the bench and I was able to guide her gently to a sitting position before she collapsed.

I rubbed her back and said, 'Take a minute. Collect yourself and then tell me what's going on.'

Like a lawnmower stuttering and then falling silent, it took her several attempts to get going. When she did she spoke a mile a minute. Swear to God, never thought a person could say so much without stopping to breathe. Even though she had sunglasses on, her big brown eyes were visible. She looked like a panicked mare; she was skittish, shocked, dazed and confused. This is what she said.

'Yesterday, I am in the park with the children. It's a nice park, a safe park frequented by the well-to-dos along with regular working people like me. The twins are playing on the see-saw and I am sitting on a bench watching them as I always do. This rather charming elderly lady comes up to me and starts talking about how adorable my children are. She asks all the usual questions and makes all the clichéd comments people do about twins, but she is complimentary and acts so sweet so I humour her. She then mentions the kids do not have my eyes. I say I think they do. She says look at me. She looks deeply into my eyes and says perhaps they do, she says, "You, my child, are a person with a kind heart; I can tell that by looking into your eyes." Then she flatters me all the more saying my eyes are a gateway to the soul and my soul is rich indeed.'

Yaritza put her hand to her chest and continued, 'Then the fucking whore witch says to me, "Listen carefully my child, I can tell you love your children deeply." I nod and say more than anything else in the world and she grabs both my hands and says, "I know; that is why you will do exactly as I say, do not look away from my eyes, my child, and listen carefully." But I looked away. My babies were gone, the see-saw was there – a perfectly balanced scale but without my little Geminis. I could not believe the power of her old gnarly hands when she squeezed my hands; I was sure she would break my bones. She said, "That is your one boon, you silly cunt, focus on me. All I have to do is raise my left hand and the boy dies; right hand the girl is kaput." This stunned me into docile numbness. "Are you with me?" she asked. I nod. She says, "Your children are perfectly safe. In a second I will tell you where they are, but remember one false move and at least one dies. Would you prefer the boy to die or the girl?" I said neither and she said good answer. She then said, "In a few seconds I will ask you to look over your left shoulder. Your beautiful children are with an old man, one in each arm. When you look, smile and wave. This will be a signal for the man to take them to the swings. He will play with them while we continue our little talk."

'I said I will give you all the money I have, please, I will even go to the bank and get more please, please, please, let may babies be. She said, "We don't want your fucking money, now just listen. Listen like a thief", she said. I remember her distinctly saying that – listen like a thief, and I was thinking I am just a nurse who has never even stolen so much as an aspirin and I am supposed to listen like a thief; what the hell does that mean?'

Yaritza finally stopped for a breath but it was a short one, 'The old woman then said to me, "Yaritza, here are some things we know about you. Last Tuesday was the last time you made love to your husband: He fucked you and then you blew him. He sucks air in through clenched teeth before he cums, looks rather comical actually. Last night you had a bath around six o'clock and then put on an old Chico Baurque record and danced in the living room with your children while your husband watched the football on the television. When you go home tonight you will find four pebbles under the pillows belonging to you and your family. The point is, Yaritza, that old man playing with your children is perhaps the deadliest assassin this country has ever produced and if you do not do exactly as we say, your children shall die. Trust me", she says. "Going to Pelanchhi or the authorities is a useless endeavor, the assassin will know and although it will break his heart he will kill at least one of your darling children."'

Again Yaritza paused for a second and then rambled on, saying, 'The old lady says, "We are only interested in the Canadian girl who is with child. All we want to do is make sure she is safe and that when the baby is born she gets home in one piece. We believe that Pelanchhi will have the girl killed once the child is delivered. You have several tasks to perform if you choose to help us, which I am sure you will when you consider the alternative." She says, "You need to memorize several questions to ask the girl. The questions are designed to be answered yes or no." She asks me if I can do that, and I say yes. "Good", she says. "Here are the questions."'

Yaritza took off her sunglasses and dried her eyes and said, 'Maddy, I will ask you the questions before I forget.'

'Okay,' I said. 'This is all so confusing, so overwhelming.'

'Tell me about it,' she replied, 'so here's the questions. Ready? Remember, just answer yes or no.'

She continued, 'Question number one. Are you safe?'

'Yes.'

'Question number two. Will they let you live?'

'No.'

I gave the question no thought. I stunned myself with the answer. I burst into uncontrollable tears and hugged my belly, I hugged my baby.

Yaritza wept afresh as well. I spied a gardener coming toward us and gave Yaritza a gentle kick in the shins. I lowered my head and pressed my palms together. Yaritza followed my cue and we fake-prayed together. Though, soon the fake prayer turned into a real one. I said, 'Dear Lord, please keep our children, the born and the unborn, safe from harm's way. Merciful and loving father we ask your blessing on not only our children but also for the children in this world who are defenseless against the tyranny of evil. Please hear our meditations.' With that we sat in silence, gathering our thoughts. I, and I imagine Yaritza as well, was taking inventory of the potential calamities that the ominous future held for us.

The gardener passed by. Yaritza said, 'Last question. After the child is born do you want us to help you escape?'

'Not without my child,' I said.

'Oh, Maddy.' Yaritza gasped, 'You are asking the impossible. Besides it is a yes or no question.'

I grabbed her by the shoulder and growled, 'You tell the old woman yes, no, not without my child. Got it?'

'You're hurting me,' she moaned.

'Yaritza, I am so sorry. I am sorry that this is happening to you. Trust me I had nothing to do with this and you can tell them I don't want their help if it means putting your children at risk, but I know these people and they are relentless when it comes to honour and protecting their own.'

'I don't blame you. I know Maximo "the spider" Pelanchhi is into all sorts of bad things, but to kill the mother of his grandchild? My God.'

She continued, 'There are two other things I am to tell you. One, you are supposed to tell me something that only you and the old lady would know.'

I thought for a few minutes and then said, 'Tell her that Inacio's cock was the first and the biggest Brazilian dick I have ever seen.'

Yaritza blushed. I actually laughed.

'He's here,' she said.

I whipped my head around fully expecting to see Maximo or Vicente but saw neither.

'Who's here?' I asked.

'The old man,' she said.

I looked at her dumbfounded, unable to conjure words.

'He said he has left the looking after of my children to his two sons. He told me that as long as I got him into the compound he would get himself out. He hid in the trunk; they don't search my trunk anymore. About halfway down the inner road I see my trunk open and he leaps out, closes the trunk, and as deft as a deer he vanishes into the jungle. He's here.'

I still could not speak. We sat in silence. Finally I said, 'We must act like nothing is going on. It is incredibly important for you to hold it together when you leave today Yaritza, I am not sure what the old man has in mind, but if it is more than just reconnaissance then there will be lots of questions, and trust me, Vicente will remember how you behaved today. Let's go back to the house and talk of this no more. Let's just follow our routine.'

She nodded. I am not sure if we would have won academy awards, but both of us did a fine job of acting like it was just another day in paradise.

However, that night I am sure my face was less than poker ready. I struggled with my conscience, wondering if I should have told Yaritza that Luiz did not have two sons to keep an eye on her children or ease her mind by telling her that Luiz and Dona Aurora would never intentionally harm children. The selfish maternal side won out as I reckoned the more Yaritza was scared the less likely she would jeopardize me, my friends and most importantly my baby's well-being. I lay in bed, eyes closed but brain fully engaged, listening to every crack and every whisper from the wind.

44

I drifted off as the sun came up. I heard nothing all night and thought Luiz must have been on some sort of a scouting trip, trying to figure out what would be the best way to rescue me.

Around nine o'clock Vicente burst into my room. It was the only time I had heard him sound flustered. He said, 'Maddy wake up, wake up immediately.'

I feigned grogginess and said, 'Please Vicente, let me sleep a little longer. This little rascal was kicking all night long, and I am exhausted.'

'My apologies, but this is urgent. If you want to live an hour after giving birth you need to get up right now.'

With that I jumped as fast as a full-term woman could and asked, 'What's wrong? I have done nothing.'

'Then explain this,' he said while handing me a note.

The note said, *If the girl dies the child dies. We will get him/her sooner than later. Before I leave I will knock three of your guards out of action. I will kill high-ranking officers one a day after the child is born if the girl is killed. It is in everyone's interest she gets home safely. Nothing will save the child from my wrath if you kill the girl. If you interrogate or torture the girl I will find out. She does not know who I am or where I live. Thank you for looking after my weapon.*

Vicente stood over me with arms crossed while I read the note. I reread and I tried to gather my thoughts while doing so. I handed it back to him.

He said, 'Well?'

I shrugged and said, 'Where did this come from? I have no idea. I have spoken to no one about my situation. I swear to God, Vicente, I have kept my end of the bargain.'

He replied, 'I see.'

'Honest to God, Vicente, I haven't a clue! This is bizarre. All I want to do is protect my baby and leave here in one piece. I am not convinced that will happen. I know chances are you will kill me. Oh my God! If you do, this monster will try to kill my baby. You must tell whoever it is I don't want that.'

'Sure, I will go to his house immediately and let him know. How can I tell him anything? He did not leave me a return address.'

'Where's Maximo?' I asked.

'He flew to Rio last night. He is on his way back as we speak.'

'Please, Vicente, you must tell him I have nothing to do with this.' I said.

'The Mauser is gone from its display case along with the scope, silencer and ammo. He left one bullet. It was sitting on top of this note which was sitting on my bedside table when I woke. There are three guards knocked out cold and tied up in the forest. Each has a black pen mark above his right eye.'

'My God,' I whispered, 'I don't want this. Those men must be terrified. Do you think he will follow through and start killing others if I die?'

'I can't imagine why he wouldn't but mark my words whatever it is he does it will not deter Mr. Pelanchhi from his agenda. I have never seen him surrender to ultimatums. I know he is undecided regarding your fate. I think he believes it would be good for you to be with the child in its infancy. He has been reading all kinds of books on raising children. Never thought I would see the day.'

I, too, found it hard to imagine Maximo Pelancchi reading up on the latest baby books.

Vicente's walkie-talkie cackled, 'Senhor Smith, we have located him.'

My heart sank.

Vicente said, 'Make sure you get the time and camera location. I will be right there.'

While making his way to the door he said, 'By the way nobody is getting in or out until I say so, that includes your nurse. You are to stay in this room and remain here until further notice. I will bring you your food. You are to speak to no one but me and Senhor Pelanchhi when he arrives.' He paused, and as he left my room I heard him speak into the walkie saying, 'Lars, please locate the nurse's car on video, I believe she arrived at the front door at 9:30 a.m.'

By locating him, I discovered they meant they found images of him on camera. Later that day I was escorted by Vicente into the only room in the house that had a television, it was a small model and it was hooked up to a VCR. I was required to watch over and over again murky tape of a man sporting a nondescript baseball cap lurk through the woods and the hallways of the house. His actions made it clear he was cognizant of surveillance cameras; there was only one shot that gave some hint to his identity. He could not resist, he handled the gun once he had removed it from the display case, pointing the barrel directly into the camera. I could imagine him cursing his vanity and carelessness the minute after such brash behavior.

45

Maximo arrived by helicopter around seven that evening. It struck me that for such a wealthy man he rarely showed his affluence. Everything, other than his looks, was understated, so to arrive via chopper meant something. I watched through my window as he made his way into the house, he was walking with purpose but appeared calm. Moments later there was a knock on my door. I said, 'Who is it?'

Without responding he walked into the room. His face was composed. 'Madeline, are you okay?'

'Under the circumstances,' I said, 'I suppose I'm fine. The baby is kicking away if that's what you're worried about.'

'A healthy mother makes for a healthy child, so I am concerned for both of you,' he replied.

I nodded.

He sat at the edge of the bed and said, 'Madeline, do you think I am a fool?'

I replied, 'I think you are many things but a fool is not one of them.'

'I am glad you do not think I am foolish. I must say, I know you are a very smart young woman, which will make our conversation much more productive and far less tedious. All I ask is that you respect my intelligence and you can be assured that I will respect yours. Okay?'

'Okay,' I said.

'So,' he said, 'Here's what I am thinking. Obviously, people outside of the compound know of your pregnancy. We are aware Bishop Matos knows. We are aware that your nurse knows. The doctor, he knows. Who else knows?'

I replied, 'The only people I have told are you, Vicente and, of course, Andres.'

He twitched ever so slightly with the mention of his dead son's name. He mulled over my response. 'So you told absolutely no one?'

'Of course not,' I said, 'I would have lost my job, not to mention the respect of all I cared for. Besides it was far too early to start telling people.'

He said, 'These people you cared for, who are they?'

'People I worked with at Saints for Sanctuary, women and children in Dona Aurora.'

He said, 'Specifics. Give me names.'

'Well,' I said, 'There was Luisa and her family. My overseer Gretchen and her driver-slash-assistant Ali. I felt close to both of them. There were also numerous women in the community and their children who I bonded with.'

'This Ali fellow, he is the huge black man?'

'Yes.'

He stated, 'Other than him, you have mentioned no men you were close to.'

'That's because there weren't any,' I replied.

'None?' he asked. 'In all your time in that shanty town, there was not one man you felt close to?'

'Apparently,' I said, 'Looking after the welfare of children and getting schools built is woman's work in Brazil.'

'Even in dire situations like this you have the capacity to be patronizing and self-righteous,' he snapped.

'If that is what you want to call truth-telling then so be it.'

He sighed and mumbled something, then he said, 'Let's get refocused. Tell me about your relationship with the priest.'

'Which priest?'

'Your answer tells me you are hiding something, Madeline. You know which priest I mean.'

'Father Lievan?' I asked.

'Yes.'

'I met him in Rio. He hitched a ride with Gretchen, Ali and me on the way up to San Salvador. I did not realize he was a priest and admit to developing a bit of a crush on him. He was supportive of me and of our cause but from an arms-length, so as not to ruffle too many feathers within the church as he was aware of our pro-contraception, pro-choice stand. He seemed like a good man but I must admit the more I got to know him the more disillusioned I became. He's more interested in towing the company line and being Matos's lackey than working for real change.'

I laughed and continued, 'I can't imagine him lurking around like a holy ninja trying to rescue a damsel in distress.'

'If not he,' asked Maximo, 'then who is our mysterious assassin?'

'I can look you in the eye and tell you I haven't a clue. I have wracked my brains trying to think who it could be and I am coming up with blanks.'

'You are trying to tell me,' he said, 'that the man risking his life, willing to kill others and anger a person whose reputation as an uncompromising cold-blooded killer is well-earned is someone you don't know?'

'Believe me,' I said, 'if I knew who he was I would tell him to cease and desist immediately. Do I want to die? Absolutely not. However, if you decide to murder me, I want my child to live. I would never agree to anything as heinous as killing an innocent child, especially my own.'

'Regardless,' he snapped, 'you know who he is. All other options are implausible. I could torture you and get his name but that might put the child in trauma. When I find him, and whoever he is connected to, they will pay dearly. My hunch is he is someone you met through your work, but I can't imagine those people having the resources to hire such an excellent assassin. Whoever he is, I have never employed him nor has he been used against me. Therefore I am thinking that somehow your father got wind of your situation, most likely through the Belgian priest. Your father seems like a resourceful man and a man who would go to any lengths to protect his family, though I doubt he would follow through and have his own grandchild killed. I have very few contacts in Canada and none in Vancouver, but it will only take a matter of days to move one of my Los Angeles people north. If I get a sense that your father in meddling in my affairs, he is as good as dead. I will be interviewing the priest, Father Van…?'

'Van den Broeck,' I said.

'Yes, him. Tomorrow, I believe, more light will be shed on our mystery guest.'

'If my father knew the truth, he would not be hiring anyone; he would be here in the flesh and you, Maximo, would be as good as dead.'

'You impress me. I swear,' he said. 'You become more Brazilian with each passing day. Perhaps you are right about your father, nevertheless let's see what Father Blue Eyes has to say.'

He left the room, quietly closing the door behind him. Confined to my room with no book or nurse to keep me company, I tried drifting off to sleep, but between the child feeling like it had dropped so low in my belly that I figured I could see its head with a mirror and a good flashlight, and my worries about what Lievan would confess to and my deep concern for my parents, sleep was illusive, teasing me with five- to ten-minute episodes perhaps twice through the night.

46

With the breaking dawn the house erupted. I was in the washroom. I could hear Maximo barking orders and seconds later I heard footsteps running toward my room. He and Vicente burst through the door.

'Jesus Christ, he's got her,' Maximo barked. 'Call the chief of police and the colonel. I want every road, every dock and every airport on the highest alert. I want her back without a scratch. I want all the dogs released and every available man on the perimeter. Once they are in position I want them to start walking toward the house. If they are still here we will flush them out.'

Before Vicente could respond I flushed the toilet. I took my time washing my hands before leaving the bathroom. Both men stood staring at me as I made my way to the bed. Maximo said, 'Don't call the chief or the colonel, but let's see if we can flush this bastard out.'

I noticed he was holding a rose and a note. He handed me the note and said, 'I will ask this once. Do you recognize the writing?'

The note read, '*I am sorry I missed you yesterday, I did not realize you were away on business. I have placed this rose picked from your wife's memorial garden as a reminder that she may not be the only loved one you will lose. If the girl lives, you and yours live. I know your pride may get the better of you, but I hope reason and smartness wins. If so, everyone wins. If not – tragedy. Your faithful servant.*'

I said, 'I'm sorry, but nothing has changed since yesterday. The man is an enigma to me. I swear on this child's life.' I immediately regretted swearing on my baby's life, but at that point in my faith sojourn I had little reason to believe there was a God who would hold me accountable. Would anyone blame me?

I gripped my stomach as I felt a sharp pain, then water cascaded down my legs. I said, 'Oh Christ!'

Vicente and Maximo, two of the three most composed men (the other being Luiz) I had ever met stood dumbfounded. Their flabbergasted looks soon changed to unproductive action. Neither seemed prepared for the inevitability that a baby would be born. All of the sudden they were transformed into flappable school boys looking at me like I had mega-girl cooties. I broke the spell by yelling, 'What the fuck are you two doing? Call the doctor or get me to the hospital, unless you want to deliver yourselves.'

Vicente said, 'I will call the doctor to come here immediately.' Simultaneously Maximo said, 'I will get the car. You get a police escort and we'll take her to the hospital.'

Again inertia took over as the men stared at each other, undecided on whose direction to take. Between clenched teeth as I was experiencing my first contraction I said, 'For God's sake, Maximo, make up your mind.'

He said, 'Right. I will get the car. Vicente call whoever it is you need to call and get a trooper to escort us to the hospital, then call the doctor. I want him and a nurse, but not the one who has been coming here, at the hospital when we arrive. Get two men to carry her to the car.'

All of the sudden these men returned to their normal selves, and before I knew it I was in the backseat of a Range Rover following a police car with its siren blasting into the early morning air toward San Rafael Hospital, the best Catholic hospital in San Salvador.

The day I anticipated and feared had finally arrived.

47

I was in labour for over thirty hours. I had always hoped than when I had a child I would give birth in my home with a midwife and the father of my child present. I imagined my parents and my sisters in the kitchen listening intently, waiting to celebrate and share in the love of a new member of the clan. I imagined all these things, and these imaginations were very realistic. Yet here I was in a Brazilian hospital with a doctor who barely knew me and a nurse who was very good, but she was not my nurse, my Yaritza. There was no one there to hold my hand or rub my back or coo in my ear; no one there to do all those male things that modern-day fathers are supposed to do no matter how inept and useless they may feel. There was just me and my pain.

I remember the doctor being reassuring, telling me over and over again that the infant's vitals were perfectly normal. He tried joking with me, saying that my womb was so perfect the little monkey did not want to come out and play.

When the doctor left, the nurse walked me to the shower, where apparently it was supposed to relax me between contractions. I could have had showers, baths and massages, and I still would not feel relaxed. My thoughts were all desperate. I felt panicked. Was the baby truly healthy? Would he or she be a golden-haired blue-eyed angel so obviously stamped with Lievan's DNA that Maximo would question the legitimacy of the

Pelanchhi lineage? If so, what be the fate of my child? When would my fate be decided? Right now was Maximo sending for a nursemaid? Was he making plans for me to be whisked off to the depths of the jungle and shot in the head, but only after torturing me until I gave up Luiz's name? My thoughts complemented by the pain made for the antithesis of everything I hoped the birth of my child would be. *Dear God*, I thought, *will they even let me see my own flesh and blood?*

But then it happened. The doctor told me he could see the crown and encouraged me to give a few final pushes. I heard him before I saw him. He let out a bombastic cry as the doctor said, 'Congratulations, Maddy, it's a boy.'

He gave my child to the nurse and while doing so said, 'She's just going to weigh and swaddle him. Hush now. Your child will be with you momentarily.'

I said, 'I need to hold him.'

He replied, 'The nurse and I will clean ourselves up and then find Senhor Pelanchhi. I think it will take us some time to get clean.'

The nurse handed me my baby boy. The doctor kissed me on the forehead and said, 'You did good, very good indeed.'

My baby came to me swaddled in a white hospital-issued baby blanket. He was the most beautiful creation I had ever laid my eyes upon. The tuft of hair, the closed, almost-translucent purplish eyelids, the pursed lips, the tiny nose with nostrils flaring and the delicate ears were all parts of an immense and wondrous beauty. In that sterile room, alone and abandoned I had never felt such love. He smelled like salvation and he felt like peace. Tears ran down my cheeks and anointed his tiny head. I whispered in English, 'My beautiful baby boy, I love you with all my heart and I promise I will do everything in my power to keep you by my side. No matter what they tell you, your name is Augustine, but I'll call you Gus.'

I sat up and undid my gown. His little nostrils flared with more gusto and I could hear the barely inaudible sound of tiny lips smacking. I guided him to my nipple. His tiny, tender mouth searched momentarily for a grip and then he clamped on. I could feel him sucking the nutrition and sustenance from my body into his. Never was giving so pure. Never was giving so fulfilling. I sang to him in Portuguese a song that had been sung to me months earlier by an old woman who held me in her arms. I sang, '*On this street, on this street there is a garden, that is called, that is called loneliness, inside it, inside it there is an angel, who stole, who stole my heart.'* My baby Gus suckled robustly while I sang. Oh the joy I felt, it was simply overwhelming.

To this very day I cherish those moments above all others that I have had in my life. Nothing comes close. I can recall every second, every nuance in my child's movements and every touch between me and him. To do so causes great pain and suffering but it is impossible for me to stop myself, because it is all I have. I am a junkie to those memories.

I sensed my alone time with my little man was coming to a close and was elated when he finally opened his eyes. I stared into his, oblivious of the fact he could not see mine. In my mind he was searching the very depths of my soul and discovering my love for him was unconditional and everlasting. His eyes looked green. His eyes looked like they belonged to the Saunders clan. The green eyes darted back and forth in the purplish hue that makes up a newborn's eyelid. Without thinking, I stole my guardian assassin's prayer, saying, 'Augustine, you are purple and green, You are every colour in between, You are an endless wave on the sea, You are everything to me.'

I offered him my other breast but he had satiated himself and tired himself out in the process. I heard a gentle knock on the door and Maximo entered the room. He quietly walked toward me. He stood above my shoulder and looked down at my baby boy. He whispered, 'He looks like his mother, he is absolutely beautiful.'

To this day I believe that Maximo did not realize he was stroking my hair while looking adoringly at who he thought was his grandson.

I almost felt sorry for him as he cooed, 'Estefan, Estefan, Estefan.'

48

Looking back at things it seems evident that the decisive Maximo Pelanchhi was at a loss as to what to do with me. He made excuse after excuse to keep me around but he implied that sooner rather than later I would have to leave the compound and leave my child.

I suppose I should thank all the trendy baby books that emphasized the importance of breast feeding and the significance of a healthy mother-and-child bonding experience. Maximo used quotes from several of his sources to justify my existence in his world. I am certain that, for one of the few times in his life, he wrestled with his conscience.

Maximo decided Gus's name would be Estefan Americo Pelanchhi. There was no consultation with me. I had hoped he would have thrown in a name that either had a connection to me or at the very least, Canada. I always called my baby Augustine or Gus whenever it was just the two of us. However, being alone with my baby was rare indeed. There was always a guard with me during the day. Maximo and Vicente were diligent in ensuring that the infant was never out of sight of an experienced bodyguard. Two were assigned to Gus and me. One was named Felicia; she was a cold, hard bitch who liked to wear her handgun high on her hip. She also liked to wear sleeveless blouses; her arms were toned to perfection. She showed no warmth toward Gus and treated me with absolute disdain. I once overheard her say to her partner, 'Never thought I would miss riding shotgun on merchandise runs up the coast to Aracaju, but that is pure excitement compared to babysitting this foreign bitch and her child.'

Pedro, her partner, was the wiriest man I had ever seen. He was at least six foot but must have weighed under one-twenty. He was not exactly Mister Personality, but compared to Felicia, he was at least civil. He reminded me of an anxious border collie on caffeine. He seemed nervous all the time and could never stay in one place for too long. I found it hard to fathom how a person could be so alert all day long. I was permitted to take Gus for as many walks as I liked but I was not allowed to do so without dragging Pedro and Felicia with me. Both were required to be available if I wished to leave the confines of the house, if for some reason they could not escort me, the walk simply did not happen until they could. During the evening one guard was posted outside my window and another was posted outside my door. These men rotated on a regular basis, I think less than ten words were passed between me and them during my tenure at the compound. They were stoic to say the least.

I was kept in the hospital for three nights. I learned that during that time Maximo stayed in a hotel very close by and that there were two guards posted outside my door. Maximo visited me and the child every few hours. I discovered that Yaritza, along with the Archbishop Matos and Lievan had been interviewed by him in regards to Luiz's forays onto the compound. I suppose Yaritza must have held her composure, he seemed convinced she wasn't involved but still did not permit her to return to the compound.

In his opinion there was no reason to think the priests were involved, although weeks after I had returned to the house he brought Lievan up in a conversation. His analysis of the man led him to believe he was hiding something, but that he had nothing to do with the assassin. He said he found Lievan to be edgy and that his quavering voice and darting eyes convinced him there was something going on. He asked me my opinion on the man.

I responded in more depth than I did the first time he asked, saying that I felt Father Lievan had several issues going on. I suggested he was a highly conflicted individual who struggled with his role in the church, his sexuality and his character. I explained that he wanted to be an obedient servant to the Archbishop but at the same time was aware that the church, in order to be relevant, had to modernize its theology. I proposed that perhaps the reason he entered the priesthood was because he struggled with his sexuality and that making vows of celibacy would protect him from damnation as he would be restricted in all sexual activity – I could almost have convinced myself that this was true.

I described Lievan as a man of weak character, a person who talked the talk but was unable to walk the walk because of his cowardice. I told Maximo that the reason Lievan acted like he had done something wrong was more to do with the fear factor than it had to do with any act of wrongdoing. I went on to say that there was as much chance of Lievan being involved in my rescue as there was a host of heavenly angels descending from above and plucking me out of my sleeping bed. A knight in shining armour he was not.

When I finished my quasi-Freudian analysis, Maximo said two things. He said, 'Madeline, you seem to know this boyish man more than I thought. I am curious about that.'

He also said, 'As you know, and as hypocritical as it might seem, I am a devout Catholic. I have studied the Bible and other religious texts. There is something I don't understand. It is in regards to the seven deadly sins: lust, gluttony, greed, sloth, wrath, envy and pride. I get six of them but the one I don't get is wrath. God is wrathful and oftentimes wrath is justified. Are you telling me wrath should not have been inflicted on the Nazis? I think wrath should be replaced with cowardice. Cowardice is a sin that should buy you a ticket to hell.' With that, he left.

I could not have agreed with him more.

Upon my return from the hospital I requested to talk to my parents. I explained to Maximo and Vicente they would be worried sick if I did not call soon and that letters would no longer suffice in remedying their anxiety. Vicente asked, 'What could have changed? There is no indication from the letters we received from them that they are particularly concerned. Surely they have no information regarding the birth of the child?'

I replied, 'I suppose. Perhaps you're right. It is more about me. I just want to hear their voices.'

Maximo chimed, 'Impossible, Madeline. Although our man from LA reports there is nothing to indicate that your father has anything to do with the intrusion and threats made toward myself and my grandson, I am still not convinced of his non-involvement. You must continue to write and let them know that under the auspices of your spiritual pilgrimage, you are still rejecting electronic technology.'

So I continued writing to my parents, making up drivel about this saint or that and how reading ancient texts was helping me reconnect with my faith. Maximo had a seemingly endless supply of religious books I could draw on. He gladly lent them to me. I think he was secretly hoping that I would rediscover my faith so I would be heaven bound when he killed me. When Gus and I were sleeping, my dreams would often go to dark places: The most recurring and powerful one was based on Shakespeare's *Othello*. In that dream Maximo said, 'If you bethink yourself of any crime, unreconciled as yet to heaven and grace, solicit for it straight.' I replied, 'Death's unnatural that kills for loving. Alas, why gnaw you so your nether lip? Some bloody passion shakes your very frame.' He replied, 'Pray Madeline, and be brief; I will walk by: I would not kill thy unprepared spirit; No; heaven forfend! I would not kill thy soul.' To which I replied, 'Fuck you, Maximo, I want my soul to rot in hell, because it will be worth seeing you there when your day comes. No repentance will be enough to justify the murder of your grandson's mother.' I watched from above as he put a pillow over my face, drew a handgun with a silencer attached and put a bullet into my temple. It became so that I feared sleep.

Nevertheless my days were filled with joy. Gus was my everything. I spent hours holding him, delighted in feeding him and I even enjoyed changing him. Though I had nothing to compare him to I think he was an excellent baby. He rarely cried, slept well and took vigorously to my breast. He was rarely fussy and when he was he was easily relieved. He was active and very alert. He would spend hours cooing. I relished the many times he would fall asleep against my chest. I swear there is nothing more comforting than having a baby sleep in your arms. I was jealous of time itself when he was not with me.

Maximo spent hours with him and subsequently me. Our conversations focused on every slight change in behavior Gus had. Maximo would ask question after question regarding my family history. He wanted to know about any genetic diseases or disorders. He wanted information about family history and politely tried to find out if depression, alcoholism or schizophrenia were rampant in the Saunders clan. I assured him we had a few drunks and mentally ill people in the closets but overall we were an above-average healthy bunch. We lived long and for the most part we prospered.

Maximo was incredibly gentle with Gus. I know this would have surprised many of his peers and I am certain that the people in Dona Aurora would be astounded that the 'spider' was capable of such sensitivity. But they had not seen him prune his wife's memorial garden. I saw first-hand the capacity for love the man had. I wondered how his life may have been different if his wife had not died so young.

While helping Vicente with his archiving I came across a box of photos of Maximo and his very pregnant wife. His grin showed unabashed joy and his eyes revealed a softness that no longer existed, not even Gus could completely eradicate the hardness of his grandfather's eyes, but by God he came close.

Vicente peered over my shoulder while I was looking at the photos. He said, 'Ahh those were happy days.'

I asked, 'What was she like?'

He remained silent for quite some time and then said, 'She was a force; her hunger for life was insatiable. She was curious about everything and smart as a whip. And beautiful? My God, was she so. These pictures don't do her justice. Everyone felt better about themselves when she was around. She was compassionate and loving.'

'Is that so?' I asked.

'That is so,' he replied. 'Why?'

'I am curious how a woman so full of brains, virtue and love could, well, marry a man who was part of a family forged by hate and lust for power.'

'I see,' he said. 'She loved him, it was that simple.'

I said no more and went back to organizing the photos. Out of the blue Vicente said, 'Things were going to be different. The plan was to move the family's interest completely out of the illegal realm and entirely into legitimate businesses. Easier said than done, I know, but with her at his side I think he could have done it. Then she died and a darkness fell over Senhor Pelanchhi. He took his grief out on his competitors, both legal and illegal, and made the empire stronger.'

He then said, 'Have you sorted the photos?'

I nodded.

He asked, 'Can you hand them to me please?'

I gave them to him and he put them in a black shoe box, which he then hid at the back of the filing cabinet.

Just then Gus woke with a little cry. I said, 'Feeding time,' and made my way to the baby.

As I was getting ready to feed him, Vicente said, 'I sense that Senhor Pelanchhi will try once more to completely overhaul his business. He wants his grandson to inherit a fortune that is built on helping Brazilians. I just hope it is not too late to get out of the other corporate interests unscathed.'

Before leaving I asked Vicente, 'Would you have shot me back in Andres's lair?'

He took off his fedora and looked me in the eye, 'With great regret, yes.'

49

I recall waking feeling very groggy, somewhat discombobulated, almost feeling like I was hovering in midair. The room seemed different. I swore I heard the whir of a ceiling fan. I fell back to sleep, but before doing so I nodded to my faithful but depraved bodyguard, Felicia.

I went back to the deep sleep I had briefly surfaced from and wished for dreams that were much more pleasant. For how much longer I slept I am unaware.

I woke again, screaming, 'Gus! Gus! Gus! Where is my baby? Where the fuck am I?' I lunged at Felicia, who was sitting in a nondescript chair at the foot of the strange bed I was sleeping in. Before my nails found her eyes the wiry Pedro had his arms wrapped around me. I desperately tried to sink my teeth into his forearm, but he was smart enough to keep far from my face. He squeezed like a boa. In an instant the panther-like Felicia was out of her seat, her gun was out of her holster and its barrel was staring at my face. She said, 'Shut up or I will do you in right here, right now.'

I spat at her and screamed. I barely saw the butt of her gun strike my temple.

I woke for a third time. This time sitting in Felicia's chair, hands and feet bound, mouth gagged and head throbbing. I tried screaming for Gus but every time I tried opening my mouth Pedro stuffed the gag further down my throat. I tried to no avail to untie myself, squirming as best I could. All that I accomplished was tipping the chair back. While flailing like a turtle on its back, Felicia stood over me and put her foot on my throat. She drew her gun again and said, 'Bitch I'm losing my patience. The boss wants us to fill you in on what is happening, but if you keep this shit up I will plug you right between the fucking eyes.'

Pedro got down on one knee and said, 'D'you want to live? I think so, yes? Because dead means you will go from less than one percent to zero percent of seeing your kid again. Compared to zero less than one can look pretty good, right?'

'He makes a point,' said Felicia.

Pedro said, 'I am going to lift your chair back up. I am going to ungag you. I will give you some water and aspirin for your head. I don't want you to say a word until I see the aspirin are down your gullet. But here's the thing, you scream, you fuss at all, and Felicia gets to do it her way. It makes very little difference to us, although the boss said if you cooperate you live. Nod if you understand.'

I nodded.

'Good girl,' he said.

He lifted the chair back up and for the first time I realized I was in a generic hotel room. He said, 'Remember inside, quiet voices only.'

He undid the gag and gave me three pills. I didn't see what they were so I bit into one and realized it tasted like aspirin. He gave me water and I swallowed. As calmly as I could muster I asked, 'Where's my baby?'

Felicia said, 'In Brazil. Safe and sound.'

I thought for a moment. 'Where am I?'

'Miami, Florida,' replied Pedro.

I threw up. Because I could not lean forward the vomit landed on my shoulder, arm and part of my leg.

'Jesus Christ,' bemoaned Felicia, 'it's going to stink in here.'

Pedro made his way to the bathroom and came back with two towels, more water and more aspirin. He said, 'Here, let's clean you up some.' He used one of the dampened towels to wipe the vomit off of me and the floor. He then gave me more water and demanded I drink most of it and then gave me the aspirin and the rest of the water. He then said, 'I am going to wrap this nice cold towel around your head. Then we will try again. Okay?'

I didn't respond. He placed the towel on my head. It did give me some physical relief. He then went to a small table and grabbed a dining chair. He placed it in front of me and sat down.

He said, 'Senhor Pelanchhi has asked we get you here safe and sound. We have done our duty and now the rest is up to you. As I said to you before, you can choose life, you can choose death. Felicia will hand you a letter and we have been instructed to stay here until you read it. When you have finished reading it you are to give us some information. What this is we haven't a clue. For you to read it means I will have to untie your hands. Do I have your word you will cooperate if we untie you?'

I whispered, 'Yes.'

Felicia said, 'Pardon me? Didn't catch that?'

I repeated louder, 'Yes.'

She said, 'Much better.'

With that she re-holstered her gun and began to roughly unbind my arms, but they kept my legs firmly tied.

Pedro reached into his jacket and pulled out a letter. Before handing it to me he said, 'Please note the signature of Maximo Pelanchhi across the back and observe the letter is indeed sealed.'

I nodded. He handed it to me. I tried opening it but my hands were shaking. I had little control over my muscles. After several attempts Felicia said, 'For fuck sake,' and snapped the envelope out of my gelatin-like fingers and opened it. She tossed it back on my lap. I fumbled but was finally able to get the letter out. I unfolded and read through blurry eyes.

Dear Madeline,

It is with regret that I write this letter. As I am sure you realize, I have fretted over what to do with the situation we have enmeshed ourselves in. I would like to begin by thanking you for the most precious of gifts you have given me. I realize you would not consider it giving and respect your opinion on that matter; however, I am also confident that you realize Estefan is indeed a blessing that has been bestowed upon me. Furthermore, I must thank you for being an excellent mother to my son. Yes, my son. It is official, the adoption papers arrived via Archbishop Matos's orphanage with an expedience I will be forever indebted to him for. He was able to process the legalities of my adoption papers that even men like me who are used to having things done quickly would still find hard to fathom. Estefan is now my legal son and will inherit all that is mine.

You once said I was a man of my word. I appreciate that you think so.

I promise to you that I will do my very best to raise my son with love and compassion. It is my goal that he will grow up in a world free of violence and corruption. It is my hope that he will love Brazil and that his endeavours and the endeavours of our enterprises will help make our country and the people who claim it as their home a nation focused on human progress, where education, health, justice, freedom and prosperity for all is the goal.

I do this in honour of the two most important women who have entered my life. I do this to honour my first wife. If she had lived and I had not fallen into despair I believe I, and by proxy, all I owned and touched, would have been so different. We would have created a world as vibrant as the roses I nurture in her honour. The other woman is you, Madeline. It is uncanny how much you remind me of Estefani. However, the first time you visited my home I saw in front of me a capricious and immature woman-child, distracted by the sound of her own voice and the allure of Brazilian beer on a hot day.

I saw these distractions as an impediment to you reaching your full potential and to be honest, wrote you off as fluff, a trifle light as air, who did not understand the complexities of my Brazil. You gave me and others cause to underestimate you. However, as circumstances unfolded, unfortunate for you as they may have been, I was able to see you in a different light. I suppose it's true: duress and trauma will reveal one's true colours.

From the day of the tragic death of my son to your last night in my home, I was able to witness your transformation into a woman who found meaning and substance in her life. The real Madeline emerged, a person who showed great resolve and composure under very trying circumstances. When I named my son Estefan I did so in honour of you both. Truth be told I think I was falling in love with you, Madeline. This could not be so. I could not permit myself to fall in love with a woman who had carnal relationships with my other son.

Did you know Andres's middle name is Americo? I named Estefan so in his honour. I know that Andres was a monster. I also recognize that I am responsible more than anyone else for making him the monster he became. I pledge to make sure my second son's rearing will be antithetical compared to my first son.

I deliberated night and day about creating a world in which all three of us could live. I realized it was impossible. The selfless thing to do would be to let you and Estefan leave and return to your loving family in Canada. I could not do so; I so love the child. The longer you stayed the more anxious I felt that you or your interlopers (whoever they might be) would steal my son from me. I know your friends would not kill my son even if I did have you permanently removed. I know this because they could not kill Vicente and they could not kill me. Having said that, there is little doubt they would come for me if terrible misfortune happened to you. Many, however, have come for me before, yet here I stand. I believe this is the best for all as in essence there are too many complications when looking at the alternatives.

You are young and beautiful, Madeline, and though there will always be a hole in your heart that will never be completely filled, you will fall in love and start a family where love will shine. Trust me. I know this to be true. So here's what you must do.

You must return to Canada. I have taken the liberty of talking to your father. I apologized to him profusely, telling him that I had innocently connected you to a group of spiritual sojourners and did not realize they had cult-like characteristics. Once discovering this I tried to talk you out of joining them, but you seemed already brainwashed. I contacted an anti-cult expert who was experienced in such matters and he suggested we perform a physical intervention and remove you from their compound. I told your father we had to sedate you to get you on the plane out of Salvador and into Miami. This part, as you can imagine, is true. I told him I would have two of my employees fly with you, wait until your head was clear and wait with you until they see you are boarded on a direct flight to Toronto – also true.

Your father was furious. He is a man whose company, I think, I would have enjoyed. He told me he and your mother would be waiting for you in Toronto. He insisted on paying for your flight from Toronto to Vancouver. Madeline, I do not wish to harm your family; I truly don't, but I will if they come after my son. For everyone's sake you must not tell them the truth. There is no doubt in my mind your father is brave and foolish enough to come after me.

I have also contacted a Ms. Maryanne Lucas and informed her of your return. The story I told her is the same one I told your father. I told her that I would be donating $500,000 Canadian dollars per year to her organization with the understanding they would expand their operations into more countries in need of help. I also informed her I would become the sole benefactor for the school in Dona Aurora for perpetuity and that all employment, facility and equipment costs would be covered. I had one caveat: In order to receive funding the school must continue to service students who come from impoverished homes, no matter how good its reputation grows. She seemed very pleased with this arrangement.

I have hired Carlos's son, Fabricio, to work on the compound. He will be helping Vicente with the books. I made an effort to visit his mother and his grandmother to let them know you are well. I explained what was happening and told them I would do my best to ensure you returned to Vancouver. Luiza regretted not seeing you, and the old crow Dona Aurora was remarkably subdued but gruffly admitted she has missed you.

Madeline I hope for all our sakes you heed my words. I have one last request. If this letter appeared to be tampered with before opening it, please tell Felicia and Pedro something that only you and I would know. If it did not seem to be tampered with please tell them something about my family that you believe to be true.

Now please ask Pedro for a lighter; he is expecting you to do so. Burn this letter immediately.

Take care of yourself.

Love,

Maximo.

I re-read the letter several times and attempted to put it in my pocket. Pedro gently tapped my head. He said, 'C'mon.'

I said, 'Give me some more time.' For the next half hour I continued to read it.

Felicia said, 'Time's up.'

Pedro handed me the lighter while Felicia grabbed a garbage can and removed the battery from the smoke alarm. My last physical connection to my life in Brazil became ashes.

That night I sat in bed and watched American TV in numbed, shocked silence. I fixated on MTV and was mesmerized by a kid running around in a field dressed as a bumble bee as some hippy-dippy-looking singer with a weird falsetto voice crooned about no rain. Clearly I had been drugged to get me through the night. It must have been put in my coke or my quarter-eaten McChicken.

The next morning I was taken to the Miami International Airport in a rental car. From the parking lot to the gate Felicia linked her arm around mine while Pedro carried my bags. By the time we arrived at the gate I was all but lucid. Felicia said, 'Do yourself a favour, kid, and don't make a scene.'

I had no intentions of doing so, I felt utterly defeated. Pedro said, 'Once you enter that gate you cannot leave. We have a person in there already; he will not board until you do. You are flying first class so you should get on right away. Now off you go.'

I walked toward the gate and then stopped dead in my tracks. I walked back to my unwelcomed escorts and said, 'I almost forgot. Your asshole of a boss told me I am supposed to tell you something specific about his family. You tell him this. Unless you were a blind fool it is obvious that his real father was his Uncle Americo. Tell him he is the bastard child of his mother and his uncle. Tell him his entire family must be riddled with children who don't know who their real daddies are.

'If you don't tell him this he will think you read his precious fucking letter and he will have you killed.'

Felicia said, 'Madeline, perhaps there is another message you could send him.'

I replied, 'No, there isn't.' I gathered them in close and said, 'Mark my words, you two will pay for this.'

There were low clouds the day I left Miami. I distinctly remember my thoughts as the 737 broke through grey and into the blue and strove upward toward the glaring sun. Dona Aurora's words echoed in my head, 'Your pride and ambition are getting the best of you. Don't fly so close the sun my child.' Pride and ambition. While in Brazil or before leaving for Brazil for that matter, I never perceived myself as ambitious or full of pride. I, however, was wrong. As the plane leveled out at its cruising altitude, I began to curl myself into my luxurious seat. Fetal I remained for all but the descent into Toronto's Pearson Airport. Thoughts of my immaturity, whimsical disregard for the advice of my mentors and my open, unabashed arrogance in my own sense of Western entitlement rattled through my mind. I believe at one point I muttered 'What have I done, what have I done?' but otherwise remained silent and contemplative.

My ego put up some kind of fight, telling me to think of all that had been accomplished while I was in San Salvador. No one could question the success of the school. No one could question my role in its establishment. I silenced that voice, realizing I was but a cog in the wheel. My efforts compared to those of Gretchen, Ali, Luisa and Dona Aurora, not to mention the hundreds of mothers who fought for the rights of their children was nothing more than what I should have expected from myself. I persevered on my covert and overt defiance of those who had warned me of potential dangers. Gretchen, bitch that she might be, was right about Lievan. Dona

Aurora's begging, how hard that must have been for her, of me not to involve myself with Andres was a prophecy a wiser, more humble person than I would have listened to.

'What have I done, what have I done?' became my mantra as the plane hurtled over the Appalachians and into Pennsylvania. I know I was not to blame for Andres's assault, I know I was not to blame for Lievan's betrayal and I know I was not to blame for Maximo's stealing of my child, but I also know in my heart of hearts that there was opportunity for me to take pause, to listen, reflect and heed advice and by doing so, would have stopped the unmitigated disaster that had become my life. My life? What life? I had no life without my child. My child, my baby would wake up without me. Would he cry? How long would he hold me in his memory?

Saudades, suadades, suadades … oh God, what have I done?

Acknowledgments

My thanks go to Laurie Brown, Ami Kambo, Dean Palfreyman, Lee Greengrass, Vici Thompson, Diane Christiansen, Laurie Richardson, Suhki Sahota, Maria Davradou,Connor Brown and Jane Maskell, Brenda Gilson, Gordon Thomas, Cheryl Wilson, Ed Griffin, Jon Ross, Judy Forster, Mary Baker, and Patti Frazee. Also to the men and volunteers of the writers group in Matsqui Prison

Special thanks to Lorrayne Norris for sharing her expertise on Salvador, Brazil.

Maddy's story continues in *A Hungry Heart*

In the follow-up to *A Hard Land*, Maddy Saunders returns to Canada feeling "kidnapped" back to her homeland with an empty heart. She holds her secret close for fear that her family could pay the consequences.

Every day feels as if she is walking with the dry, cracked earth of Brazil stuck to her feet. Every day she lives with *suadades.*

But then she meets Sean, a detective whose own journey back to his homeland of Ireland has left him struggling for meaning. When Sean and Maddy meet, their inner journeys lead to an outer quest to return to Brazil and help Maddy get back all she has left behind.

Excerpt from *A Hungry Heart*

Although interrupted by bumps in the road and unpleasant dreams, Maddy and Sean, exhausted from their travelling, did sleep on the drive from Aracaju to Salvador. The roads were clear and dry and Ali pushed the van well past the speed limit. Around three in the morning Ali pulled over to the side of a road and turned off the engine and lights. He reached round and shook Maddy's knee while whispering her name. Maddy woke, as did Sean. Ali said, 'Maddy we're here. I have parked a block away; it's safer that way.'

Maddy nodded and Sean said, 'Where are we?'

Maddy said, 'Never mind.' She slid open the van door, reached for Sean's hand and said, 'Come with me.'

The night was all but silent and the faint smell of papaya filled the tropical air. A slight wind whispered through the leaves and Maddy's sandaled feet were caressed by the fine dirt that swirled with every footstep she took toward her second home. Though dark and unlit, the moon and the silhouettes of corrugated roofs of the favela guided her down the road she walked so many times. She stood in a spot where she had witnessed a poor gay prostitute get beaten to within an inch of his life. It seemed a lifetime ago. She stared at the only unnatural light on the block. A candle flickered in the window of the one-room abode that stood beside Luiza's home. Maddy whispered to Sean, 'Come.'

She crossed the street and stood outside the window and said softly, 'Yemanja, you are purple and green, You are every colour in between, You are an endless wave on the sea, You are everything to me.'

Seconds later the door opened and a hand motioned for them to enter. Sean followed and saw Maddy in the arms of an elderly man. Sean's eyes averted to a small bed by the window and could see the lined face of an old lady lying on her back. Her eyes were open but stared straight at the ceiling. Her mouth was agape and if not for the subtle and infrequent movement of her chest, Sean would have taken her for a corpse. He figured she weighed less than ninety pounds. He looked back to see that Maddy and the old man were no longer embracing but were also staring at the old woman. The old man said, 'I will wake Luiza.'

Sean saw Maddy nod but was oblivious to what was said. He did not have to be told, however, that he had just met 'Cardoso the Kid' and that the old woman on her death bed was Dona Aurora.

Maddy made her way to the bed. She kneeled down and sought the old lady's hand that was under a thin blanket. Dona Aurora squeezed her hand and whispered, 'Maddy.'

Maddy replied, 'Yes.'

'You have come for what is yours.'

'Yes.'

'Good,' replied Dona Aurora. She took a gasp of air. 'Please bring your face in front of mine as it troubles me to turn this wretched old head of mine.'

Maddy straddled the bed with her arms so her face hovered in front of the old woman. Sean noticed an attempt of a smile cross the old lady's face and assumed that she was saying something sentimental and profound when Dona Aurora said, 'You look like a whore. Finally our angel has got rid of her halo.'

Maddy laughed but then began to cry, oblivious of her tears falling on the ancient face below her. Maddy wiped her eyes and said, 'May I introduce to you my fiancé?'

The old lady nodded her head said ever so slightly and said, 'Please, but I want to see him. I hope he isn't squeamish.'

Maddy instructed Sean to do what she had just done. He leaned over the old lady and heard a faint gasp, she reached her frail hand to his face and said, 'Say hello to Americo for me Englishman.'

There and then Maddy had thought, Brazil. Brazil is magic and nothing really dies for whatever dies someday comes back in the land of Candomble, in the land that embodies the lusciousness of life.

Before Sean had an opportunity to ask what the old woman had said, Luiza burst into the room. She threw her arms around Maddy and the two women wept uncontrollably for a long time. Luiza grabbed Maddy by the shoulders and gently pushed her away from herself. Luiza looked Maddy in the eye and said, 'Tomorrow I am coming with you, this is indisputable as I must be certain my Fabricio is safe. Now go before the neighbourhood wakes.'

Maddy nodded, but as she turned to leave she heard the old woman say, 'Luiz, it's time. Hold my hand my love. Luiza my feet, rub my feet.'

Maddy made her way to the old woman and kissed her forehead. She said, 'Thank you for all you have done for me, Dona Aurora. I would not have the strength to be here if you had not given me such profound lessons in resilience.'

Barely audible, Dona Aurora said, 'Don't thank me, my child, thank Brazil and her hard lessons learned. Now go.'

As Maddy and Sean left they saw Luiz kneel beside the love of his life and hold her hand and saw Luiza gently rub oil into her mother's withered feet.